FOR BETTER OR WORSE

For better or worse, Marietta was the wife of Christopher Thorning, Viscount Sheridan, notorious gambler, infamous womanizer, legendary rake.

For better or worse, Marietta was the mistress of a mansion staffed with slovenly and rebellious servants and awash in the debris of years of disorder.

And now for better or worse, Roger Thorning, Christopher's younger brother, had returned, to tempt Marietta to do a turnabout on her faithless husband by proving that two could play at the game of love à la mode.

Marietta had vowed to take her husband for better or worse—but never had a young wife better reasons to do the very worst. . . .

A
MARRIAGE
OF
INCONVENIENCE

SIGNET Regency Romances You'll Enjoy

A
MARRIAGE
OF
INCONVENIENCE

Diana Campbell

A SIGNET BOOK
NEW AMERICAN LIBRARY
TIMES MIRROR
PUBLISHED BY
THE NEW AMERICAN LIBRARY
OF CANADA LIMITED

NAL BOOKS ARE AVAILABLE AT QUANTITY DISCOUNTS
WHEN USED TO PROMOTE PRODUCTS OR SERVICES. FOR
INFORMATION PLEASE WRITE TO PREMIUM MARKETING
DIVISION, THE NEW AMERICAN LIBRARY, INC., 1633
BROADWAY, NEW YORK, NEW YORK 10019.

First Printing, November, 1982

2   3   4   5   6   7   8   9

 SIGNET TRADEMARK REG. U.S. PAT. OFF. AND FOREIGN COUNTRIES
REGISTERED TRADEMARK - MARCA REGISTRADA
HECHO EN WINNIPEG, CANADA

SIGNET, SIGNET CLASSICS, MENTOR, PLUME, MERIDIAN
and NAL BOOKS are published in Canada by The New American
Library of Canada, Limited, Scarborough, Ontario

PRINTED IN CANADA
COVER PRINTED IN U.S.A.

A
MARRIAGE
OF
INCONVENIENCE

1

MARIETTA HAD IMAGINED innumerable versions of her arrival at Twin Oaks. Her favorite scenario was one in which the chaise drew to a halt, and Roger Thorning bounded eagerly through the forest of pillars guarding the portico. As Roger handed her out of the coach, Marietta observed a veritable army of servants arrayed behind him. Roger led her amongst the grooms and scullery maids, the footmen and valets and lady's maids, performing introductions.

"This is my fiancée, Miss Chase," Roger announced proudly. "Who, as you know, is shortly to be mistress of the household."

Marietta nodded to each, warmly yet regally, and they bowed or curtsied and smiled in return.

In Marietta's *least* favorite variation of the scene, Roger emerged alone from the pillars, wearing a frown of puzzlement because he did not quite recognize his wife-to-be. This, Marietta owned grimly, was by no means unlikely, for she had met her future husband under a month since and had seen him no more than a dozen times.

As it happened, neither of Marietta's extreme visions, nor any in between, came to pass. The hired chaise stopped at the top of the long semicircular drive, and Marietta first noted that the house did not look at all as she had dreamed it. To begin with, the portico was situated on the first floor instead of the ground level; the entrance was an unpretentious, rather narrow arch flanked by long, stark windows. In the second place, Twin Oaks was not the gleaming white edifice

she had pictured; it was constructed of brown brick
and conveyed an impression of sturdiness rather than
elegance. The aura of simplicity was enhanced by the
severely rectangular lines of the house: except for the
pointed roof atop the center wing, it resembled nothing
so much as a large, elongated box.

The other factor which differed dramatically from
Marietta's numerous rehearsals was that no one, no
one at all, came forth to welcome her. The chaise had
halted behind a curricle, but the latter was unattended,
its matched bays tied to a metal post in front of the
left-hand wing. She had written to Roger that she
would arrive in midafternoon on July 1, and the
church clock in Braintree had chimed two as they
changed horses. Braintree was less than an hour from
Twin Oaks, which was located almost squarely in the
middle of Essex, so it must be nearing three. Three
o'clock, Marietta decided, was as near to "midafternoon" as she could conceive.

She glanced rather irritably at the front door, and at
that precise moment it flew open, and her heart
crashed into her throat. But it was not Roger who
strode through the archway and down the shallow
stairs to the drive; it was a plumpish man of medium
height with an astonishing shock of white hair. Marietta
assumed him to be Roger's elder brother—Christopher
Thorning, Viscount Sheridan, the owner of Twin
Oaks—whom Roger had described as "a crotchety fellow of middle years." Marietta would have judged the
Viscount somewhat beyond his middle years, but he
certainly seemed crotchety enough to fit Roger's por-
trayal: his face was flushed an alarming shade of scarlet, and as he smashed his beaver hat upon his head,
Marietta feared he might well break his neck. She reminded herself that she would be compelled to get on
with Roger's difficult brother, and she cautiously lowered the coach window.

"Lord Sheridan?" she called. He stalked on, glaring
stonily ahead. "Lord Sheridan!" she ventured again.
But he had evidently elected to ignore her: he untied

his horses, leaped into the curricle seat, and slapped the bays to a smart trot. The carriage raced between the oak groves bordering the drive, disappeared, and Marietta sighed.

"Well, miss." Marietta hadn't seen the postboy dismount, and she started. "It seems ye weren't expected."

"I *was* expected," she corrected, with as much dignity as she could muster. She stole another glance at the front door, which the Viscount had left open, but detected only darkness beyond. "If you will but wait a moment, I shall go inside—"

"I ain't paid to wait, miss." The postilion flashed a cool, crooked, and largely toothless smile. "I was paid to drive ye from Stowmarket to here."

"So you were," Marietta agreed stiffly. "Perhaps you might just unload my bags, then, and . . ." She had been at the point of suggesting that he carry her luggage into the house, but his smile had grown distinctly frozen round the edges. "And set them in the drive," she concluded lamely.

"Yes, miss."

He jerked the door open, tugged down the steps, then rushed to the other side of the chaise, leaving Marietta to alight unassisted. She had been in the coach for the better part of six hours, and she clambered awkwardly out and attempted to smooth the wrinkles from her brown bombazine carriage dress. She was just plucking a bit of lint from one of the Spanish puffs near the bottom of the skirt when the postboy dumped her trunk and valise unceremoniously at her feet.

"That settles it, miss. I trust you enjoyed your journey."

He did not actually extend his hand, but his gap-toothed grin rendered his words unmistakably clear. Marietta opened her reticule. She had left Suffolk with exactly two pounds, and she reluctantly proffered a shilling.

"I normally receive half a crown, miss," the postilion said.

"*I* normally receive baggage service," Marietta snapped.

In fact, this was the first time she had traveled unaccompanied in her entire life, but the postboy touched his hat, as if to concede a draw. He remounted the left-hand horse and, with a final wave and wink, sped down the drive.

Marietta peered hopefully back at the house, but the doorway remained a black, empty hole. There had obviously been a misunderstanding, she thought. Roger had no doubt instructed the butler to watch for her, and the butler had retired to take tea or some such thing. He would be enormously embarrassed to discover that he'd missed his new mistress, but Marietta would generously forgive him.

She climbed the front stairs and, feeling quite foolish, knocked on the open door. There was no answer, and she stepped inside. In contrast to the brilliant July sunshine, the interior was dim, and Marietta could only surmise that she was in a large entry hall.

"Roger?" she said softly. "Roger?"

Silence. Marietta's eyes began to adjust to the gloom, and to her right she made out a plant stand with a fur rug tossed rather haphazardly in front of it. She looked toward the left and had just identified a bow-fronted commode when she felt something cold and damp pressing against her right fingertips. She lunged away, stumbled into a side table, and realized that the fur rug had come alive: it was a large, curious, and hopefully friendly dog.

"Nice dog," she said nervously, regaining her balance. "*Nice* dog."

Marietta proceeded gingerly to her left, the dog nosing at her brown chamois sandals, and opened the first door she encountered. It was clearly a library—shelves towered from floor to ceiling on every wall—and she started to step inside. But there were dogs here as well, two retrievers and a spaniel, and they greeted her with undisguised suspicion and low, threatening growls. Marietta hastily closed the door and patted the sleek head of her companion.

"Nice dog," she reiterated. "Sweet dog."

Where was Roger? she wondered frantically. Her personal dog—a spaniel-retriever mix, she now saw—seemed amicable enough, but apparently Twin Oaks abounded in vicious canines. She stood perfectly still for a moment and thought she heard a murmur of male voices in the rear of the house. That was it, of course: Roger had invited some friends to meet his fiancée, and, the butler having shamelessly neglected his duties, Roger and his cronies were still passing time in the drawing room. Marietta decided she might well reprimand the butler after all.

She was just in front of the staircase—a straight flight, separating, at the first landing, into two curved tiers. There was a pair of identical doors beyond the stairs, and Marietta walked to the nearer one. It was ajar, and she nudged it open and beheld a dining room. Well, she amended, it had originally been a dining room; the great mahogany table was now littered with books and papers, and half a dozen hunting dogs reclined beneath it. One of them, a particularly large Labrador, snarled and lumbered to his feet, and Marietta slammed the door to.

That left but one final door, and as Marietta approached it, she observed that it was three-quarters open. She paused on the threshold, uncomfortably aware that the dog was now licking her fingers, and peered inside.

She had located the saloon, she collected: the ceiling was exquisitely molded, and there was a great marble fireplace on the far side of the room. However, the chairs and couches and occasional tables had been shoved carelessly against the walls, and an ancient dining table was situated immediately beneath the chandelier. Around the table, occupying chairs in various stages of dilapidation, were some half a dozen men, each holding a playing card, each with stacks of coins and banknotes arranged in front of him.

Marietta's eyes flew around the table, and her knees fairly sagged with relief when she spied Roger, his back to the door, hunched intently over his hand. As she stepped eagerly across the threshold, the man in question turned his head a degree or two, and she realized she had been deceived. The player possessed Roger's chestnut hair, but that was all; in profile, his nose was quite pronounced, totally unlike Roger's snub-nosed, rather flat features.

Marietta glanced about again, but none of the other men resembled Roger in the least: three of them had gone distinctly gray, one was blond, and the man at the head of the table had black hair, shot here and there with silver. The dog licked her hand in especially ecstatic fashion, and Marietta eased away. The man at the head of the table glanced up and examined her with cool gray eyes; if he was surprised to find a strange young woman lurking in the doorway, he betrayed no sign of it.

"None of us was dealt a winner, then," he said. "Do you wish a card, Sir Hugh?" He transferred his gaze to the player at his left, who took a card and immediately threw down his hand with a moue of disgust.

"Eleven," the dealer commented, sweeping up the abandoned hand. "And you, Sutton?"

Marietta was hard put to quell the notion that she had wandered into a peculiar dream. The dog had now planted its forepaws approximately at her waist and was panting up at her, whether with hunger or adoration, she could not determine. Meanwhile the macao game continued: "Sutton" seemed pleased with his hand, but "Cooper," sitting just to his left, was compelled to throw in as well. Was it possible that the dealer had not seen her, that those pale, chilly eyes had looked quite through her? Marietta thought not, and she debated whether to march boldly into the saloon or to slink away.

"I fancy I have reached nine, gentlemen." The dealer

exposed his cards and, to the accompaniment of low groans around the table, raked in the stakes. "Nevertheless, I fear I shall be forced to pass the deal, for I have a bit of business to attend. If you will do the honors, Purcell?"

He handed the deck to the player Marietta had mistaken for Roger, stood, and sauntered toward the door; and Mr. Purcell began to shuffle.

"Miss Chase?"

Though Marietta had watched his approach, his arrival somehow startled her. Perhaps, she thought, it was because he was so very tall: well over six feet, she judged, with broad shoulders that accentuated his leanness. At close range, his gray eyes were nearly silver, matching the threads in his hair. That could be an illusion, of course—the contrast of pale eyes to sun-darkened skin . . .

"Miss Chase?" he repeated sharply.

"Yes," she murmured; "yes, I am Miss Chase."

"I am Viscount Sheridan." His bow was so abbreviated as to be effectively nonexistent.

"But . . ." She had started to say that he could not be, then realized that she must have confused the identity of the middle-aged man in the drive as well. The Viscount was absently patting the dog, who had left Marietta to scamper round its master's feet. "I did not intend to interrupt your game, Lord Sheridan," she said. "If you will but summon Roger before you return to the table—"

"I daresay we should be more comfortable in my study," his lordship interjected.

The Viscount seemed inclined to deafness as well as blindness, Marietta reflected dryly. But before she could protest, he had moved past her and begun to stride down a dim, narrow corridor paralleling the drawing-room wall. The dog trotted along behind him, and Marietta trailed the dog. She would never have guessed Lord Sheridan to be Roger's brother, she marveled. The Viscount was scarcely a man of "middle years"; indeed, he was far more attractive than his sib-

ling. Taller, thinner, darker, except for those unsettling
eyes. . . .

His lordship reached a door, opened it, and beckoned Marietta in before him. She was unsurprised to
find two Irish setters flanking a large and exceedingly
untidy writing table. Apparently these dogs were
friends of her canine companion: the three of them
greeted one another enthusiastically and gamboled into
the hall. The Viscount nodded Marietta to a chair in
front of the writing table, from which she was compelled to remove two books and a ledger before she
could sit. Lord Sheridan plucked another ledger from
his own chair, placed it carefully on the floor, and lowered himself into the chair. It occurred to Marietta that
his lordship's person and his home were singularly at
odds. The Viscount was impeccably clad in pantaloons
of dark blue, a white waistcoat, trimmed in the same
shade, and a pale blue frock coat. However, as he
propped his elegant, superfine elbows on the table, a
book crashed off the left side, and several sheets of paper cascaded down the right.

"Miss Chase," he said again. "As I recall, your
Christian name is Marietta."

"Yes," she confirmed, "Marietta. Now if you would
kindly direct me to Roger, I shall take no more of
your time—"

"A most unusual name," Lord Sheridan remarked.
"I do not believe I have encountered it before."

Marietta found his habit of interruption exceedingly
annoying, but she again recollected that she must live
in peace with Roger's elder brother. A prospect, she
thought darkly, which appeared increasingly unlikely
with every passing moment.

"It is not my real name," she said, as politely as she
could. "My name is Maria Henrietta, but when I was a
baby, a young cousin of mine garbled it up, and I have
been Marietta ever since. I should have supposed Roger might have informed you—"

"Maria Henrietta," his lordship mused. "And what
is your real *surname*, Miss . . . ah . . . Chase?"

He had assumed a sardonic smile, frosty as his eyes, and Marietta did not pause to consider why he should have posed such an odd inquiry. "My real surname is Chase," she snapped. "My father was Sir Henry Chase, of Rosefields, near Stowmarket, Suffolk. Papa died three years ago, and as I was the only child, the title became extinct."

"Sir Henry Chase." The Viscount frowned. "I fancy I have never heard of him." He seemed to imply that since he was not familiar with Sir Henry, Sir Henry could not possibly have existed.

"I daresay it is entirely conceivable that Papa never heard of you either," Marietta said coolly. She thought she detected the ghost of a smile at the corners of his lordship's rather thin mouth, but she could not be sure. "Be that as it may, I should like to speak with Roger."

"Roger." The smile, if there had been one, abruptly faded. "Yes, I am extremely interested in your acquaintance with my brother. I am given to understand that the two of you met in London during the recent Season. At Lady Everleigh's ball, was it not?"

"I believe it was." Marietta's three weeks in town had been so frenetic that she could not distinguish one ball from another, could hardly separate the breakfasts from the dinners, the boating trip from the opera party.

"Surely it was not your come-out, Miss Chase?" The Viscount lifted one eyebrow; his brows, Marietta noted, were untinged with gray and seemed therefore darker than his black hair.

"I collect you are referring to my age, Lord Sheridan," she said warmly. "You will be delighted to learn that your surmise is correct: I am not eighteen; I am one-and-twenty. I am quite certain you will next ask why I did not come out at the proper time, so I shall spare you the trouble. Papa died just after my eighteenth birthday, and he instructed my stepmother to bring me out the following year. However, Agnes, my stepmother, was in no rush to do so—she is exceedingly clutchfisted, you see—and it was only after she took up with Mr. Hewitt that she elected to escort me to London. We arrived in the latter part of May—"

"Who is Mr. Hewitt?" his lordship interposed.

"You might obtain more information were you as eager to listen as to talk," Marietta suggested testily. "Mr. Hewitt is Agnes' new husband. Her *very* new husband, I should add; they were married just this morning. In any event, Mr. Hewitt had made it abundantly clear that he did not wish to support Agnes' stepdaughter, and she—"

"Mr Hewitt told you this directly?"

Marietta could not read Lord Sheridan's expression; he might have been curious, skeptical, sympathetic, or any combination of the three. At any rate, she was not unduly displeased by his latest interjection, for she had been at the point of blurting out that Agnes had dragged her off to London specifically to snare a husband.

"No, he did not," she replied. "I am not personally acquainted with Mr. Hewitt, but my stepmother conveyed his sentiments quite well."

"I see. Does your Mr. Hewitt have an occupation?"

Marietta strongly suspected, based on Agnes' random comments, that Ambrose Hewitt was a smuggler, but she elected not to reveal her supposition to his lordship. "He is not *my* Mr. Hewitt," she responded. "I presume he is in business, but I do not know what his business is." She persuaded herself that, literally, at least, she had stated the truth.

"In any event, you traveled to London with your stepmother and met my brother, and the two of you fell over head and ears in love."

His face was blank now, and Marietta wondered if she had only imagined an undertone of sarcasm. Perhaps she was reacting with excessive sensitivity, she conceded, staring down at her hands. The fact was that she did not love Roger Thorning at all. Roger was handsome and amusing, and—as Agnes had pointed out at least fifty times per day—his family was one of the oldest and wealthiest in England.

"You could do considerably worse, Marietta," Agnes

would conclude. "But far be it from me to push you into an unhappy marriage. You may prefer Lord Riverton . . ."

Agnes' voice would trail provocatively off, leaving Marietta to ponder Lord Riverton's stooped shoulders, balding pate, and foul breath. In the end, of course, Marietta agreed that Roger was much the more desirable of her suitors and accepted his offer. Agnes whisked her back to Suffolk, financed a modest trousseau (the carriage dress, one walking dress, one evening gown, and miscellaneous underthings), and began planning her own wedding to Ambrose Hewitt.

Marietta raised her eyes and caught a derisive grin on Lord Sheridan's lips. He sobered at once, but it was too late: he had given her an opportunity to dissemble.

"Evidently you find the subject of love highly entertaining," she snapped.

"Highly," he acknowledged. "I suspect that love is the insidious invention of poets and novelists; *I* certainly have not experienced any such distressing emotion during my five-and-thirty years."

"Do you solicit congratulation or commiseration, milord?" She had intended to wither him, but the Viscount threw back his black-and-silver head and laughed. "I fancy we have chatted long enough," Marietta continued stiffly. "I must insist that you advise Roger of my arrival."

"Roger." Lord Sheridan sighed heavily and shook his head. "I regret to inform you that Roger is not available." His sighing and head-shaking notwithstanding, there was no trace of regret in the cold gray eyes. "I need not elaborate; Roger left a message."

He pawed through the precarious stacks of paper on his writing table and quickly produced an envelope. Too quickly, Marietta decided; he had known where the envelope was all along. He passed it across the writing table, and Marietta observed her name scrawled upon the front. It occurred to her that she had never before seen Roger's handwriting; it was bold, confident, but exceedingly uneven. She tore the envelope open, dismally aware that her fingers were trembling.

Marietta [the brief missive began],

I can scarcely bring myself to report my actions, and I certainly cannot justify my behavior. The fact is, I have come to recognize that I am not yet prepared to enter into a bond so permanent, so sacred, as the holy bond of matrimony. In view of my deep and painful reservations, I felt I had no recourse but to leave the country. Which I have done.

I wish you much happiness in the future. I am sure Chris will attend your immediate needs.

Yours truly,
Roger Thorning

Marietta read the note a second time, a third, but there was no hidden meaning; Roger had expressed himself dreadfully well. She looked up, belatedly realizing that she had crumpled the message into a tiny ball.

"It appears you are overset, Miss Chase," his lordship said.

"Overset?" Marietta croaked. She cleared her throat. "Have you read the note, sir?"

"No, I have not. However, Roger did advise me, just prior to his departure, that he felt compelled to cry off your engagement. I presume he so stated in his message."

"When . . . when *did* Roger depart?" Marietta asked.

"As I recollect, it was the day before yesterday. Though it might have been Friday."

"I see," Marietta murmured. She wanted to read the note again, but the Viscount's pale, chilly eyes were flickering over her face. She smashed the paper into an even smaller ball.

"I suggest, Miss Chase, that we resolve this unfortunate situation in a civilized manner. I daresay Roger assured you of my cooperation."

"Yes; yes, he did."

"I *shall* cooperate, of course." He was speaking very smoothly now, very pleasantly. "I shall provide a carriage to return you to Suffolk tomorrow—"

"But I can't go back to Suffolk!" Marietta protested. "As I mentioned, my stepmother remarried only this morning, and she and Mr. Hewitt have left for an extended honeymoon. We stayed last night in Stowmarket—Agnes and I—because she has closed the house and discharged the staff. There is no one there; no one at all."

"How very inconvenient," his lordship drawled. He seemed remarkably unconcerned. "To what idyllic locale have the happy newlyweds repaired?"

"I . . . I don't know," Marietta said.

"That is most unfortunate." The Viscount shook his head again, but his frosty eyes remained fastened on her face. "Perhaps you have other relatives, Miss Chase?"

"Only my cousin; the one I told you of. She married an American some years since, and they live in Virginia."

"America." Lord Sheridan flashed a benign smile. "I am compelled to confess a certain fondness for that troublesome little country; Papa was granted our title as a reward for his service in the American rebellion."

"How nice," Marietta mumbled absently.

She had heard the story before; more to the point, she had just begun to comprehend the magnitude of her dilemma. Roger had jilted her, Agnes had disappeared, and Cousin Joan (with whom, truth to tell, Marietta had never got on) was thousands of miles across the sea. She felt as though her rib cage had been encircled in an iron vise, and she struggled for breath.

"America," the Viscount repeated. "If I may be permitted another suggestion, Miss Chase, it strikes me that you would do well to join your cousins there."

Marietta recollected Cousin Joan's thin, pale face and Cousin Herbert's fleshy, sallow one and narrowly suppressed a shudder. But she was forced to own that she had no alternative, and she clenched her hands.

"I fancy you are right, Lord Sheridan. However . . ." Her mouth had gone quite dry, and she coughed and licked her lips. "However, I have insufficient funds with which to pay my passage."

"Insufficient funds." His lordship drew the syllables out, as if these were esoteric words foreign to his vocabulary. "You seem to imply that *I* should pay your passage, Miss Chase. It would be small recompense, would it not? You could, after all, sue the Thorning family for breach of promise."

Marietta's cheeks warmed with humiliation, and she gazed once more at her hands. "You may do as you deem fit, milord," she murmured.

"I deem fit not to give you a groat!" the Viscount hissed. His abrupt attack took Marietta so completely by surprise that her eyes flew up, and her jaw sagged. "I shan't pay you a single farthing," he reiterated; "not now and not ever. I therefore leave it to you, Miss Chase, to propose an alternative solution."

Marietta's mind was fairly whirling with confusion; indeed, she had developed a severe headache. She reflected that Viscount Sheridan was "crotchety" in the extreme, surely the most difficult person she had ever encountered—dangling opportunities, snatching them back, studying her, all the while, with those terrible gray eyes. She cast desperately about and did, in fact, glimpse a solution.

"Roger had arranged for me to reside with your uncle and aunt prior to our marriage," she said. "The Marquis and Marchioness of Cadbury—"

"Had he indeed?" his lordship interrupted. "I wonder, then, why he instructed you to meet him here at Twin Oaks."

"I don't know," Marietta replied, swallowing an infuriating threat of tears. "I know only what Roger told me: that I was to stay with Lord and Lady Cadbury. Perhaps I could yet do so, temporarily, of course. I shall immediately write my cousin in Virginia, and she will forward my passage." Marietta judged it entirely possible that Cousin Joan would refuse to send her an American nickel, and she groped for another possibility. "In the interim, Agnes might well get in touch with me."

"I'm afraid your proposal is altogether impractical," the Viscount said. "Uncle Ralph was here this afternoon; he departed just prior to your own arrival. I am sorry to say that his visit ended on a rather unpleasant note. I fancy he would not be at all amenable to accepting a house guest for—what?—upwards of three months?"

Marietta collected that it was the Marquis of Cadbury she'd seen in the drive, but she perceived no reason to mention this surmise to his lordship. Indeed, she could think of nothing further to say at all, so she merely watched as the Viscount leaned back in his chair—ignoring the papers he dislodged from the writing table—and laced his fingers over his stomach.

"There is but one honorable alternative," Lord Sheridan said at last. The papers had settled on and around the book he had earlier placed on the floor. "I should like, Miss Chase, to extend an offer."

"An offer?" Marietta gasped. "An offer of *marriage?*"

"That was my intention, yes," the Viscount confirmed dryly.

Marietta's head pounded so painfully that her vision started to blur. Within the space of half an hour, she had been jilted, then proposed to by an utter stranger. She was astonished to discover that she was not prepared to refuse Christopher Thorning out of hand; if he was the most difficult man she'd encountered, he was also, by far, the most attractive. Furthermore, as she had recognized, as he had pointed out, her options were painfully limited. But she would not make an impulsive decision, not while her head was throbbing and splitting.

"I am exceedingly flattered, milord," she murmured. "However, I am sure you will understand that I require

some time in which to consider your . . . your . . ."
Her mouth was now so dry that she could not finish.

"You will have all the time you wish." His lordship
straightened, and another half-dozen papers glided off
the writing table. "I shall have your bags taken to one
of the guest bedchambers."

"Here?" Marietta asked redundantly. "I fear that
would be most improper. Unless there is a chaperon of
whom I am not aware—"

"There is no chaperon." The Viscount's voice, his
eyes, had frozen again. "If you prefer not to remain at
Twin Oaks, I shall dispatch you to the inn in
Chelmsford. Where you may stay, at *your* expense, as
long as you like."

Marietta's silence served as her response, and Lord
Sheridan rose, strode to the door, opened it.

"Crawford!" he yelled into the corridor. "Ho! Crawford!"

Marietta stood as well, but a wave of dizziness assailed her, and she sat abruptly down again. She would
wait for Crawford in the chair, she decided. Yes,
Crawford would be along at any minute; in the mean-
time, she'd close her eyes and perhaps her headache
would go away.

2

MARIETTA COLLECTED THAT she had dozed, for she
was next aware of a powerful hand shaking her shoulder.

"Come, Miss Chase. I cannot seem to locate Crawford, so I shall escort you up myself. Come along,
now."

Marietta stood, swayed, and Lord Sheridan sighed and took her elbow. He propelled her back the way they had come, but Marietta's legs were so weak with exhaustion that she soon began to stumble against him. Indeed, by the time they reached the entry hall, the Viscount was compelled half to carry her, and Marietta distantly noted that despite his leanness, he was exceedingly strong. They mounted the left-hand flight of stairs and proceeded along a seemingly endless corridor to—or so Marieta surmised—the guest wing. His lordship opened a door, pushed Marietta in ahead of him, and dropped her arm. Her skin felt peculiarly warm, even beneath the fabric of her sleeve, and she resisted an inclination to rub the spot where his fingers had gripped her.

Marietta shook her head and was rewarded by a stab of pain, which served, at least, to render her a trifle more alert. She gazed about and observed that she was in a bedchamber of moderate size, furnished with an uncurtained four-poster bed, a smallish mahogany wardrobe and matching chest of drawers, a rosewood washstand and dressing table. The furniture was of excellent quality, as was the Aubusson carpet, but the upholstered armchair in the corner, the counterpane, and the drapes at the window betrayed unmistakable symptoms of age. Marietta speculated that the room had not been used for some time: the late-afternoon sunlight revealed a thin veneer of dust on the various wood surfaces.

"Here we are, Miss Chase," Lord Sheridan said gratuitously. "I shall return to the game now, so if you wish anything further, you may ring." He indicated a frayed bell rope near the bed. "I shall have your luggage brought up at once . . ." He stopped and frowned. "I do not recollect seeing your luggage in the foyer."

"No," Marietta agreed; "it was left in the drive."

"In the drive." His lordship appeared to attach some peculiar significance to this; he quirked his black brows before he nodded. "Very well; I shall send it along. Good afternoon, Miss Chase."

He tendered his abbreviated bow and stepped back into the hall. As soon as he had closed the door, Marietta rushed to the bed and threw herself upon the counterpane. She fancied she could still hear the rapid tattoo of the Viscount's footsteps as she tumbled into a deep, dreamless sleep.

She was awakened by a knock at the door and bolted upright, momentarily disoriented. She peered fuzzily about, remembered her location, and looked toward the window. She calculated that she had been asleep an hour or more; the sunlight had paled, and shadows had begun to creep along the carpet. There was a thud from beyond the door, and Marietta had just lowered her feet to the rug when the door opened and a figure crossed the threshold.

"I knocked," the figure announced querulously, "but no one answered. I've brung up your bags, miss."

He dropped her valise, with a resounding crash, on the floor, then turned and dragged her trunk—thump, thump—across the doorsill. He straightened and dusted his hands, as if he had completed an exceedingly difficult and rather distasteful task.

"You must be Crawford," Marietta said.

"Oh, no, miss, I'm Bailey, the second footman. Mr. Crawford is the *butler*." A position, his tone suggested, which ranked Mr. Crawford only slightly below God.

"Thank you, Bailey."

"Yes, miss. If there won't be nothing else, I'll be on my way."

"As it happens, Bailey, I should like . . ."

But he had already whirled around, and Marietta was scarcely able to note his ill-matched coat and pantaloons, his scuffed and dusty shoes, before he fled into the corridor and disappeared.

Marietta sighed. She had been at the point of asking Bailey about the dinner hour at Twin Oaks, for her nap had left her ravenous. She glanced at the clock on the mantel above the fireplace, but it reported a time of half-past two, and she guessed it had not been wound in months. At any rate, Lord Sheridan would surely dispatch someone to summon her to dinner. In the interim, she would unpack.

Marietta set her valise on the bed but hesitated with her fingers upon the clasps. At this juncture, she judged, she had not been irreparably compromised. She had, it was true, spent several hours in the Viscount's home, totally without benefit of a suitable chaperon; she had even rested in one of his bedchambers. However, she thought her behavior, if it came to light at all, would be regarded as a minor indiscretion. Whereas, if she actually stayed a night under his lordship's roof . . .

She shuddered, jerked her hands away from the valise, and cast desperately about for some alternative which had not occurred to her before. Perhaps she might return to Suffolk and throw herself upon the mercy of a neighbor. What neighbor? The Tappans were on holiday in Europe; the Bishop property had been sold and was temporarily vacant; and Agnes had engaged the Lawsons in a bitter feud concerning a Lawson cow who had dared to graze in a Chase pasture. In fact, Agnes had managed to alienate *all* their neighbors in one fashion or another; none of them was likely to take Marietta in for a period of months.

An inn, in Chelmsford or anywhere else, was equally out of the question: Marietta would be able to pay her way for ten days, two weeks at the outside, and would then be cast, literally penniless, into the street. She considered Lord and Lady Cadbury; they had agreed to house her during the interval preceding her and Roger's wedding. But Roger had jilted her, and Marietta could not suppose the Cadburys would so readily accommodate their nephew's *former* fiancée. Not for months on end. Not if the Marquis, as seemed to be the case, had quarreled with said nephew's elder brother.

There was, in short, no alternative, and Marietta reluctantly opened the valise and removed her lingerie to the chest of drawers. She could not lift the trunk, so she laid it open on the floor and scurried back and forth to the wardrobe, hanging her dresses and gowns. Not that much scurrying was required, she conceded wryly: aside from her tiny trousseau, she possessed but two walking dresses and three evening gowns purchased for her come-out. When everything was put away, Marietta placed the trunk and valise under the bed and looked again at the window.

It was after six, she estimated, perhaps closer to seven. In the course of stooping and rising and running about, she had discovered that her headache was gone, but her stomach was rumbling with hunger. Lord Sheridan should have called her to dinner by now; should, at the least, have advised her of its hour. She went to the door, opened it, peered into the hall, but there was no sign of Bailey or any other messenger. Her stomach emitted a particularly demanding gurgle, and she strode to the bell rope and gave it a rather peevish tug. She waited, by her reckoning, for five minutes, rang the bell again, waited ten minutes more. But there was no response, and faced with the prospect of imminent starvation, Marietta marched into and down the corridor.

She had been too tired to observe her surroundings earlier in the day, and she was now too hungry to give them more than an idle glance. She did note that there were three doors on either side of the corridor—six bedchambers then—and she assumed that the right wing of the house was similarly designed. The hall led to a morning room, decorated in cheerful pastels, and an identical corridor issued from the opposite side. There was another room to Marietta's right, at the front of the house, but she pounded down the stairs without stopping to look inside.

The dining-room door was closed, and Marietta tapped upon it and turned the knob. A familiar chorus of growls emanated from within, and she hastily secured the door again. She proceeded halfheartedly to the drawing room, but as she had expected, it was dim and deserted.

The kitchen must be situated on the understory, Marietta thought, and she did not recollect a staircase between the saloon and his lordship's study. She walked back to the dining-room door, passed it, and discovered a narrow hall like that on the drawing-room side of the house. She ventured along the corridor, spotted a stairway on her right, and hurried down the steps. She paused at the bottom and collected that she had, indeed, located the kitchen: there was a range directly in front of her, a cooking hearth at her left, and, scattered all about, shelves and tables laden with blackened pans and kettles and skillets.

"And just what might *you* be wanting?" a disembodied female voice demanded.

Marietta started, peered around, and spied a woman seated at a sagging oak table beside the range. Hardly a disembodied woman; she appeared to weigh every bit of fifteen stone.

"I am Miss Chase," Marietta said rather lamely.

"I'm Mrs. Sampson," the woman retorted. "The cook." Marietta would have guessed this, for Mrs. Sampson's apron was splashed and spotted, dashed and dotted, with souvenirs of a hundred meals. "What is it you want, Miss Chase?"

"I am a guest at Twin Oaks," Marietta murmured.

"Indeed?" Mrs. Sampson sniffed and crammed something into her generous mouth—a piece of bread or a pastry, Marietta believed, her own mouth watering. "And what do you want with me?"

"Dinner," Marietta blurted out. "That is to say, I fancy it is approaching the dinner hour, and as no one has yet informed me of the specific arrangement, I came down to inquire—"

"Lord Sheridan is out this evening," Mrs. Sampson interjected.

It might have been a non sequitur, but Marietta grasped the horrible implications at once: since his lordship was away, there was to be no dinner. She looked at Mrs. Sampson's plate, but even as she watched, the enormous cook devoured the last morsel of whatever it was.

"I see," Marietta gulped. "Perhaps you might just give me some leftovers, then."

"It is not my responsibility to feed every wanderer who happens along," Mrs. Sampson said.

The cook spoke with considerable dignity, and Marietta might have bowed to this perverse whim of fate had Mrs. Sampson not chosen, at that precise moment, to deliver a great, satisfied belch. Marietta's empty stomach roared in response, and she felt her temper snap.

"Quite the contrary," she said frigidly. "It is *entirely* your responsibility, Mrs. Sampson; you are the *cook*. I am, as I have stated, a guest; I am hungry; and I wish something to eat. *At once!*"

Mrs. Sampson's multiple chins fairly quivered with indignation, but she lumbered out of her chair.

"I don't have much," she said sullenly. "A bit of beef, left from his lordship's lunch, and I don't mind telling you I'm sick to death of cooking for a horde of gamesters day after day—"

"Thank you, Mrs. Sampson," Marietta interrupted firmly. "When you have finished, please ask someone to bring the plate to—"

"There's no one to take it anywhere," the cook said. "I told you Lord Sheridan was from home. The staff is off."

"But surely Crawford has not yet retired," Marietta protested.

"Mr. Crawford is indisposed. And it isn't *my* responsibility—"

"Never mind," Marietta said wearily. She was compelled to own that it was not, in fact, Mrs. Sampson's duty to deliver food about the house. More to the point, she did not believe the ponderous cook could survive a journey up two flights of stairs. "I shall take the plate myself."

Mrs. Sampson waddled around the kitchen, continuing to mutter under her breath, and eventually presented a plate: several ill-carved chunks of roast beef, a hard-cooked egg, a slice of bread, and—by some miracle—a tart. Marietta asked for silverware and a napkin, a request which elicited Mrs. Sampson's keen displeasure as it necessitated a visit to the adjoining scullery. Marietta would have liked a glass of wine as well, but Mrs. Sampson's face was now quite scarlet—whether with fury or unaccustomed exertion, Marietta could not determine—and she elected not to press her luck.

"Thank you, Mrs. Sampson," she said again. But the cook had already collapsed, with a great, martyred sigh and greater thud, back into her chair.

Marietta soon decided that her contretemps with Mrs. Sampson had been a battle fought for a cause long lost. The meat was overdone and stringy, the bread stale. She took one bite of the egg and determined it might well be classified an antique. She thought the tart was gooseberry, but she could not be sure: there was no more than a spoonful of filling inside the thick, soggy crust.

But, famished as she was, she consumed all but the egg, set the plate on the floor beneath the dressing table (where she had, so to speak, dined), and uttered a tremulous sigh of her own. She realized that much of her concern with unpacking, with eating, had been in the way of procrastination. She had spun these mindless activities out as long as she could, and now she must contemplate the wretched bumblebath into which she had so abruptly been thrust.

She considered Roger for a moment, but only a moment. She would not pretend, even to herself, that his abandonment had left her heartbroken. She had agreed to marry Roger because she had to marry someone, and Roger had seemed to promise a comfortable, pleasant, uncomplicated union. Instead, Roger had placed her in a terrible predicament—a predicament, it appeared, which only Lord Sheridan could resolve.

This conclusion brought Marietta, more quickly than she might have wished, to the matter of the Viscount's astonishing proposal. *He* certainly was not the man she would have chosen either, she reflected. She reviewed their conversation, recalled his frosty eyes, his mocking smiles, his nasty little innuendos. Indeed, she recollected, at one juncture he had actually seemed to imply that Marietta was some sort of impostor. He couldn't possibly believe such a thing, of course, so his remarks must have been just another instance of his sardonic wit.

He *did* have wit, Marietta conceded, and that was perhaps the most winning of his positive characteristics. She remembered the one occasion on which he'd laughed, remembered that the laugh had brought his dark, thin face alive. He should laugh more often, Marietta thought, for amusement enhanced his singular good looks. Though his lordship probably fancied that he was quite sufficiently attractive as it was. Marietta recalled their long walk through the house and up the stairs, recollected the Viscount's warm fingers on her arm, and could not suppress a small, indelicate shiver.

Furthermore—Marietta swiftly redirected the drift of her deliberations—Lord Sheridan had splendid prospects. His and Roger's father, the third son of the ninth Marquis of Cadbury, had purchased a commission in the army some forty years before. As Roger had explained and his lordship had mentioned, the heroic Captain Thorning had become a viscount at the conclusion of the American rebellion. What the present Viscount had *not* mentioned, but Roger had dwelled on at considerable length, was that the second brother ("Uncle Alfred, a rather unstable chap") had shot himself to death following an unhappy love affair; and that Uncle Ralph, the eldest son and tenth Marquis, was childless.

"Which means," Roger concluded, "that Chris will one day be the Marquis of Cadbury."

"How unfortunate that *Roger* has no hopes of a title," Agnes later lamented. "Still, my dear, you could do far worse than to claim a marquis as your brother-in-law."

Marietta wondered what Agnes would say if she knew her stepdaughter's present circumstances. Foolish speculation: Agnes would deem it a magnificent opportunity and speedily take credit for providing it. And not without justification, Marietta owned dryly, for Agnes was, at bottom, liable for her hobble. Sir Henry had instructed Agnes to provide for Marietta; Agnes had promised to do so; and Sir Henry, ever a trusting soul, had left his entire modest estate to his wife. Now that Agnes had reneged, had effectively banished her from Rosefields, Marietta had no option but to contract a marriage of convenience. No option except to enter a convent, and she was not *quite* ready for that.

So, Roger having removed himself rather dramatically from the picture, Marietta was left with the choice of Lord Sheridan or Lord Riverton. She gazed into the mirror above the dressing table, and Lord Riverton's blackened teeth smiled back at her. Marietta shuddered, then realized, with a horrid start, that even Lord Riverton might no longer have her. No, if word of her visit to Twin Oaks got about (and the remark of a scullery maid traveled faster than the royal mail), she would be altogether cut from polite society.

It seems I shall *have* to marry you, Lord Sheridan, she thought, and she felt a peculiar sense of relief. She started to stand, but there was a final question in her mind: why had the Viscount presented his incredible offer? He had alluded to honor, but he did not strike Marietta as the sort of man who would permit his behavior to be dictated wholly by convention. Of course he wouldn't; she was here, shamelessly unchaperoned, in his house.

She studied her image in the mirror, but she looked much as she had from the age of fourteen onward: not unhandsome, not beautiful; dismally average. Her face was rather too round, her nose a bit too short, her chin a trifle recessive. Added to which, her hair was a vile hue—something between dark blond and pale brown. Marietta liked to think of it as "honey-colored," but it remained something between dark blond and pale brown.

On the positive side, her skin was unblemished and unusually dark; in the summer, it was sometimes darker than her hair. And—her only truly commendable feature—her eyes were huge and thickly lashed and so deep a brown as to be, for all practical intent, black.

On this day, the first of July, she looked her very best, Marietta thought objectively. Though, in view of the London Season, she had spent scant time in the summer sun, her hair was at its fairest, her skin at its duskiest, and her black eyes resembled two great embers in her face. She was of a nice, medium height, she assured herself, and only a *little* too thin. So perhaps Lord Sheridan found her genuinely attractive . . .

But it didn't signify; the decision had been made. She jumped up, nearly upsetting the chair, began to fumble with her buttons, and heard an odd noise at the door. It didn't seem to be the knock of a servant, but in view of the Viscount's peculiar staff, she could not be sure. Maybe Mrs. Sampson had crawled, gasping and wheezing, along the corridor.

"Yes?" she called. "Yes . . . who is it?"

There was no answer, and Marietta cautiously crossed the room and cracked the door. The dog, *her* dog, bounded in and, with a prodigious leap of joy, managed to plant a wet kiss on Marietta's chin.

"You!" Marietta said. She tried to sound annoyed, but she somehow regarded the dog as a favorable omen. "Oh, very well; you may stay."

She closed the door and stripped off her carriage dress, donned her nightgown and climbed into bed. The dog jumped up beside her.

"I didn't mean *here,*" Marietta said. "You can't stay in the *bed.*"

But the dog snuggled against her, appropriating the spare pillow, and after a while Marietta threw her arm around it, and they both fell asleep.

3

WHEN MARIETTA WOKE, she wanted nothing so much as a bath, and she tugged the bell rope energetically but with little hope of response. Her pessimism proved well-founded, and at the end of fifteen minutes she sighed and went to the washstand. She had found a few inches of ancient water in the pitcher the day before, and she had carefully hoarded most of it against just this contingency. She washed her face and hands, dabbed her body as best she could, and proceeded to the wardrobe.

She decided, for some reason, to save her one new walking dress, so she donned the peach ensemble: a jaconet dress over a sarcenet slip, with a spencer of white lutestring. She then sat at the dressing table and despairingly studied her hair. Agnes had insisted, prior to their departure for London, that Marietta adopt a new *coiffure:* loose ringlets in the front, spilling from a center part, and, in the back, a long braid wound around the crown. But the braid had fallen hopelessly apart during the night, and Marietta could not begin to repair it. She brushed the braiding altogether out, re-pinned the back hair in a loose knot, and adjusted the side curls over her ears. The result was far from perfect, but it would have to suffice. She rose, stepped into the hall, and started toward the morning room, the dog trotting behind her.

Marietta had determined to inform Lord Sheridan of her decision at once, and she had somehow fancied that he would be pacing about in plain view, impatiently awaiting her word. However, the morning room was empty, and Marietta, a trifle deflated, paused to consider where his lordship might be at this hour. The breakfast parlor most likely, but she did not know where that was. She was attempting to visualize the plan of the house when a man emerged from the adjacent room, the one she had bypassed the previous evening.

The man did not appear to see her; indeed, he did not appear to see anything well, for he promptly stumbled into an arc-backed chair and stopped to massage his injured knee. Marietta observed that his black pantaloons and coat were reasonably well-tailored and that his neckcloth was *almost* white and *almost* tied in a Mathematical. He seemed, in short, a distinct cut above Bailey, and Marietta guessed she had at last encountered Crawford. He continued toward her, hobbling a bit, and Marietta detected a powerful odor wafting ahead of him. She further surmised that the "indisposition" Mrs. Sampson had reported had stemmed from an excessive intake of spirits and that the butler was frequently "indisposed" in this particular fashion.

"Crawford?" she said sharply.

He stopped again, focused his eyes, drew himself up, swayed, grasped the back of a mahogany sofa for support. "Yes?" he intoned.

"I am Miss Chase. I am a guest at Twin Oaks."

"A guest?" The butler straightened his shoulders still further but left his fingers firmly planted on the couch. "Lord Sheridan did not advise me of any guest." His voice was deep and resonant, his words, astonishingly, unslurred, and he had assumed a haughty frown.

"Perhaps that is because Lord Sheridan was unable to find you," Marietta suggested coolly.

"Ahem. Perhaps so. I shall certainly inform his lordship that you are here."

"His lordship *knows* I am here," Marietta snapped. "Where, pray, is he?"

"Lord Sheridan?"

"Yes, Lord Sheridan!"

"You needed but ask, Miss Guest," Crawford said indignantly. "His lordship is riding, as he always does at this hour of the day. He will shortly return for breakfast. Would you care to join him?"

"I should indeed," Marietta replied.

"Then might I propose that you wait in the breakfast parlor?" He tossed his head toward the door behind him and winced. "I shall apprise Lord Sheridan of your arrival."

He bowed and walked carefully to the stairs, clutching, in turn, an Adam chair, an upholstered stool, and a satinwood card table. Marietta watched his difficult progress with fascination, and only after Crawford had disappeared did she proceed to the room at the front of the house. She peered inside and beheld a small round table, surrounded by half a dozen Hepplewhite chairs, and a miniature sideboard. The table was set for four, and Marietta initially supposed the Viscount was expecting other guests for breakfast. However, she soon noted that the tablecloth was spotted, the settings unevenly placed; and she collected that, in the interest of time, the table was laid every six days, and his lordship moved from one position to another until all the settings were exhausted. She calculated that it did not much signify what place she occupied, so she took a chair facing the door, and the dog lay down at her feet. She gazed at the stairs, her stomach beginning to growl again with hunger.

"Good morning, Miss Chase."

The Viscount had approached from the right wing, taking Marietta unawares, and she started.

"Good morning, Lord Sheridan," she murmured.

He looked exceedingly handsome, she observed. He was wearing buckskin breeches, a brown riding coat, white-topped boots; and *his* neckcloth, positively snowy, was tied in a perfect, complicated Oriental. His dark skin was still ruddy from the outdoors, and his slightly windblown hair lent him a rather boyish aspect. He glanced around the table, selected the place just across from Marietta, and sat down.

"I trust you slept well?" He laid a copy of *The Times* beside his plate.

"Yes, very well; I slept extremely well indeed."

"Excellent." He unfolded his newspaper and began to read.

The moment was not proceeding at all as Marietta had imagined. She waited for him to scan the front page—to ascertain that Napoleon had not again escaped, that London was not afire—and look up. But he read the front page at length, then turned to the second, and Marietta cleared her throat.

"Before I retired, however, I considered your . . . your . . . that is to say, our conversation. Our conversation of yesterday." She belatedly recalled that they had *had* no other conversation. "I came to the conclusion that—"

She was interrupted by the entry of a footman, who panted into the room and crashed an enormous tray upon the table. Apparently this was the first footman, Marietta speculated; in any event, his clothes were quite as splattered with food as Mrs. Sampson's apron. He set several bowls and platters on the table and, leaving the tray behind, departed as abruptly as he'd come. His lordship served himself from the various dishes and started to eat, continuing, as he did so, to read *The Times*.

The Viscount had not taken all the food—an oversight, no doubt, Marietta thought grimly—and she helped herself to two rashers of bacon, a kidney, and a muffin, gingerly avoiding the eggs. She was not surprised to find the muffin soft in the middle, but she did count it odd that one slice of bacon was burned to a crisp while the other was raw. She decided not to eat the kidney after all. She stole a glance at his lordship; he was impartially wolfing down the items on his plate as if he judged every one of Mrs. Sampson's offerings equally delicious. Marietta cleared her throat again.

"I was at the point of saying, Lord Sheridan, that I have pondered our discussion. As a result of my deliberations, I have determined to . . . to accept your offer."

"Indeed?"

The Viscount looked up at last, but except for a slight quirk of his black brows, his face was blank. She might as well have pronounced her opinion of the bacon, Marietta thought, might as well have declared (in all truth) that the coffee was far too weak.

"Evidently you were not attending," she said stiffly. "I stated that I have decided to marry you."

"I *was* attending, Miss Chase, and I heard you quite well. When do you wish the ceremony to be conducted?"

She had expected some display of emotion. Perhaps a negative emotion—disappointment or resignation or alarm—but *something*. Something beyond this mild, pragmatic inquiry. "When?" she repeated lamely.

"Yes. Shall we wait for the banns to be posted, or shall I procure a special license?"

"I . . . . Roger and I were to be wed on the fifteenth." A date which had absolutely no meaning now, and Marietta bit her lip, wondering why she had mentioned it.

"That is another matter, Miss Chase. Are we to inform the world of your previous liaison with my brother?"

"I should not suppose that question is mine to answer." Marietta's mouth felt numb, and she moistened her lips. "I daresay everyone in the neighborhood knows I was engaged to Roger."

Lord Sheridan's gray eyes flickered, narrowed. "Be that as it may, if you have settled on the fifteenth, I shall make the necessary arrangements."

Marietta had not "settled on" anything, of course, but she perceived no advantage in issuing a correction. The Viscount stabbed his fork absently at the bacon platter, tilted it up, frowned.

"There is no more bacon," he commented gratuitously.

It was the most unromantic thing he could possibly

have said, and Marietta—dangerously, inexplicably close to tears—succumbed to fury instead.

"There is no more bacon because I ate your second portion," she hissed. "I ate your second portion because you did not instruct Mrs. Sampson to prepare any breakfast for me."

"Mrs. Sampson?" His lordship's frown deepened. "You are acquainted with Mrs. Sampson?"

"I am *intimately* acquainted with Mrs. Sampson because I was compelled to go to the kitchen last evening and literally beg her for my dinner. I was driven to this extreme measure after I had rung repeatedly, and with repeated lack of success, for a servant. I was similarly ignored this morning when I rang for a bath. I had to make do with a few drops of water which were fairly yellow with age."

"Water does not yellow with age, Miss Chase. Nor does it curdle or mold."

"You know quite well what I mean! You have failed to extend me the most rudimentary courtesy. I do not demand an abigail, but I should like for *someone* to be advised of my presence. Someone besides Crawford, who no doubt forgets his name from one minute to the next."

"I am sorry you find my domestic organization so inadequate," the Viscount said frostily. "As it happens, I am a bit short of staff just now."

It suddenly occurred to Marietta that the Thornings might not be so wealthy as she, as Agnes, had assumed. Many prominent families had fallen on hard times since the end of the war, and if Lord Sheridan was an habitual gamester . . .

"Nevertheless," his lordship continued, "I shall appoint '*someone*' to respond to your summonses." He managed to imply that Marietta's summonses were probably quite frivolous, and she bristled again. "Is there anything else, Miss Chase?"

"Yes, there is," she snapped. "If we are to be married, I should think you might stop addressing me as 'Miss Chase.'"

"Very well. Is there anything else, *Marietta?*"

"No, there is not. Good day"—she coughed— "Christopher."

She rose and marched around the table, and the dog overtook her at the door, thrusting its cold, wet nose into her hand.

"It seems you have also become acquainted with Poppy," Christopher remarked. "Her latest litter recently left home, and she invariably adopts a human being in lieu of her departed pups. I should warn you that she may well insist on moving to your bedchamber."

"I trust you would not object," Marietta said coolly. "I have noted that dogs reside in every *other* corner of the house."

"Am I to add that to your roster of complaints?"

Marietta stalked into the morning room without reply and heard, behind her, an angry rattle as his lordship returned to his paper.

Marietta passed the day, and those immediately following, largely in her bedchamber. Fortunately, she had packed several books in her trunk—novels by Miss Austen and Mr. Beckworth and Miss Burney—and these occupied much of her time. She spent the remainder pondering her very odd engagement and observing the Viscount's schedule.

The latter, Christopher's schedule, was not difficult to ascertain. His lordship rode between eight and nine, at which time he took breakfast and began poring over *The Times*. As he was normally still immersed in the paper when Marietta left the breakfast parlor, she was not sure exactly how long his morning reading required. In any event, at eleven o'clock precisely, carriages began to roll up the drive—a gig, a barouche, and a high-flier phaeton, in various sequences. The carriages disgorged Christopher's gambling cronies, and they strode into the house while a harried groom drove the vehicles to the coach yard at the rear.

Hours elapsed, and at five or six the players

emerged, looking sometimes triumphant, sometimes overset, sometimes merely befuddled. In any case, the groom brought their carriages round again, and the men departed. An hour or so after that, Christopher, unaccompanied, raced a spanking new curricle out of the coach yard and down the drive. Marietta did not know when his lordship returned; it was, apparently, after she fell asleep or before she rose.

If the Viscount's habits were easy to deduce, his demeanor remained an impenetrable mystery. He seemed to take their engagement very lightly, seemed, indeed, to regard it as a matter of no consequence at all. He did not invite Marietta to participate in his evening activities, but she realized there might be a reason for this: his lordship might well be visiting his latest barque of frailty. Far more puzzling was his evident unconcern about their scandalous situation. The peculiar circumstances of their marriage would no doubt generate a great ripple of *on-dits* as it was, and Marietta could scarcely conceive the furor if it became known that she and Christopher had *lived* together for nearly two weeks prior to the wedding. Yet the Viscount did not counsel the slightest discretion; Marietta took it upon herself to lurk in her bedchamber and avoid the curious eyes of Christopher's neighbors.

Marietta had initially perceived one advantage to her shocking circumstances: she and his lordship would be able to develop a close relationship despite their very brief betrothal. However, Christopher displayed no inclination to encourage any such development. She saw him only at breakfast, and even then he appeared deliberately to evade any but the most desultory conversation.

"I wish to thank you for assigning a servant to attend me," Marietta said politely on the second morning.

"Umm," the Viscount grunted. "I hope you find her performance satisfactory."

Actually Marietta found the girl, April, barely passable. She had, it was true, delivered Marietta's evening meal and morning bath, but both had been quite tepid when they arrived. Following the bath, April had fairly jammed Marietta into her clothes, then whined that she was "much too busy" to assist Miss Chase with her hair. (Which, judging from the lamentable state of April's own *coiffure,* was probably a blessing.) But Marietta elected not to mention these deficiencies to Christopher.

"She is fine," she murmured.

"Splendid. I myself hold May in high esteem."

"Her name is April," Marietta corrected.

"Ah, yes. May is her sister, the parlormaid."

"Do you also employ January, February, and March?"

She thought a smile tickled the corners of his lordship's mouth, but if so, he suppressed it and pointedly turned the page of his paper. As though, Marietta reflected, he did not *want* to be amused, but she couldn't fathom why, and she choked down a leathery bit of ham.

On the following morning, they ate in silence for the first quarter of an hour, and eventually Marietta tried another tactic.

"Is there anything of interest in the news?" she asked.

"What do you term 'of interest'?" Christopher responded absently. "There is a description of the Lapland Eskimos who are presently touring the country."

"I was wondering about the Bilston Moor colliers. I understood they were marching on London to protest their unemployment."

The Viscount glanced sharply up, a quizzical expression on his face. "Do you follow politics then?"

"I don't regard it as politics." He was watching her intently, and her cheeks began to warm. "It seems to me that the colliers represent certain problems which must be solved if any of us are to have a proper future."

"As it happens, I quite agree with you." Christopher

leaned back in his chair, his dark features animated in a way she had not observed before. "I have presented several speeches in the House on that very subject. We must address the grievances of the lower and middle classes, and I believe the best means is an extension of the franchise."

Marietta felt her eyes widen; she had fancied his lordship entirely occupied with horses and hunting and interminable games of chance.

"Apparently that surprises you, Marietta."

"I . . ." She wanted to say that, as little as she knew him, *nothing* could truly surprise her; wanted to enlarge the tiny chink in his armor. But it was too late.

"Never mind." His face went blank again. "The colliers continue their march; I shall leave the paper for you if you wish."

He looked firmly down and flipped to a new page, creating a barrier quite as effective as if he had erected a wall between them.

There was a similar incident the next morning. It began when April brought Marietta's bath fully half an hour late, then compounded her sin by spilling water all over the peach ensemble, which Marietta had laid out on the bed.

"We shall have to select another garment, miss," April announced. "We" suggested that Marietta somehow shared responsibility for the soggy mess on the counterpane.

"Get the new dress then," Marietta snapped, rinsing the soap from her body. "The purple one."

She leaped out of the tub and dried herself, donned her underthings and dashed to the wardrobe. April tugged the gown over her head, and Marietta noted with dismay that the fit was most uncomfortable. She peered down and perceived that April had somehow managed to get the dress on backward.

When the gown was at last put aright, Marietta could not locate her left shoe; April finally found it under the bed, where April had obviously kicked it. It was now quarter past nine, and Marietta frantically examined her reflection in the mirror above the dressing table. The gown was becoming enough, she decided—a lavender silk with violet lozenges round the bottom—but April's clumsy ministrations had left her hair in utter disarray. Marietta shoved in half a dozen additional pins and sped down the corridor, dismally aware that her hair was still half tumbling down her back. She could not but wonder why she was in such a rush to meet his lordship, who would no doubt fail to notice if she burst into the room stark naked.

She did, in fact, burst into the breakfast parlor, and Christopher glanced up from his inevitable *Times* and granted her a cursory nod. She hurried on around the table, but before she could take her chair, she sensed that the Viscount was watching her again.

"I apologize for my tardiness," she said breathlessly. "Pray continue your reading."

But he did not; he continued, instead, to study her, his eyes oddly dark, until Marietta felt quite naked indeed.

"You look very handsome this morning," he said at length. "Lavender suits your coloring." Praise was the last reaction Marietta had anticipated, and she could think of no reply. "Is your hair not different as well? Yes, I fancy I prefer it loose."

"Thank . . . thank you," Marietta stammered.

She might, once more, have broken some peculiar spell: the Viscount dropped his eyes and rose. "In view of your delayed arrival, I took the liberty of beginning without you. As I have finished my meal, I trust you will excuse me."

He bowed and walked out, and Marietta sank into her chair. He had refused to own that she might be amusing or clever; now he had apparently chosen to deny her modest physical attributes as well. She gazed despondently at her hands. She was no longer a flighty girl, and she had never entertained the adolescent notion that Christopher Thorning would fall suddenly, overwhelmingly in love with her. She had hoped they could build a marriage of respect and affection rather than passion, but she realized that *any* bond would prove impossible if Christopher was determined to hold her at arm's length. Surely the nuptial bed would temper his reserve . . . The thought rendered Marietta's face exceedingly warm, and she looked quickly up and fumbled for a blackened piece of toast.

Marietta had set her mantel clock to correspond with the clock in the morning room, and it was exactly three when she finished her final book. She briefly thought to ring for April and instruct the girl to bring an additional supply of volumes from the library, but upon consideration she judged it unlikely that she and the chambermaid shared similar literary tastes. And who was to see her if she ventured downstairs for just a moment? The game was long since under way and would not adjourn for several hours.

Nevertheless Marietta fairly crept along the corridor and down the circular steps, and she paused on the landing, peeping out from behind a great urn and pedestal. The foyer was deserted, and Marietta was further reassured by a sudden, loud oath emanating from the drawing room. She descended the final flight and was halfway across the entry hall when the front door flew open. A man charged through, leaving the door to creak in the summer breeze, and literally ran her over.

"Oh, I say," he panted. He caught her up just before she hit the floor, drew her to her feet, and peered down at her. "Miss Chase? Oh, I am sorry indeed; I do hope you are not injured."

In fact, he had nearly driven the breath from her body, but Marietta was more startled than injured. She gasped for air, meanwhile squinting up at him, and eventually identified the man she had mistaken for Roger. His neckcloth was damp and spilling untidily down his waistcoat, and he wore an expression of acute alarm, far in excess of that warranted by their minor accident. Since it was entirely too late to avoid him, she elected to behave as normally as she could.

"It is quite all right," she said, still wheezing a bit. "I am not hurt in the least. Mr. . . . Mr. Purcell, I believe?"

"Sir Mark," he corrected distractedly. "Sir Mark Purcell. I am looking for Chris." His eyes did, indeed, roll rather wildly about the foyer.

"I should think you might be aware, Sir Mark, that Christopher is playing macao in the saloon." Even as she spoke, it occurred to her that she had not observed Sir Mark during her twice-daily reconnaissance at the window; evidently he was only an occasional participant.

"The saloon; yes, of course, the saloon. I shall fetch him at once. Good day then, Miss Chase." He bowed, and his beaver hat, which he had failed to remove, tumbled off his head and landed on Marietta's right toe. He stooped and plucked it up. "Good day."

He bowed again and rushed past her, and Marietta frowned after him. She had taken one further step toward the library when he whirled around and stared at her.

"But you cannot be seen here, Miss Chase," he whispered. "May I suggest that you return immediately to your bedchamber? I shall wait until you have . . . er . . . disappeared."

"Your discretion is most commendable, Sir Mark," Marietta said dryly. "However, *you* have seen me already, and Christopher takes my presence quite for granted."

"But Chris does not . . ." He stopped and mopped his brow with a limp handkerchief. "*Please,* Miss Chase; I assure you I have only your interests at heart."

It was all very odd, Marietta thought, but Sir Mark certainly seemed sincere; indeed, he seemed positively hysterical. At length she shrugged, retraced her way, and with a last, puzzled nod at Sir Mark, started back up the stairs. As she reached the landing, she heard his footsteps pounding toward the drawing room.

Very, *very* odd, Marietta reflected, walking into the

first-floor corridor. Perhaps Sir Mark had just learned of her and Christopher's living arrangement and had come to advise his lordship of its horrifying impropriety. Though in that case, Sir Mark's concern appeared a trifle tardy; if the news had circulated about the neighborhood, there was little, nothing, to be done.

In any event, Marietta concluded, opening her bedchamber door, Sir Mark's intervention had left *her* with nothing to do. Poppy, comfortably ensconced on the bed, wagged her tail in greeting, and Marietta idly patted her head. If only you could talk, she mused, what a fascinating conversation we should have. I should tell you what it is like to accept the offer of a stranger, a man who chooses to remain a stranger. . . .

Poppy lifted her ears, as though she quite understood, but Marietta detected the sound an instant later. A commotion in the drive. She went to the window, tweaked the drapes apart, and collected, to her astonishment, that the game had ended. The players were gathered on the front steps—two of them counting wads of banknotes, two gazing morosely at their boots—and soon the gig pulled up. The gig driver was one of the winners; he climbed quite jauntily into his vehicle and, with a cheerful farewell wave, trotted down the drive. Marietta dropped the curtains and noticed that they had developed a slight, telltale gap in the center.

"Marietta!"

Her bedchamber door crashed against the wall, and she spun around. She had recognized the Viscount's voice, but she hardly recognized *him:* he was leaning upon the jamb as if for support, and his dark face had paled to a distinctly yellowish hue.

"I was not spying," she said stiffly. "I chanced to hear a noise—"

"You must pack." Christopher strode into the room, running his fingers through his black-and-silver hair. "You must pack at once; I shall assist you. Where is your luggage? May will help as well; where is *she?*" He gave the bell rope a vicious jerk.

"Her name is April," Marietta reminded him.

"April, May; where *is* the damned girl?" Five seconds had elapsed since his summons.

"I fancy she will be along momentarily," Marietta said coldly. "In the interim, I should like to know just what it is I am packing for. Where am I to be sent?"

"You are not to be *sent* anywhere; you are to stay with Uncle Ralph and Aunt Charlotte. Under the bed, no doubt." He fell to his knees, popping one of the buttons off his pearl-gray waistcoat, and wrestled out her trunk and valise. He staggered up and threw them on the counterpane. "I daresay we should begin with the wardrobe—"

"I am quite capable of packing my own things," Marietta snapped. "However, I find the entire undertaking extremely curious in light of your recent insistence that Lord and Lady Cadbury would not receive me."

"The situation has changed." Christopher threw open the wardrobe doors. "I have dispatched Mark to Cadbury Hall, and he will inform my uncle and aunt of our imminent arrival. Shall we start with this?" He began tugging at the carriage dress.

"Do not touch my clothes!" Marietta shrieked.

Poppy, evidently overset by her mistress' tone, jumped off the bed, and at that very moment April dashed through the door. Dog and girl collided in the middle of the Aubusson carpet and went down in a great tangle of calico and fur.

"Get out," Marietta hissed to the Viscount. "Get out; April and I shall pack." Assuming, of course, that April was still alive.

"Very well, but you must be ready within a quarter of an hour. I can give you fifteen minutes, no more."

"I can be ready in ten if you will only *get out!*" Marietta screeched.

"Very well," he mumbled again.

He backed through the door, altogether neglecting to bow, and Marietta began to heave April off the floor.

4

In fact, Marietta's packing required twelve minutes, for she was compelled to work entirely alone; April perched on the edge of the bed, insisting that her ankle was surely broken.

"Broken in several places, I daresay," she moaned. "Do not forget your hairbrush, miss." Since she had managed to walk *to* the bed in quite lively fashion, Marietta was not unduly concerned.

As if to underscore the extreme urgency of her departure, Bailey arrived before the packing was half done and paced, with visible impatience, just outside the door. The instant the valise was closed, the trunk lid secured, he dashed into the room, snatched up the bags, and fairly sprinted down the corridor. Marietta glanced about and spotted Poppy, who, though apparently unhurt, had taken refuge in the remotest corner of the bedchamber.

"I shall be back," Marietta said gently. "I promise that I shall return."

She wondered, even as she spoke, what she could possibly *promise* at this peculiar juncture, but Bailey was already clattering down the stairs, and Marietta hurried to catch up.

Christopher was waiting in the drive, standing beside his curricle, and he literally hurled her luggage into the rear compartment before shoving her unceremoniously up to the seat. She noted, as he leaped up himself, that his lordship had evidently been too rushed to change his damaged waistcoat; his shirt was poking through the gap left by the missing button. He slapped the horses to a start, and the carriage raced down the drive.

"Now that we are under way, milord," Marietta said crisply, "I should like to know just what you are at."

"At?" he echoed. He exhorted the team—a splendid pair of matched grays—to even greater speed, and though he was an excellent driver, Marietta closed her eyes. "I believe I explained that you were to spend the remainder of our engagement with my uncle and aunt."

"You *explained* nothing," Marietta corrected, forcing her eyes back open. "You mentioned, barely mentioned, that the situation has changed, and I demand to know the particulars."

"The particulars." The Viscount coughed, and as if this were a signal, the horses lengthened their stride. "The fact is that Mark pointed out to me, pointed out in no uncertain terms, that our circumstances, yours and mine, were highly . . . ahem . . . irregular."

"I pointed out precisely the same thing several days since," Marietta said coldly.

"So you did." Christopher coughed again.

"I can only collect, then, that Sir Mark's word carries considerably more weight than my own."

"I should prefer to phrase it somewhat differently." The Viscount tugged at one of his shirt-points, which had begun decidedly to wilt. "I should prefer to say that Mark alluded to certain factors I had not previously considered."

It was a specious rejoinder, clearly designed to evade the issue, but Marietta elected to let it pass. "Has it not occurred to you," she said instead, "that you are locking the stable door well after the steed has been stolen? I have been at Twin Oaks four full days, and I should suppose that word of my presence has circulated about the entire neighborhood."

"I think not."

He spoke so quickly, so firmly, that he seemed to be speaking the truth, and Marietta responded in kind.

"*How* can you think not?" she pressed. "The news had traveled to Sir Mark at least."

"No, it had not. Mark is my dearest friend, has been so since our childhood, and I confided in him at the outset. I have no reason to believe that anyone else was aware of our . . . our . . ."

"Our 'irregular' arrangement," Marietta finished wryly.

She thought he was dissembling again, but she could not perceive how or why. He was obviously sincere about his friendship with Sir Mark, and insofar as Marietta knew, none of the other neighbors *had* observed her. Which left only the servants, and in this respect his lordship's lamentable staff was a distinct advantage. She doubted either Crawford or Bailey would recollect her name; April lacked sufficient sense to recognize that she had stumbled upon a delicious *on-dit;* and Mrs. Sampson appeared quite incapable of heaving herself beyond the kitchen. Then why had Sir Mark flown so suddenly, so belatedly into the boughs? And why had Christopher been so overset as to adjourn his game and spirit her frantically to Cadbury Hall?

She stole a glance at his lordship and observed that he was now clawing at his neckcloth, which was also beginning to sag. She decided to count herself well out of a *scandale terrible* and bit back her questions.

"Very well," she said. "I shall abide by your opinion." They galloped on, and she absently noticed the stands of elm and ash bordering the road, the shepherd's rose and honeysuckle twined amongst the hedgerows.

Christopher cleared his throat once more. "There is one further matter, Marietta. Unless you particularly wish it to be known, and I cannot conceive that you do, I suggest you not disclose your engagement to Roger."

"Not disclose it?" Marietta repeated. "But that steed has surely been stolen, milord. Lord and Lady Cadbury were initially expecting me to come as *Roger's* fiancée—"

"No, they were not. Roger did not advise my uncle

and aunt of your betrothal. Nor, insofar as I am aware, did he inform anyone else."

"But why?" Marietta gasped. "Why did he choose to keep it a secret?"

"At the risk of distressing you, I might speculate that Roger determined, early on, to terminate the engagement. Perhaps he sought to spare the both of you unnecessary embarrassment."

"How very kind of him!" Marietta snapped. She thought his lordship gave her a sharp sideward look, but she continued to stare at the road.

They reached the drive shortly thereafter, turned in, and trotted between two rows of great oaks so perfectly aligned as to resemble a disciplined corps of sentries. They rounded a bend, and Cadbury Hall loomed ahead—enormous, pristinely white, with pillars fronting each of its several entries. It reminded Marietta of her vision of Twin Oaks, a notion reinforced when the curricle stopped and a servant bounded down the stairs to meet them. He exchanged greetings with the Viscount, handed Marietta out of the carriage, and escorted them up the steps and into the foyer.

"Christopher!"

Lady Cadbury (or so Marietta assumed) had apparently been awaiting their arrival, for she fairly hurtled across the entry hall and threw herself into his lordship's arms. "You naughty, *naughty* boy; how very *mischievous* of you to engineer such a surprise! I could scarcely credit Sir Mark's information, and Ralph was altogether *overcome;* he has retired to the Green Saloon for a spot of brandy. How splendid that you are to be wed at last, and *this*, I fancy, is the lovely bride."

She turned and beamed at Marietta. She was a short, plump woman, and Marietta surmised that she had once been quite beautiful. Indeed, though she must be sixty, her face was still remarkably unlined, but her smallish eyes had faded to pale blue, and her hair had gone entirely white.

"Yes," the Viscount confirmed, "this is my fiancée. Miss Marietta Chase."

"Lady Cadbury," Marietta murmured.

"No, my dear, you *must* call me Aunt Charlotte, for
I am truly to be your aunt in . . . what? Did Sir Mark
not say the wedding is to occur Monday week? I always knew, Christopher, that when you encountered
the *right* woman, you would be utterly *bouleversé*. I
quite approve your haste; I do not subscribe to long
courtships and lengthy engagements. Ralph and I met
and married within two months' time, and we have
been *exceedingly* happy for nearly five-and-thirty years.
Though I daresay you have been acquainted for something less than two months; I collect you met when
Christopher traveled to Suffolk to see to the Fram-
lingham property? Some three weeks since, was it not?"

Marietta was not sure to whom the question was
addressed, nor, in fact, exactly what the question was.
Fortunately, Lady Cadbury did not wait for a reply.

"Be that as it may, I am *overjoyed* by the outcome.
I often wondered how Christopher was *ever* to locate a
suitable wife in view of his refusal, his *absolute* refusal,
to journey to London for several Seasons past." She
stopped, frowned at Christopher, beamed again at
Marietta. "I do hope, Marietta, dear, that you can re-
form my nephew; I observe that his dress has deteriorated to a shocking state indeed. But come; Ralph is
extremely eager to meet you."

Aunt Charlotte led them along a corridor, and Marietta noted, from the corner of her eye, that the Viscount was adjusting his neckcloth, stuffing his shirt
back through the gap in his waistcoat, and attempting,
with no success, to prop up his limp shirt-points. Lady
Cadbury threw open a door and danced in ahead of
them.

"They are here, Ralph!" she trilled.

The Marquis of Cadbury looked precisely as Marietta remembered him, though she guessed that his rosy
complexion might now be attributable to brandy rather
than fury. In any event, he strode forward, briefly
clasped Christopher's hand, and peered down at Marietta.

"Henrietta!" he boomed. "I am delighted to make your acquaintance."

"Marietta," she corrected politely.

"Marina! Of course!"

"Marietta," Aunt Charlotte said. "Ma-ri-et-ta."

Marietta collected that Lord Cadbury was quite hard of hearing, a deficiency which explained his fortunate failure to acknowledge her presence in the drive at Twin Oaks. At any rate, he seemed to have comprehended Aunt Charlotte's careful syllables, for he nodded.

"Marietta!" he roared. "And a handsome girl you are, my dear." Marietta blushed, but the Marquis had already transferred his still-keen eyes to Christopher. "Decided to heed my advice, did you, boy? Elected to settle yourself down, eh?"

"I have always heeded your advice, Uncle," the Viscount said mildly.

"No, you have not!" Lord Cadbury bellowed. "Had you heeded my advice, I should not have been compelled to threaten you with disinheritance. As I told you on Monday, I was quite prepared to disown you if you did not modify your rakeshame habits. I am happy to see that my words had such salutary, such *immediate* effect."

"Now, now, Ralph," Aunt Charlotte clucked, "let us not dredge up old differences."

She smiled at Marietta, and Marietta tried to smile back, but her mouth was stiff around the edges. Was *this* why Christopher had offered for her: because his uncle had commanded him to find a wife? It didn't signify, of course—theirs was, after all, a marriage of convenience—but she couldn't quell a surge of disappointment.

"Well!" Lady Cadbury spoke a trifle too brightly, as if she had divined Marietta's thoughts. "I ordered an early dinner, for I fancy Marietta is *quite* exhausted after her drive from Suffolk. This way, my dear."

The dining-room table was laid with a snowy linen cloth and matching napkins, sparkling china, twinkling crystal, gleaming silver. As soon as they were seated, four footmen bounded forward and served steaming bowls of soup. Marietta cautiously tasted hers and found it a thick, delicately seasoned mulligatawny. After four days of near-starvation, she was hard put not to wolf it down.

"Now," Aunt Charlotte said, "we must discuss the wedding. I believe Sir Mark indicated, Marietta, that you have no family to assist in the planning. I wish to assure you that *I* shall take full responsibility. Though I do fear it will be rather difficult to write and deliver the invitations in just above a week's time—"

"Invitations?" The Viscount dropped his spoon, and a few golden beads of soup splashed upon the tablecloth. "That is most kind of you, Aunt, but as it happens, Marietta and I have agreed upon a private ceremony." He shot Marietta a piercing glance across the width of the table, and she lowered her eyes. "Naturally we want you and Uncle to attend us, but we shall be married in Mr. Archer's home."

"In the rector's home." Lady Cadbury shook her head. "I do not understand you modern young people at all, but of course I cannot *insist* that you have a formal wedding."

She emitted a wounded sniff and signaled the footmen to remove the bowls and present the fish course. She consumed a few bites in silence, then stabbed her fork triumphantly in the air. "What we shall do, then, is conduct a ball in your honor."

"A ball?" Christopher seemed to be choking; had the fish not been salmon, Marietta would have assumed that he had encountered a bone. "Prior to the wedding?"

"Yes, indeed." Aunt Charlotte had apparently got over her miff, for she fairly radiated enthusiasm. "It will be in the way of a betrothal celebration, and it will provide Marietta an opportunity to meet the neighbors. Of course, it will also be difficult to arrange an assembly in such a brief space of time, but I daresay I am up to the task. Since the wedding is to be Monday week, we shall hold the ball on the preceding Saturday. Tomorrow week; do you concur, Christopher?"

It was clear that whether the Viscount concurred or not, the matter was settled; Lady Cadbury continued to chatter her plans through the rest of the salmon, the saddle of mutton, the mince pie. They would naturally place potted palms all about the ballroom, but did Marietta prefer red or yellow roses? One of the local orchestras was *particularly* accomplished in country dances while another favored waltzes; which should they employ? Marietta murmured her opinions, and Christopher ate in silence, occasionally pausing to mop the fine sheen of perspiration that had formed upon his brow.

"That is it then," Aunt Charlotte concluded happily, laying her napkin aside. "I shall begin the preparations tomorrow. In the interim, I shall insist that you depart at once, Christopher; dear Marietta *must* be afforded a chance to recover from her long, tiring journey."

They rose, and Lady Cadbury ushered them all back to the foyer, where the Viscount immediately took his leave. Lord Cadbury, who had uttered not a word during dinner but had consumed four glasses of wine, proceeded somewhat unsteadily back toward the Green Saloon. Aunt Charlotte led Marietta up the stairs and through a veritable maze of corridors to a corner bedchamber. It was not significantly larger than her quarters at Twin Oaks, but the furniture was in impeccable condition, and the room was spotlessly clean.

"I perceive that Alice has unpacked your things, for she has left the wardrobe doors open." Lady Cadbury marched across the Brussels carpet, peered briefly inside the wardrobe, and slammed the doors closed. "Alice is generally an excellent girl, but she suffers moments of *unforgivable* carelessness."

Marietta wryly wondered how Aunt Charlotte would judge Christopher's slipshod household. She *was* tired, though hardly for the reasons Lady Cadbury presumed, and she sank onto the bed.

"You must not care for Ralph's remarks, my dear,"

Aunt Charlotte said kindly. She walked back to the bed and sat beside Marietta on the satin counterpane. "It is true that Christopher is a bit of a rake, but Ralph's own reputation was far from spotless at the time we met. I can personally attest that a *reformed* libertine makes for an excellent husband."

Marietta could not but feel that it was rather hazardous to gossip about her fiancé with her future aunt-in-law. On the other hand, she was intensely curious, and she glimpsed no safer means of obtaining answers to her questions.

"Why . . . why do you say that Christopher is a rake?" she asked.

"Oh, my dear, the *money* he spends! He and Ralph employ the same man of business, and naturally Mr. Lloyd discusses Christopher's financial affairs with Ralph." Marietta did not think this "natural" at all, but she elected not to comment. "Christopher has the most *astonishing* gambling losses; there was one recent payment—*one* payment—of nearly five thousand pounds. I recollect the occasion vividly because Mr. Lloyd was exceedingly overset; in the very same month, he was compelled to send a substantial check to a gentleman in . . . Was it Norfolk? I believe it was. A most distressing incident: evidently Christopher had compromised this particular gentleman's daughter . . ."

Lady Cadbury bit her lip and assumed her too-bright smile. "But, as I have stated, you must not tease yourself about it. It is apparent that you dealt with Christopher in extremely clever fashion; I fancy you kept him guessing until the last possible instant. Well, of course you did. We attended a dinner party at Lord Edgerton's last evening, and Christopher did not even *mention* your arrival."

So the Viscount hadn't been visiting his barque of frailty, not last night at any rate. Yet he had not invited Marietta to accompany him to Lord Edgerton's. . .

"Indeed," Aunt Charlotte continued, "Christopher was quite as attentive to Elinor as is his custom." She stopped and bit her lip again. "Which is to say that he was not attentive in the least because his relationship with Elinor has always been a casual one—"

"Who is Elinor?" Marietta interrupted sharply.

"Lady Elinor Winship. She was widowed just above a year ago, but she was on the catch for Christopher long *before* Sir Horace expired. Not that I can find it in my heart to cast blame: Horace was a fool in his youth, and a doddering *old* fool at the end. But do not give it another thought, my dear; Christopher chose *you*, and a wise decision it was. I suspect Elinor will be *enormously* surprised when she learns the turn of events.

"Enough!" Lady Cadbury clapped her hands so loudly and abruptly that Marietta started. "I shall leave you to your rest, for I daresay Christopher will come calling at the very crack of dawn. Shall I summon Alice to help you undress?"

"No," Marietta murmured. "No, thank you; I can manage for myself."

"Very well." Aunt Charlotte stood and gave Marietta a last, fond smile. "When you wake, you've only to ring, and Alice will be up directly. Good night, my dear."

She sailed into the hall, closing the door behind her, and Marietta went wearily to the wardrobe. She removed the lavender gown and hung it up, plodded to the chest of drawers, located her nightdress, pulled it over her head. She crawled into the bed but, exhausted as she was, lay for a moment staring at the ceiling.

Evidently she had consented to wed a rake. An *impoverished* rake at that: he was unable properly to staff his home: he could not afford the London Season; he was burdened with gambling debts and conscience payments. An impoverished rake who had offered for her out of desperation, whose uncle had threatened him with disinheritance if he did not mend his ways. An impoverished, desperate rake who failed to grant her the most cursory attention. An impoverished, desper-

ate, disinterested rake who had dallied with another
woman for years.

Marietta closed her eyes and—blessedly, miraculously—fell at once to sleep.

5

As Aunt Charlotte had promised, Marietta's first
tug of the bell rope was swiftly answered by a plump,
pink-cheeked girl who identified herself as Alice. In
sharp contrast to April, Alice promptly fetched a tub,
filled it with steaming water (not spilling a drop), and
tidied up the room while Marietta bathed. When Marietta had dried, Alice deftly assisted her into the peach
ensemble, which, fortunately, had survived April's dep-
redations, and arranged her hair into quite a creditable semblance of its original *coiffure*. Alice then
escorted Marietta back along the multitudinous corridors she had traversed with Lady Cadbury and eventually ushered her into a breakfast parlor on the
ground story. Aunt Charlotte was alone at the table, a
cup of coffee at her left and a sheaf of papers at her
right.

"Good morning, my dear," she beamed. "I trust you
slept well?"

"Very well, thank you," Marietta responded politely.
She sat down, and a footman scurried forward to deliver a plate of pigeon pie, eggs, bacon, ham, and fresh,
warm bread.

"I fear that Christopher will not be coming after
all," Lady Cadbury said.

Marietta had never shared Aunt Charlotte's confidence that the Viscount would call "at the very crack

of dawn" or at any other time, but she could not suppress an irrational flicker of disappointment.

"He dispatched his butler so to advise me early this morning," Lady Cadbury continued. "Crawford stated that Christopher had an errand in Chelmsford and was then to attend a race meeting; Crawford was unclear as to exactly where the race is to be held. I have previously observed that the man is *exceedingly* forgetful."

"I . . ." Marietta had started to say that she well knew the reason for Crawford's chronic absentmindedness, but she recalled that she was not supposed to be acquainted with Christopher's tipsy butler. "I see," she murmured.

"I instructed Crawford to suggest to Christopher that we all attend church together tomorrow," Aunt Charlotte added. "I do hope he remembers to relay the message."

Marietta felt her cheeks color with embarrassment. How unfortunate, she reflected grimly, that after having been ordered to marry her, the Viscount must now be commanded to grant her an occasional moment of his time.

"Christopher's absence is probably for the best," Lady Cadbury said soothingly, as though she had again perceived Marietta's thoughts. "With the day free, you will be able to assist me with the invitations for the ball. I am just in the process of composing the list."

Aunt Charlotte indicated the stack of papers beside her. It appeared that she had already filled three pages, and as Marietta watched, she poised her pencil eagerly over a fourth. "It occurs to me, my dear, that since Suffolk is so very near at hand, your friends will be able to come as well. Naturally Ralph and I shall provide overnight accommodation—"

"No!" Marietta screeched. "That is to say, I do appreciate your thoughtfulness, Aunt Charlotte, but there is no one I care to include. Really; there is no one."

"I see." Lady Cadbury briefly frowned, then assumed her sunny smile again. "In that event, we shall invite only the immediate neighbors and a few of our own acquaintances from Suffolk and Kent and Hertfordshire, as well as those still in town for the Season . . ."

She rattled on, jotting notes upon the paper, and Marietta nervously gulped down her breakfast. She had not considered how she was to explain the abrupt modification of her plans to Agnes and Mr. Hewitt, far less to the Tappans and the Lawsons . . .

"Need I send a formal invitation to Roger?" Aunt Charlotte wondered aloud. "He will surely *assume* that he is invited."

A bit of egg slipped off Marietta's fork and dropped to the tablecloth. She hastily scooped up the offending morsel and dabbed at the spot with her napkin. "I am given to understand that Roger is abroad," she said as levelly as she could.

"Abroad?" Lady Cadbury sighed. "I do wish *Roger* would settle down as well. If only *he* could meet a girl such as yourself, my dear."

Marietta narrowly managed not to strangle on a sip of coffee.

Evidently Crawford had delivered Aunt Charlotte's message, for Christopher was waiting with Lord and Lady Cadbury when Marietta reached the foyer on Sunday morning. The four of them piled into the Marquis' splendid landau and trotted along the road to Chelmsford, Aunt Charlotte chattering that she *did* pray the lovely weather would hold for the ball and the wedding.

Marietta had rather dreaded her first public appearance as Christopher's fiancée, but as it happened, the church was nearly empty. There were but two other families in the private pews, and judging from the polite nods they exchanged with the Viscount and Lord and Lady Cadbury, Marietta collected that they were not especial friends of the Thornings. The only untoward event occurred after the service, when Christopher introduced her to the rector.

"Miss Chase." He was a large, graying man, and he

seized her hand warmly in both of his. "How delighted I am to meet you. I must own that I was quite astonished when Lord Sheridan called yesterday to advise me of your imminent wedding, but naturally I shall make the necessary arrangements."

Yesterday? Marietta thought. Why had the Viscount waited four full days after their betrothal to notify Mr. Archer of their plans? But she had long since abandoned any notion of comprehending Christopher's odd behavior, and she merely nodded and hurried back to the landau.

Aunt Charlotte insisted that the Viscount remain for Sunday luncheon, during which she happily reported that the ball invitations would be dispatched upon the morrow.

"I did wish to inquire, Christopher, dear, if you would like to ask any of your schoolmates. As I recollect, you met some *darling* boys at Winchester and Cambridge alike."

It struck Marietta that she had not previously been aware of his lordship's educational background, a dismal example of how little she knew her husband-to-be.

"No, thank you, Aunt," Christopher said quickly. "I fear I have largely lost contact with my old acquaintances; there is no one I care to include."

"Marietta said *precisely* the same thing about her friends in Suffolk." Lady Cadbury shook her head. "If I did not know better, I should be compelled to conclude that the two of you desire to keep your marriage some sort of *secret*. As it is, I can only regret the modern tendency to avoid close ties . . ."

Aunt Charlotte expounded on this theme through the rest of the meal, and as soon as the Viscount had finished his cheesecake, he begged to be excused, explaining that "guests" were shortly due at Twin Oaks.

"Your gaming confederates," Lady Cadbury sniffed. "Very well, Christopher, but I *hope* you will not continue to neglect dear Marietta. I shall plan for you to dine with us the balance of the week."

Aunt Charlotte flashed her bright smile, the Viscount bowed stiffly out, and Marietta, her face warm again, gazed at her plate.

"Do not care for it, my dear," Lady Cadbury whispered. "He is sowing the last of his wild oats, but he must be reminded of his new responsibilities. I am sorry to say that *complete* reformation may require some months."

By Monday, Marietta had exhausted her limited supply of walking dresses, and she was once more clad in the lavender gown when she reached the breakfast parlor. Lady Cadbury had evidently been sorting the invitations by destination, for some half-dozen stacks of envelopes were arrayed on the table before her. She glanced up as Marietta entered the room.

"That is a *charming* ensemble, dear," Aunt Charlotte said; "indeed, I intended to mention it on Friday. However, it does prompt me to inquire about the rest of your things."

"The rest of my things?" Marietta echoed. She sat down, and one of the ever-attentive footmen placed a heaping plate in front of her.

"Yes, the remainder of your clothes." Lady Cadbury studied several additional envelopes and plopped them atop the appropriate piles. "Did you dispatch them directly to Twin Oaks?"

"There *is* no remainder, Aunt Charlotte," Marietta replied wryly. "I have no other clothes."

"Well, that will not do at all," Lady Cadbury said. "Fortunately, there is an excellent mantua-maker in Chelmsford. I plan to visit Miss Bridger later in the day so as to order my own gown for the ball, and you shall accompany me. We shall have you properly fitted out in no time."

Marietta wondered just how much fitting-out could be accomplished with two pounds. Two pounds less a shilling, she amended, recalling the gap-toothed postboy. But Aunt Charlotte had returned to her envelopes, as though the matter were quite settled, and Marietta swallowed her objection. It would no doubt be best to go to the seamstress and simply decline to buy.

Marietta had had painfully scant experience of mantua-makers, but she judged Miss Bridger's establishment to be above the average; it was small but tastefully appointed with glittering chandeliers, delicate gilt chairs, and several fine cheval glasses. The modiste herself was a very tall, very thin woman of middle years, and a rather poor advertisement for her wares: she wore a plain black bombazine dress whose excessively long skirt threatened to trip her as she bounded forward to greet them.

"Lady Cadbury," she gushed. "It is always a pleasure to see you."

"Thank you, Miss Bridger. May I present Lord Sheridan's *fiancée*? This is Miss Chase, who, I daresay, will become one of your foremost customers."

"Lord Sheridan's *fiancée*?" Miss Bridger's mouth fell open. Her teeth were unusually large and, in combination with her other features, lent her a distinctly horsish aspect.

"I believe I so stated," Aunt Charlotte said briskly. "I shall be ordering only one gown, but Miss Chase will require a number of garments. Several carriage dresses, I fancy, half a dozen walking dresses, and as many evening gowns. If you could fetch your patterns, Miss Bridger . . ."

The mantua-maker fairly galloped away, increasing her resemblance to a bony mare, and Marietta turned to Lady Cadbury, her cheeks blazing wtih humiliation.

"I cannot order anything, Aunt Charlotte," she hissed. "I've under two pounds in all the world."

"I certainly did not suppose that *you* would pay," Lady Cadbury said. "We shall charge the order to Christopher; he can well afford it."

"Can he?" Marietta bit her lip. "As you yourself pointed out, he does have certain . . . er . . . debts—"

"Nonsense." Aunt Charlotte waved her hand dismissingly. "Christopher is extremely wealthy, and you must not permit him to persuade you otherwise, my dear. It is a common trick of men: to claim poverty when faced with an expense *they* did not contract. I assure you that Christopher can readily finance his little transgressions and a wife as well. And here is Miss Bridger with her lovely drawings . . ."

In the end, Marietta held the order to eight garments: a carriage dress, four walking dresses, and three evening gowns. After all the designs and fabrics had been determined, Miss Bridger produced a tape and measured the critical portions of Marietta's anatomy.

"You are considerably thinner than Lady Winship," the mantua-maker commented idly.

"Then I daresay Miss Chase and Lady Winship would not look at all well in the same garment," Aunt Charlotte snapped. "I trust you will ensure that neither of them is subjected to that particular embarrassment, Miss Bridger."

The seamstress insisted that she exercised *every* precaution in this regard, and Marietta blushed again. At last the ordeal was over, and after stops at the florist and the caterer, Marietta and Aunt Charlotte set out for Cadbury Hall. Marietta devoted the drive to a consideration of how she might explain her purchases to Christopher, but she reckoned without Lady Cadbury, who opened the dinner conversation with a detailed description of their trip to town.

"And so," Aunt Charlotte concluded, "Marietta commissioned eight *stunning* ensembles. I've no doubt she will make a great hit in the neighborhood—"

"*Eight?*" the Viscount interrupted. "Eight new gowns?"

"Had it been left to me, I should have ordered a dozen," Lady Charlotte said. "Marietta was *very* prudent."

"How comforting." His lordship looked across the table at Marietta, and his gray eyes narrowed. "I daresay I should count myself most fortunate then."

"Indeed you should."

Aunt Charlotte signaled for the entrée, and Marietta hastily attacked her roast beef.

The rest of the week flew by in a flurry of ball preparations and further shopping. On Tuesday, Lady Cadbury directed some half-dozen maids and footmen to polish "every single luster of every single chandelier" in Cadbury Hall's great ballroom, which occupied the entire ground floor of the far north wing. This awesome task required the full day, and on Wednesday Aunt Charlotte instructed the staff to clean the windows, draperies, and furniture and to wax the floor, though the latter was already sufficiently agleam that Marietta could see her reflection in the smooth, dark wood. Lady Cadbury supervised the operation throughout the morning, then declared that as things were proceeding *quite* well, she and Marietta could dare another journey to Chelmsford for final conferences with the florist, the caterer, and the orchestra. While they were in town, Aunt Charlotte escorted Marietta to the milliner, where, to the proprietress's delight, her ladyship insisted that Marietta purchase three *toques* and four bonnets.

It was late when they returned to Cadbury Hall, and Christopher arrived just as two footboys began bearing Marietta's parcels into the house.

"Has Miss Bridger completed your order then?" he asked, tossing his reins to a waiting groom.

"You have a great deal to learn," Aunt Charlotte laughed. "No, dear boy, those are hatboxes; Marietta has bought some *lovely* headdresses."

"*Hats?*" One of the footboys chose that precise moment to drop his share of the load, and several boxes tumbled down the front steps and scattered about the drive. "They are all *hats?*"

"Do not carp, Christopher," Lady Cadbury said sternly. "I am sure you wish dear Marietta to have a proper trousseau."

"So I do."

His tone was light, but his eyes had narrowed again. He did not seem exactly *angry*, Marietta reflected; in any other context, she would have defined his expression as one of suspicion. But there was no time to

puzzle it out; Christopher bent to retrieve one of the
boxes, and Aunt Charlotte beckoned them both
through the front door.

On Thursday, Miss Bridger's order *did* come, and
Marietta perceived at once that Chelmsford's resident
mantua-maker—her unfortunate appearance notwithstanding—was a modiste of considerable talent. Lady
Cadbury, watching from the bed as Alice unpacked the
boxes, somehow found a different adjective for each
emerging garment: the blue carriage dress was "elegant," the primrose walking ensemble "exquisite," the
apple-green evening gown "magnificent." When everything had been hung up, Aunt Charlotte proceeded to
the wardrobe, now quite stuffed, and studied its contents for a moment.

"The raspberry is my favorite," she announced,
"and you *must* wear it to the ball." She closed the
wardrobe doors. "I fancy you now have enough to see
you through the summer; we shall return to Miss
Bridger in a month or so and order your *winter*
wardrobe."

Marietta inwardly shuddered to contemplate the Viscount's opinion of this program, but one did not argue
with Lady Cadbury.

"Yes, Aunt Charlotte," she said obediently.

At the conclusion of dinner that evening, Lady Cadbury proclaimed that preparations for the assembly
were virtually complete and that they could all rest assured that it would be a "*splendid*" event. The Marquis
did not, of course, hear this assurance, and Christopher's reaction was to spread the remnants of his
blancmange about his plate.

"However, Christopher, dear," Aunt Charlotte
added, "there is one final matter to attend, one in
which you have been *sorely* remiss."

"What matter is that, Aunt?"

"Marietta's engagement ring. Your mother's ring."

"Mama's ring?" the Viscount said sharply.

"How *could* you have forgotten? I distinctly recollect
dear Margaret's statement, long before she died, that

her engagement and wedding rings were to proceed to your wife. I am certain you want Marietta to have the engagement ring before the ball, so, lest you *continue* to forget, allow me to propose that you bring it along tomorrow."

"It" was an enormous burst of rubies and sapphires and diamonds, and when Christopher laid it in her palm the following evening, Marietta suppressed a gasp. It was quite the loveliest thing she had ever beheld, but she could not but wish that the circumstances of its presentation had been somewhat different. She had long imagined her future husband slipping an engagement ring upon her finger, sealing their troth with a tender kiss . . .

"Well, put it on, dear," Lady Cadbury said impatiently.

Marietta's imaginings had *not* included the presence of a third party, but she managed a smile and pushed the ring onto the third finger of her left hand.

"It is a *perfect* fit," Aunt Charlotte sighed. "Margaret would be *so* pleased."

"I trust Marietta is pleased as well," the Viscount said. "Perhaps Mama's ring is just the thing she has always wanted."

His eyes were pale and cold and slitted with that same odd suspicion. Marietta clenched her hands, and the stones of the ring bit painfully into her adjacent fingers.

On the morning of the ball, Marietta was awakened by a rhythmic tattoo upon her windowpanes, and when she peered between the drapes, her horrid conjecture was confirmed: it was raining.

"But it can*not* rain," Aunt Charlotte insisted, as Marietta entered the breakfast parlor. "I have instructed the caterer to place the refreshments on the terrace, and everything will be *quite* ruined if they are moved inside. It *must* clear." She stamped one of her tiny feet and firmly drew the curtains.

Evidently the Almighty Himself was subject to Lady

Cadbury's iron will, for by noon the rain had stopped, by one the sky had begun to lighten, and by two the sun was fairly blazing down. Having been confined largely indoors for the better part of two weeks, Marietta seized the opportunity to stroll in the garden, nodding to a veritable army of gardeners engaged in last-minute pruning and weeding and raking. Within the hour, however, she spotted Aunt Charlotte waving to her from the terrace, and she reluctantly walked back to the house.

"You must wash your hair *at once,* dear," Lady Cadbury admonished, "so that it will have ample time to dry."

The ball was not scheduled to begin until nine, and six hours seemed rather more than "ample." But Marietta recognized the futility of protest, and she was soon luxuriating in the hot, fragrant tub which Alice brought to her bedchamber.

Alice returned at half-past six, stating that it was time for Marietta to dress: her ladyship desired Miss Chase to come to the ballroom *no later than* half-past eight.

"I believe Lady Cadbury said you wished to wear the raspberry gown, miss," Alice said, opening the wardrobe doors.

Actually Marietta preferred the apple-green, but she was not prepared to debate this point with Aunt Charlotte either. "Yes, that will be fine," she agreed.

The dress was not really raspberry, she decided, examining her reflection in the mirror above the dressing table; it was a paler, subtler hue, just a shade darker than deep pink. And it *was* a lovely gown—a net frock over a satin slip, cut daringly low in the front and trimmed in a deep flounce of blond lace. Alice gently pushed her into the dressing-table chair and began brushing her hair.

"I suppose you want it up, miss?" the maid asked, after she had rather painfully unsnarled the tangles.

Marietta recollected Christopher's comment and

shook her head. "No, I should prefer it left rather loose in the back."

Alice frowned with some disapproval, but she followed Marietta's directions and bound up only a part of the back hair, leaving a cascade of curls to tumble nearly to Marietta's shoulders. "It may do, miss," she said hesitantly when she had finished. "Let us just try the headdress . . ."

She went to the wardrobe and scampered back with the Kent *toque,* which was fashioned of a natural gauze precisely matching the lace trim of the dress. She set the *toque* on Marietta's head, fussed for a moment with her side curls, stood away, and smiled. "It does very well indeed," she declared. "If I may say so, miss, you look exceedingly handsome."

Marietta was compelled to own herself pleased as well. She had long since realized that she would never be a great beauty, but she thought she looked as well as ever she had; Christopher would have no reason to be ashamed of her. "Thank you, Alice," she murmured.

"If you are satisfied then, miss, I fear I must attend Lady Hockaday. Her abigail took ill on the journey from London; the poor girl has been retching and heaving from the moment of her arrival."

Marietta, who was feeling somewhat queasy herself, hastily nodded, and Alice hurried to the door. She was halfway into the corridor when she turned and snapped her fingers.

"I nearly forgot, miss; Lady Cadbury wanted to lend you these." She rushed back across the room, fumbling in the pocket of her skirt, and withdrew a velvet bag. "She believed they would complement the dress," Alice added, thrusting the pouch into Marietta's hands. "If you'll excuse me, then . . ."

She bounded out again, closing the door behind her. Marietta opened the bag and extracted a glittering amethyst-and-diamond necklace and matching earrings. A smile tickled the corners of her mouth even as a lump swelled in her throat. Aunt Charlotte's heart was surely made of gold, but she was determined to have her way. Thank *God* Marietta had not chosen the green gown.

The clock on the mantel read twenty-seven minutes past eight. Marietta put on the jewelry, donned her gloves, stood, studied her mirrored image one final time. No, she could do no better. She stepped into the hall, made her way along the now-familiar maze of corridors, and paused at the top of the steps. Her stomach was positively churning, but she had already diagnosed her "illness": she was suffering an attack of sheer terror. Once she entered the ballroom, there would be no turning back, no chance for reconsideration.

But there never had been. Marietta squared her shoulders, grasped the banister, and proceeded down the long marble staircase.

6

CHRISTOPHER WAS ALONE in the ballroom, gazing through the open terrace doors. The scene beyond appeared to be one of chaos: some half-dozen men scurried about, bearing great platters and chafing dishes, while an invisible Lady Cadbury issued shrill instructions.

"Not *there*, Mr. Mead; I wish the oysters immediately next to the lobster patties." A pause. "Well, you will simply have to *make* them fit: it is not *my* fault that you elected to use such extremely large platters."

Marietta looked back at Christopher, observing that his evening attire served to emphasize the differences between his physique and Roger's. The Viscount's knee breeches and wasp-waisted coat made him appear even taller and leaner than he was, and the calves beneath his white silk hose were slender and finely shaped, totally unlike Roger's rather stocky legs. She started across the room, and Christopher turned and walked to meet her.

"You are here then," he remarked, his gray eyes flickering down upon her.

"Of course I am here," Marietta retorted. "Where did you suppose I should be?"

"Never mind; it doesn't signify."

The raw state of Marietta's nerves had evidently sharpened her perceptions, for she suddenly understood his peculiar suspicion. "It *does* signify," she snapped. "You have behaved throughout the week as though you somehow expected me to . . . to escape. To abscond with my gowns and my hats and your mother's ring. Obviously I did not, nor did I steal away and sell the ring in secret. It is here under my glove, which I shall be happy to remove if you care to check—"

"*Please,* Marietta," the Viscount hissed. He glanced over his shoulder at the terrace, where Aunt Charlotte could be heard upbraiding Mr. Mead about the curried crab. "I spoke very thoughtlessly, and I apologize."

Marietta detected a disturbance overhead and, from the corner of her eye, saw the orchestra striding into the gallery. It was no time to quarrel. Christopher had probably encountered numerous fortune hunters in the past and had found it difficult to dismantle his defenses.

"Very well," she muttered.

"May I say that you look quite lovely this evening?"

She could not determine whether his compliment was sincere or in the way of a sop, for at that moment Lady Cadbury marched through the terrace doors and across the ballroom.

"I have entirely lost patience with Mr. Mead," Aunt Charlotte announced. "He invariably attempts to increase his profit through the use of *giant* serving dishes which require only the occasional replenishment.

They are fairly *crammed* upon the table, and the oysters have already spilled over twice. I shall never employ Mr. Mead again; regardless of the expense, I shall deal with a London caterer."

"I believe you so stated on the occasion of your Christmas assembly," the Viscount said dryly.

"This time I shall *not* relent." Lady Cadbury peered past Marietta and clapped her hands with vexation. "*Where* are we to locate the receiving line?" she demanded rhetorically. "I *distinctly* told Mr. Pierce to leave the left-hand side of the entry free, but he has placed palms on *both* sides. Apparently I shall be compelled to rely on a city florist as well . . ."

Aunt Charlotte eventually decreed that they would form the line in front of the intrusive palms; she herself would take the head position and would be followed, respectively, by Christopher, Marietta, and Lord Cadbury. The latter, somewhat flushed with his pre-ball portion of brandy, arrived just as Aunt Charlotte pronounced her final decision, and they were all in place when the orchestra began to tune up and the first guests entered the ballroom.

Despite her nervousness, Marietta experienced only three distressing moments during the ensuing hour. The first occurred when she recognized "Sutton," one of Christopher's gaming cronies. As it turned out, he was actually Major Sutton, a veteran of the recent war, and when he bowed over Marietta's hand, she could not but recall the many times she had spied upon him from the window of her bedchamber at Twin Oaks. She fully expected the Major to drop her hand, level an accusing finger, and roar out the truth about Miss Chase's shocking conduct. However, Major Sutton merely murmured his "best wishes," a sentiment echoed by his pale, homely wife, and joined the growing crowd in the ballroom.

Marietta's encounter with Major Sutton bolstered her confidence sufficiently that when Sir Hugh appeared, some five minutes later, she was able to greet him with considerable aplomb. She was utterly taken aback when he stepped away and raised his quizzing glass.

"But have we not met before, Miss Chase? You look exceedingly familiar."

Marietta belatedly recalled Sir Hugh's position at the table on the day of her arrival: aside from Christopher, he was the only one of the players who might have glimpsed her.

"Perhaps you saw Marietta in London," the Viscount interjected smoothly. "You were in town for the Season, were you not, Sir Hugh?"

"For a short time." Sir Hugh was now squinting through his glass.

"That explains it then," Christopher said firmly.

"I fancy so." Sir Hugh did not seem altogether convinced, but additional guests had gathered in an impatient knot behind him, and he was forced to move along.

The ormolu clock in the anteroom had just begun to strike ten when the final incident occurred. The stream of arrivals had steadily dwindled over the past quarter-hour and now appeared to have ceased entirely, a circumstance which prompted Lord Cadbury to slip to the terrace for a fortifying glass of champagne. Marietta glanced at Aunt Charlotte, hoping her ladyship would permit them to disband, and at that moment a woman swept through the entry and seized Lady Cadbury's hand.

"Charlotte!" Her voice sounded quite piercing, but Marietta fancied that was because the guests nearest the door had fallen silent. "And there is Christopher, in all his devious splendor. How *dare* you perpetrate such a surprise, you shameless man!"

Lady Winship (for Marietta had no doubt that it was she) grasped the Viscount's arm with her free hand and drew him toward herself and Aunt Charlotte. The cozy semicircle thus formed neatly excluded Marietta, which, she suspected, had been precisely Lady Winship's intention. Her ladyship continued to chatter, her dark eyes darting from Aunt Charlotte to Christopher, and the nearby guests, evidently despairing of a dramatic Scene, resumed their own conversations.

Elinor Winship's hair was dark as well, Marietta observed; nearly as dark as the Viscount's. Marietta had inferred from Miss Bridger's comment that her ladyship was a trifle plump, but she was now compelled to own that "voluptuous" was a far more accurate word. Though Lady Winship was almost exactly Marietta's height, she outweighted her by at least a stone, every ounce of which was most advantageously located. And displayed, Marietta further noted. She had counted her own gown daring, but Lady Winship's ample bosom threatened literally to burst from the tight bodice of her dress. And her skirt clung so closely to her shapely hips and thighs that Marietta could not but suspect it had been dampened.

"Marietta?"

Christopher cleared his throat, and Marietta realized that they were all looking expectantly at her. Lady Winship did not await an introduction; she dropped Aunt Charlotte's hand, Christopher's arm, and bounded forward.

"Miss Chase!" she said warmly. "Since the very instant I received dear Charlotte's invitation, I have been quite beside myself in my eagerness to meet you." So much so that she had lingered in the entry for upwards of five minutes, Marietta thought dryly. "Be that as it may, I am sure you are anxious to join the festivities, so I shan't delay you any longer. I *do* hope we can talk later." She inclined her head, bare except for a string of pearls twined artfully amongst the dark tendrils, and stepped on into the ballroom.

"Well," Lady Cadbury said, "as Elinor is always the last to arrive, I daresay we *can* safely join the festivities. I instructed Mr. Taylor to postpone the first waltz until the two of you could lead it out, and if I can but catch his eye . . ."

Aunt Charlotte walked past them and waved discreetly through the potted palms on the right-hand side of the entry. The orchestra ended the current quadrille, then played a flourish which rang, in Marietta's ears, like the strains of the last trumpet. She was fairly feverish with embarrassment, but Lady Cadbury was beckoning them frantically forward, and Marietta allowed Christopher to take her elbow and escort her onto the floor. Fortunately, they had executed only a few bars when the rest of the dancers took up the rhythm and began to whirl around them. Nevertheless . . .

"Everyone is watching us," Marietta whispered.

"Indeed they are," the Viscount whispered back. "Consequently, I shall attempt to display a suitably lovelorn countenance."

He smiled brilliantly down at her, and Marietta felt a tremor in the vicinity of her rib cage. He would shortly initiate her into the physical mysteries of marriage, and it was a prospect she regarded with a curious blend of anticipation and apprehension, excitement and terror.

"You must return the favor, my sweet," Christopher said through his teeth.

"Yes, of course." Marietta smiled as well, but her mouth was quivering at the edges. She had nearly forgotten that his attention was an act, that their union was to be one of sheer convenience.

"You have behaved extremely well this evening," the Viscount said abruptly.

His words conveyed the unmistakable implication that he had somehow expected her to *mis*behave, and Marietta started to bristle. However, she spotted Lady Winship at the perimeter of the ballroom, assessing their every step, and she widened her shaky smile instead.

"Thank you," she murmured.

"And you *do* look lovely." His gray eyes narrowed appraisingly. "I particularly like your hair."

"Yes, you mentioned that before. I chose this style because I knew you preferred it."

"Did you?" He seemed uncharacteristically pleased, and Marietta wanted to believe that he drew her a bit closer, though that might have been a flight of wishful thinking.

Marietta stood up for the following sets with a variety of partners, all of whom expressed (though in somewhat subtler terms than had Lady Winship) the considerable surprise occasioned by Lord Sheridan's precipitate decision to wed.

"Though, having met you, Miss Chase, I *quite* comprehend his enthusiasm," Major Sutton added gallantly.

When her boulanger with Major Sutton had ended, Marietta looked about for Christopher but, to her dismay, encountered Sir Hugh's quizzing glass instead. The floor had become so crowded that a rapid escape was impossible, and Marietta could only watch with resignation as Sir Hugh hurried toward her and requested the honor of a dance. As she had feared, he at once renewed the subject of their previous acquaintance.

"I daresay Sheridan is correct," Sir Hugh said dubiously. "I must have glimpsed you in London."

"You must have," Marietta agreed. "I understand that you live nearby, Sir Hugh—"

"Though I am puzzling as to precisely where," he continued doggedly. "I was in town but a few days; my wife fell ill—"

"Oh, I am sorry," Marietta cooed. "I do trust she has recovered?"

"Quite so. Perhaps it was at Lady Weatherley's assembly."

As it happened, Marietta well recollected that she had *not* attended the Countess of Weatherley's rout: Agnes had been highly incensed by their failure to receive an invitation. But she was desperate to put an end to Sir Hugh's inquiries.

"Perhaps so," she dissembled. "I am sure you understand, Sir Hugh, that after three *busy* weeks in London, I find it difficult to recall just where I went and whom I encountered."

"Of course." Sir Hugh bobbed his gray head and smiled down at her paternally. "Under the circumstances, however, you no doubt remember Roger Thorning."

Marietta missed a step, but Sir Hugh, a sorely unaccomplished dancer, did not seem to notice. His remark had jolted her to consideration of a horrible factor she had somehow overlooked: sooner or later, Roger would reappear. He might stay away for months, years, but eventually—thinking her long gone and long forgotten—he would return to Essex. And he would have no reason to pretend that they were strangers.

"I fancy I *did* meet Mr. Thorning," she said as casually as she could. "But let us talk of you, Sir Hugh: you have not yet told me the precise location of your estate . . ."

Sir Mark claimed Marietta for the next set. It was a decision, she thought, which he must soon and bitterly have regretted, for—unnerved as she was by the specter of Roger—she trod on his feet three times within the first fifteen seconds.

"You seem a bit . . . tired, Miss Chase," he said at last. She had just kicked him in the ankle, and he was valiantly suppressing a grimace of pain. "Might I propose a glass of champagne?"

Marietta nodded gratefully, and he guided her through the throng on the dance floor and outside to the terrace. The refreshment tables were quite besieged, but Sir Mark seated Marietta on one of the stone benches at the edge of the terrace, bowed away, and, miraculously, elbowed his way back within five minutes, bearing two glasses. He passed one to her, then sat beside her, and Marietta drained half the wine with indelicate speed.

"Do you feel better now?" Sir Mark asked.

To the contrary, the champagne had rendered Marietta distinctly dizzy, reminding her that she had eaten nothing since breakfast. She started to reply with a bright lie, to say that she felt much better indeed. But

Sir Mark was regarding her sympathetically, and she recalled that he was the only person in all the world in whom she could confide.

"The fact is, Sir Mark, that I was not tired, not in the physical sense. Sir Hugh brought to my mind a most oversetting circumstance . . ."

The wine had loosened her tongue sufficiently that she was able to speak with little hesitation, and she poured out her intense alarm at the prospect of Roger's inevitable return. When she had finished, Sir Mark sipped thoughtfully at his own champagne.

"I must pose a potentially painful inquiry, Miss Chase," he said at length. "Are you in love with Roger?"

Marietta searched his face for any hint of a devious motive, but there was none. "No, I am not."

She thought he drew a deep breath, as though of relief, but she could not be certain. "Then it would seem to me that Roger's return is a matter of no consequence at all. I suggest you look ahead: forget entirely about Roger and your unfortunate relationship."

"But—" Marietta wanted to ask if Christopher could so readily forget the past, but she was interrupted by Aunt Charlotte's commanding tones.

"There you are, dear!" Lady Cadbury materialized before them in a cloud of scent and silk. "You cannot monopolize Marietta, Sir Mark," she scolded; "there are others waiting to speak with her. Come, dear; I *particularly* wanted you to exchange a few words with Lady Weatherley, who has just arrived."

"Lady Weatherley?" Marietta entertained a grim vision of the Countess and Sir Hugh discussing the guest list of her ladyship's recent assembly. She hastily rose and, with an apologetic nod at Sir Mark, trailed Aunt Charlotte back into the ballroom.

As it turned out, Marietta had nothing to fear: Lady Weatherley claimed that the "enchanting" Miss Chase had definitely been "the hit" of her rout. "And do extend my best wishes to your dear father," she concluded. Marietta smiled and sent a silent message to Sir Henry, wherever he might be.

Following her conversation with Lady Weatherley, Marietta was compelled to stand up with Colonel Mortimer Thorning, a distant Hertfordshire cousin. The Colonel regaled her with tales of his war exploits, though insofar as Marietta could determine, he had mapped the proceedings from the safety of a London office. When the interminable set was over and Cousin Mortimer (as he had insisted Marietta should address him) showed no inclination to release her, Marietta pleaded fatigue and hurried to the ladies' withdrawing room. She was, in truth, tired by now, and she sagged against the door, thankful to be momentarily free of scrutiny.

"And did you observe her hair?" The voice issuing from beyond the door was unmistakably that of Lady Winship. "Spilling all about her neck." A loud sniff. "Someone should advise her that that style fell from favor twenty years since."

There was an indecipherable murmur of response, and then the doorknob jammed into Marietta's back. She leaped away but not in time: Mrs. Sutton literally stumbled over her feet.

"Miss Chase!" she squealed. Marietta fancied she paled; in view of her already waxen countenance, it was difficult to tell. "Oh, dear." Mrs. Sutton hiked her skirt nearly to her knees and fled down the corridor toward the ballroom.

"Miss Chase," Lady Winship echoed. Her dark eyes met Marietta's in the mirror above the long dressing table. "As you no doubt overheard, Mrs. Sutton was just discussing you."

Lady Winship tugged at one of her perfect side curls, and Marietta wished she possessed but a tenth of her ladyship's brash composure. To say nothing of her generous curves.

"But I daresay you were prepared for a good bit of gossip," Lady Winship continued. "You must have been aware that Christopher's engagement would generate a considerable furor."

Marietta distantly realized that every second she hovered in the doorway, shuffling her feet upon the China carpet, was a second of surrender. She was assuming the role in which Lady Winship so cleverly sought to cast her—that of an intruder. She closed the door and marched across the withdrawing room, took the chair next to Lady Winship and pretended to adjust her own hair.

Lady Winship extracted a tiny bottle from her reticule and dabbed a drop of perfume behind either ear. "One of the *on-dits* you will certainly hear—perhaps have heard already—is that Christopher has sparked me quite assiduously since the death of my husband." This was rather different from the story Aunt Charlotte had related, but Marietta elected to let it pass. "I should like to assure you that I bear you no ill will, for I could *never* have married him. Indeed, I wish you the very best of luck, Miss Chase; you will need it."

She was obviously supposed to ask why, Marietta thought, but she would not tumble into her ladyship's trap. "Thank you, Lady Winship," she said smoothly. She deliberately drew one of her back curls to its maximum length.

"As I say, you will require a great deal of luck." To Marietta's perverse delight, her ladyship's tone had turned distinctly peevish. "Perhaps you do not know, Miss Chase, that Christopher's reputation is that of an incorrigible rake."

"So I understand." Marietta released her curl, and it sprang back into place.

"And you choose not to believe it?"

"I choose to believe that no one is *'incorrigible,'* Lady Winship. I fancy Christopher and I shall get on quite well."

"Evidently you do not share my other concern either then." Lady Winship closed her reticule and began to put on her gloves. "My dear husband was well into middle age at the time we wed."

Marietta did not see what possible bearing the late Sir Horace had upon the matter at hand, but she nodded.

"He was, in short, a man of limited physical appetite. Totally *unlike* Christopher. I do hope you will be able to satisfy him, Miss Chase."

Lady Winship rose, flashed a chilly smile, and sailed out of the withdrawing room, leaving Marietta to stare at her own reflection. She could not determine whether Lady Winship was personally familiar with Christopher's "physical appetite" or had merely attempted to embarrass her. If the latter, her ladyship had quite succeeded: Marietta's cheeks were a brilliant shade of scarlet. She fussed with her *toque* and her jewelry until the furious blush had faded, then picked up her reticule and sped back to the ballroom.

The orchestra was on intermission, and the room relatively empty; apparently most of the guests had retired to the terrace to partake of Mr. Mead's refreshments. Marietta glanced around and spotted Christopher but a few yards away, engaged in conversation with some half-dozen other men. She felt her face start to color again, and she stepped to a corner of the entry, a position from which she could observe without being seen. The ormolu clock behind her began to chime, and Marietta counted the strokes: nine, ten, eleven, twelve.

"Midnight," Cousin Mortimer announced jovially. "You've but one full day of freedom left, old chap."

"So I have."

The Viscount smiled, but his eyes were those of a man condemned, a felon doomed to mount the gallows in six-and-thirty hours and await the fatal fall of the noose about his neck.

7

WHEN MARIETTA WOKE on Monday morning, she leaped out of bed, hurried to the window, and drew the heavy drapes. To her relief, the sky was blue and utterly cloudless, and she pushed the window open and leaned outside. The air was cool, and she surmised that by afternoon it would be balmy, not unpleasantly hot. It was, in short, a perfect day. Her wedding day.

Marietta shivered a bit and, attempting to attribute her reaction to the morning chill, hastily closed the window. She went to the wardrobe and donned her dressing gown, but its thin fabric in no way warmed her. Nor could it have, she admitted, for her icy hands and feet, the gooseflesh upon her arms, had nothing to do with the weather. She had been unable to forget Christopher's bleak expression, and she could not quite persuade herself that his feelings were normal, the classic reluctance of a bachelor facing the imminent responsibilities of marriage. She shook her head and tugged the bell rope rather more sharply than she had intended.

To Marietta's surprise, it was Lady Cadbury who answered her ring, bearing a silver tray, which she deposited awkwardly on the dressing table.

"It was a tradition in our family," Aunt Charlotte explained, turning to smile at Marietta. "For centuries, or so I was told, the mother of the bride delivered the bride's breakfast on the morning of the wedding. And as you've no mother to be with you, dear . . ." Her eyes were suspiciously bright, and Marietta felt the swelling of a lump in her own throat.

"Sit down now," Lady Cadbury commanded gruffly. "I am sure you are far too nervous to eat, but you must *try*. A bite or two is all I ask."

Marietta obediently took the chair in front of the dressing table. The mere sight of the eggs and the kidney rendered her faintly nauseous, but she thought there was hope for the toast and bacon. As she began to nibble at a rasher of the latter, Aunt Charlotte paced about the room, flicking imaginary specks of lint from the upholstery and painstakingly rearranging the pitcher and basin on the washstand.

"Speaking of mothers, dear . . ." Lady Cadbury cleared her throat. "One purpose of the family tradition was that it permitted the mother to instruct the bride in . . . ahem . . . the ways of the world. My mother described the subject as that of 'wifely duties.' "

Marietta choked on a small morsel of toast.

"You must not let it overset you, dear," Aunt Charlotte said firmly. "Though it may initially prove a shock—"

"There is no need for instruction, Aunt Charlotte," Marietta wheezed. The toast had lodged in her chest, and her complexion had turned quite purple. "I am well aware of what is expected of me."

"Excellent." Lady Cadbury's own cheeks were a trifle pink, but she managed one of her brilliant smiles. "We can immediately proceed to the matter of your attire then, after which I shall summon Alice to help you dress and pack."

On this occasion, Marietta and Aunt Charlotte agreed upon an appropriate gown: a petticoat of white jaconet, trimmed with narrow welts at the bottom; a matching open robe, edged with lacy scallops; and, surmounting the whole, a spencer of pale blue. The decision made, Lady Cadbury rang for Alice, who fetched Marietta's bath, assisted her into the chosen ensemble, and dressed her hair in the fashion Lady Winship had so lamented.

When Marietta's toilette was complete, Aunt Charlotte returned to supervise the packing. Her ladyship insisted that every garment be folded and refolded, placed and replaced in the trunk so as to avoid the slightest unnecessary crease. As a result, the task required above an hour, but at last it was finished, and only the velvet jewel pouch remained upon the dressing table.

"Your necklace and earrings," Marietta said, extending the bag to Aunt Charlotte. "And I do thank you for allowing me to wear them."

"I wish you to keep them, dear. Regard them as a wedding gift."

Marietta wanted to protest, but her throat had closed again. She nodded and tucked the pouch in her trunk, and Alice secured the lid.

"I fancy it would be best to send your bags along to Twin Oaks," Lady Cadbury said. "Your abigail can unpack them yet this afternoon, and everything will be in readiness when you arrive."

Marietta could hardly bear the thought of April tearing through her clothes, but upon consideration she judged it unlikely that April would unfasten the first clasp. "Yes, Aunt Charlotte," she murmured.

"I shall see to it then." Lady Cadbury marched to the door. "Now put on your hat, dear, and come down at once; we ourselves must be under way."

Mr. Archer's house was just beside the church, and the street which fronted them was deserted. Marietta immediately concluded that the Viscount had decided to cry off after all, and she hoped he had been kind enough to dispatch a message to the rector. If not, they would be compelled to wait for endless hours while Aunt Charlotte sent to Twin Oaks and word came back that Lord Sheridan had joined his brother abroad. Oh, the humiliation of it: to be jilted twice, and once nearly within sight of the altar . . . There was a clatter of hooves behind her, and Marietta whirled around just as Sir Mark brought his curricle to a halt.

Whether by design or no, Christopher and Sir Mark were identically dressed in black pantaloons and frock coats and waistcoats of solid white. Had their gloves been black rather than white, Marietta might well have collected that they had come to town to attend a funeral.

"Good afternoon," Sir Mark and the Viscount said simultaneously.

"Good afternoon." Marietta and Aunt Charlotte responded in unison as well.

"Good afternoon!" Lord Cadbury boomed. He had apparently failed to hear the previous exchange.

They stood in the street for a moment, but as no one could seem to think of anything further to say, they trooped up the walk to the rectory door.

Inside, all was in readiness: Marietta was touched to observe that Mrs. Archer had placed great urns of flowers on either side of the fireplace, where, evidently, the ceremony was to take place. The rector's wife asked if they might like a cup of tea before the vows were said, but Christopher replied that he would prefer to "get on with it." Marietta wished he had expressed himself in somewhat gentler fashion.

At any rate, Mr. Archer assumed a position directly in front of the hearth, Mrs. Archer arranged the rest of them in a facing semicircle, and the wedding rite began. The first of several unsettling moments occurred almost at once, when the rector inquired whether anyone present knew a reason why the man and woman before him could not be joined in marriage. Christopher had not yet taken Marietta's hand, but she felt him stiffen, and then, to her dismay, the Viscount actually started to turn his head, as though he feared (or hoped) that an objector would bound through the door of Mr. Archer's modest drawing room. The rector coughed, Christopher looked ahead again, and Mr. Archer hurried on.

Shortly thereafter, the rector asked who gave "this woman" in marriage. Lord Cadbury had been assigned that duty, but the Marquis, quite unable to follow the proceedings, was gazing out the nearest window.

"Lord Cadbury!" Mr. Archer hissed.

"Eh?" The Marquis jumped to attention, and Marietta's hand almost slipped off his arm.

"Who giveth . . . ?" The rector carefully repeated the question.

"Eh?"

Lord Cadbury frowned, and Aunt Charlotte nudged him in the ribs. *I do,* she mouthed frantically; *I do.*

"I do!" the Marquis roared.

Mr. Archer jumped as well, nearly dropping his prayer book, and Mrs. Archer led Lord Cadbury to a nearby chair.

The final incident was, by comparison, rather minor: Marietta had neglected to remove her gloves, and her wedding ring would not fit over the fabric. The Viscount pushed and shoved until she was hard put to maintain her balance, but he eventually gave up. Marietta gazed down at the ring—a circlet of gems matching those in her engagement ring—and, perhaps because of the odd way it was perched above her knuckle, found it difficult to believe that she was truly married.

But she was; they were. The rector intoned the closing words, then offered his best wishes, and Mrs. Archer insisted that the wedding party accept a cup of tea to celebrate the happy event. She seated them in the dining room, where Aunt Charlotte at once began to relive the "*lovely*" ceremony. Sir Mark did not appear entirely to share her ladyship's enthusiasm, but he smiled and nodded at the appropriate points in her discourse. The Marquis, for his part, glowered into his tea, no doubt wishing it were a snifter of brandy instead. Marietta stole a glance at Christopher and thought he seemed rather dazed. Perhaps he, too, could scarcely conceive that a few minutes, a few words, had bound them irrevocably together.

"Ah." Mrs. Archer poured her own tea and sat down. "Since you are now a member of the parish, Lady Sheridan, I do hope I shall be able to interest you in some of our charitable activities."

Marietta waited for Lady Sheridan to respond, then

realized that the rector's wife was looking directly at her. She had quite forgotten that *she* was Lady Sheridan.

"I am sure you will," she murmured. She picked up her cup, but her hands had begun to tremble, and she sloshed a good bit of tea over the side. She hastily replaced her cup in the saucer and moved the latter to cover the brown pool on the tablecloth.

The clock in the church tower was striking five when they emerged from Mr. Archer's house and started down the walk to their carriages. Aunt Charlotte announced that she had planned a "little supper" for the newlyweds, one she hoped Sir Mark would be able to attend as well. But the baronet murmured his regrets, claiming a prior engagement; Marietta suspected he had enjoyed Lady Cadbury's company sufficiently for one day. In any event, Sir Mark clambered into his curricle and galloped off, and the rest of them piled into the Marquis' landau.

"Everything proceeded *perfectly*," Aunt Charlotte declared as they rounded the first corner and the rectory disappeared from view. "I do not recollect a *single* hitch." Marietta hoped she might eventually be able to cultivate Lady Cadbury's splendid, selective memory. "Naturally I wish you had elected to be wed in church, but under the circumstances it was a *beautiful* service. Do you not concur, Christopher?"

"I do indeed, Aunt," the Viscount said politely. He was twisting his beaver hat round and round in his fingers, and Marietta feared the brim would be rubbed quite bare by the time they reached Cadbury Hall.

But the hat was still intact when Christopher handed it to Hawkins, the forbidding butler, who unbent to the astonishing extent of mumbling his congratulations to Lord and Lady Sheridan. Uncle Ralph at once guided the Viscount in the direction of the Green Saloon.

"We shall have a spot of brandy," Lord Cadbury trumpeted. "One can hardly conduct a proper celebration with *tea*. And I have a small gift for you, my boy . . ."

They continued along the corridor, and Aunt Charlotte fondly shook her head. "Ralph is teasing," she whispered. "He intends to present Christopher a very substantial check. Not that Christopher *needs* it, of course, but I fancy Ralph views it as something of a reward."

A reward for execution of an exceedingly distasteful task. Marietta bit her lip, but fortunately Lady Cadbury did not appear to notice.

"Go freshen up now, dear, for I shall direct supper to be served immediately. I know you are *most* eager to journey on to Twin Oaks."

In fact, Aunt Charlotte's "little supper" required nearly three hours, and Marietta soon perceived that the Viscount was deliberately delaying their departure. He dawdled at excruciating length over each course; indeed, at one juncture Lady Cadbury snapped that if he continued to "toy with" his turbot, the filet of veal would be "altogether frigid." His food at last consumed, Christopher accepted two successive glasses of port, each of which he swallowed drop by tiny drop. He was at the point of permitting the Marquis to fill his glass a third time when Aunt Charlotte intervened.

"You really must go, Christopher," she said firmly. "You may have forgotten that you are to borrow one of our carriages. I instructed Henderson to be ready at eight, and it is now approaching half-past nine."

Was it truly so late? the Viscount marveled. He had quite lost track of the time. Lord and Lady Cadbury ushered them out of the dining room, through the foyer, and into the drive, where two footmen assisted them into the landau.

"We shall not intrude upon you, dears," Aunt Charlotte called as Henderson clucked the horses to a start. "We shall respect your privacy absolutely, so do advise us when you are prepared for guests."

Marietta's cheeks grew extremely warm, and from the seat beside her Christopher emitted a small, strangled cough.

They trotted down the drive and into the road.

Marietta's hands had become hot and damp as well, and she stripped off her gloves and began to fumble with her rings. She had told Lady Cadbury that she was well aware of her "wifely duties," and in a technical sense she had stated the truth. However, she had been given to understand that the experience could range from rather pleasant to utterly horrifying, and the Viscount's obvious reluctance was scarcely calculated to bolster her confidence. Though the night was cool, she felt beads of perspiration forming on her brow, and having forgotten to bring a handkerchief, she indelicately mopped her face with one of her gloves.

There was, of course, no one at Twin Oaks to greet them. Christopher alighted from the carriage and stepped round to Marietta's side of the vehicle just as Henderson opened her door. Each of them extended a helping hand, then elected to defer to the other, as a result of which Marietta tripped on the step and tumbled toward the drive. Christopher caught her at the last instant, fairly wrenching her arm from its socket, muttered a "Good evening" to Henderson, and propelled Marietta up the front stairs and into the entry hall.

Marietta was initially surprised to find the foyer looking precisely as it had upon the day of her arrival at Twin Oaks; she then recalled that despite all that had transpired in the interim, she had traveled down from Suffolk only two weeks since. The Viscount tossed his hat on the bow-fronted commode and flashed a rather weak smile.

"I believe I shall retire to the library for a glass of brandy," he said. "Would you care to join me?"

"I fancy we have had quite enough to drink," she replied.

"Which is to say that *I* have had quite enough to drink. Spoken like a true wife, and you've had but a few hours' practice."

"I am sorry, Christopher; I did not mean . . ."

But he had already stalked to the library door, and

Marietta realized that if their marriage was not to begin with a quarrel, she must follow. She reached the door just as the Viscount opened it, and three enormous hunting dogs bounded forward, barking and yelping a canine welcome.

"Down, Juno; down, Merlin," he instructed. "Resume your places."

Juno, Merlin, and their unidentified companion loped back across the room and jumped on the threadbare couch in front of the hearth. Christopher proceeded to a mahogany cabinet near the window and withdrew the stopper from a crystal decanter.

"You wish nothing?" he asked.

"No, thank you."

The Viscount nodded and, it appeared, added Marietta's unwanted portion of brandy to his own. Reluctant to suggest the slightest degree of criticism, Marietta averted her eyes and gazed about the library. In sharp contrast to the disreputable sofa, the tattered chair, and the faded carpet, the shelves were quite jammed with expensive leather-bound books. So jammed indeed that Marietta wondered how his lordship could possibly locate a particular volume: many of the books were situated upside down or back to front, and numerous volumes were strewn haphazardly atop those standing upright on the shelves.

Marietta glanced idly up and beheld two portraits above the mantel, clearly those of the first Viscount and Lady Sheridan. How odd that their sons resembled them individually rather than collectively, she mused. Christopher was the very image of his father, a dark-haired man whose painted eyes looked quite silver in the lamplight. Roger, on the other hand, much favored Lady Sheridan, a pretty, snub-nosed woman with gleaming chestnut hair and hazel eyes.

"Papa and Mama," Christopher said. "They were killed fifteen years ago."

Roger had told Marietta this story as well, but she did not feel it a propitious moment to mention her knowledge. "I am sorry," she murmured.

"Yes, it was a tragedy, though I daresay they died under the best of circumstances. They were en route to a house party in Hampshire, and the night before they were due to arrive, the inn at which they had stopped caught fire. They were overcome by smoke, I'm told; it was all very painless. They died together and at a time of happy anticipation; I fancy it happened exactly as they would have willed it." He took a long sip of his brandy.

"It must have been very difficult for you though," Marietta said.

"I often assure myself of that," Christopher agreed ruefully, "for I fear I reacted in exceedingly childish fashion. I was only twenty at the time, of course, but my youth does not entirely excuse my behavior. I closed the house, went up to London, and roistered about for the better part of a year. Perhaps I learned a difficult lesson: I have scarcely been able to bear the city from that day to this."

Marietta could not suppress the thought that the Viscount's dislike of London had impelled him to go "roistering about" the countryside instead. But for the first time in their acquaintance, he seemed open, vulnerable, and she merely nodded.

"I returned to Twin Oaks," Christopher continued, "but it was never the same. I have formulated excuses for that as well: I remind myself that the staff had dispersed and the war made it difficult to find replacements. The truth is, however, that since Mama and Papa died, I have not regarded Twin Oaks as home. It is a place to live; it is not a home."

The Viscount drained his snifter and unstopped the decanter again. Little as she knew him, Marietta had observed that he did not normally drink to excess, and it suddenly occurred to her that he might be quite as nervous as she. Despite his sophistication, his experience, it was his first wedding night no less than hers.

"Would you prefer something other than brandy?" he asked, filling his own glass back to the rim. "I have

an excellent port, a respectable sherry, a Tokay I myself have not tasted . . ."

He went on enumerating the various alcoholic offerings within his cabinet, and Marietta impulsively decided to seize the initiative.

"I really want nothing." She interrupted his description of an especially savory claret. "I should like to
dress for bed. I should therefore appreciate it if you
would direct me to the . . . er . . . appropriate chamber." It sounded terribly stiff, but this was possibly due
to the fact that her lips had gone quite numb.

"Bed." Christopher capped the decanter with a resounding clang.

"Yes; I am tired. That is to say, I—"

"You needn't explain, Marietta; in light of our very
brief acquaintance, I can well conceive your distress.
Indeed, I have given the matter considerable thought,
and I wish to assure you that I shall not take advantage
of the situation. When your bags arrived, I had them
sent to the room you previously occupied; I daresay
you will continue to find it comfortable."

He had said so much, and in so few words, that
Marietta did not at once collect his meaning. When she
did, she felt a wave of humiliation so intense as to be
almost physical. That tantalizing moment of intimacy
had been but the talk of wine; their marriage of convenience was to be a union in name alone as well. She
clenched her hands, and her mortification turned to
fury.

"It is quite satisfactory to me if you choose for us to
sleep apart," she hissed. "However, I shall not permit
you to hold me up to ridicule. I demand that you place
me in the family wing; at least the servants will have
no reason to suppose that anything is amiss—"

"I'm afraid that would prove most awkward," the
Viscount interjected. "The family wing has been
largely closed since the death of my parents; the only
available bedchamber is Roger's. If you like, I shall
have your things moved there."

"I shall not sleep in Roger's bed!"

"So I assumed," Christopher said mildly. "I fancy my arrangement is the only alternative then."

There was no advantage to be gained by further argument; to the contrary, every second she lingered could but increase her embarrassment. "Very well," she said stiffly. "If you will excuse me then, I shall retire."

"I shall see you up—"

"Do not trouble yourself," Marietta snapped. "I know the way!"

She exited the library with as much dignity as she could muster; only when she judged herself well out of the Viscount's sight did she lift her skirt and run across the foyer. She raced up the curving stairs and down the corridor to her bedchamber, threw open the door and scurried inside, slammed the door and leaned against it. As she had surmised, her bags lay unopened in the middle of the carpet, and she rushed to them and savagely jerked up the lid of the trunk. Fortunately, her nightgown was near the top, and within the space of five minutes she had removed her clothes, donned her nightdress, and crashed the trunk lid shut again. She tore back the counterpane and the bedclothes and was at the point of leaping into the bed when she detected a sound at the door.

Christopher? Had his lordship reconsidered? Despite her rage, her heart bounded into her throat, and she drew a deep, steadying breath. She went to the door, cautiously cracked it, and a cold, damp nose thrust through the crack and sniffed joyfully at her ankles.

"Ah, it is you, Poppy," Marietta sighed. "Well, come in; it seems I shall have no one else to share my bed."

They crawled beneath the bedclothes, and Marietta extinguished the candle and snuggled against the dog. Her wedding night, she thought, and she had a sufficient sense of the ridiculous that she could not quell a laugh.

8

MARIETTA WAS A firm believer in the mysterious powers of sleep, so she was not surprised when she woke the next morning and discovered that during the night an idea had taken root in her mind. While she might be Christopher's wife solely in name, she was, in fact, Lady Sheridan. More to the point, she was mistress of Twin Oaks, and she possessed both the authority and the funds to reorganize the Viscount's lamentable household. She did not think his lordship would object to such a program: he had seemed, last night, sincerely to regret the conditions of his existence. Indeed, he might be so grateful that he would come to regard Marietta with considerable favor, true affection . . . But she would not spin gossamer dreams; she would concentrate on the task at hand.

Marietta got out of bed and glanced at the mantel clock. It had obviously not been wound since her departure; it read half-past five. A small symptom of neglect which served to harden her resolve. Though she did not know the time, she wound the clock, tugged the bell rope, donned her dressing gown, and perched on the edge of the bed to wait.

"Good morning, Miss . . . er . . . Lady Sheridan." April had opened the door, but she remained in the corridor, peering across the threshold. "I fancy you'll be wanting a bath—"

"I should appreciate it if you would knock in the future, April," Marietta interposed pleasantly.

"Yes, ma'am. I'll fetch your bath now—"

"My bath can wait a moment," Marietta said.

"Indeed, it *has* waited for quite some time already. Are you aware, April, that exactly twenty-two minutes have elapsed since I rang?"

"Well, I came as quickly as I could, ma'am."

"No, you did *not* come as quickly as you could." Marietta stood, and Poppy—evidently recognizing the person who had previously wreaked such havoc in the bedchamber—emitted a sleepy growl. "I myself have traversed the distance from the understory to this room in three minutes, and *I* was carrying a plate."

"Yes, ma'am," April gulped.

"Do you wish to be my abigail, April?" Marietta spoke with studied abruptness.

"Your abigail?" April frowned. "I fancy it would be a good deal of work."

"It would indeed," Marietta agreed kindly, "and if you are not up to the mark, I daresay I can find someone else. Fortunately, I shall not have to discharge you, for we are in need of a scullery maid."

"A scullery maid?" April's blue eyes widened with horror. "Perhaps I *could* be your abigail, Lady Sheridan."

"Excellent," Marietta said. "Then let us be clear upon several points. When I ring, you will be here within five minutes, no more. If it is morning, you will bring a tub, which you will immediately fill with *hot* water. You will have complete responsibility for my room, my clothes, and my personal effects, and they must be immaculate at all times. Do you know how to dress hair, April?"

"I . . . I fancy I could learn." The newly appointed abigail had gone quite pale.

"You *will* learn," Marietta said grimly. "Now fetch the tub, and while I am bathing, you can begin to unpack my luggage."

Marietta was clean, clad, and coiffed within half an hour, and as she studied her reflection in the mirror above the dressing table, she was compelled to own that April had done quite a creditable job. Her hair was not perfect, but it surpassed anything Marietta could have accomplished alone, and she flashed the abigail a warm smile.

"Thank you, April; I believe we shall get on very well. When you have finished unpacking, please clean the room, and do not forget to set the clock."

Marietta smiled again, rose, and left the bedchamber. She could not but observe, when she turned to close the door, that April was removing each garment from the trunk as though it were a sacred relic.

The morning-room clock read ten past nine when Marietta entered, and she hurried on to the breakfast parlor, but it was deserted. The table was set for three today, she noted, and one of the empty places was marked by a few scattered crumbs of bacon. She sighed and started to step inside but was interrupted by a great crash behind her. She whirled around and watched as Crawford replaced a three-branched candelabrum on one of the occasional tables, stood back to admire his handiwork, then proceeded unsteadily toward the stairs.

"Crawford?" she called.

He turned and slammed his shin into the arc-backed chair, which seemed to be his nemesis. But he walked gamely forward, squinting a bit and managing to avoid the rest of the furniture.

"Yes?" he intoned when he had reached the breakfast-parlor entry. "Ah, yes; Lady Sheridan. Yes, his lordship advised me that he was to be married yesterday." He said it in the same tone he might have employed to announce that Christopher had stated a preference for toast rather than muffins with his breakfast.

"I see," she said dryly. "And has his lordship not yet returned from his morning ride?"

"He had no time for a morning ride, ma'am. He left very early for town."

"For Chelmsford?" Marietta said.

"No, ma'am, for London."

"London?" Marietta repeated disbelievingly.

"Yes, ma'am. I now recollect that he desired me to

tell you so and to inform you that he would be back on Friday."

"I see," Marietta said again. She felt a familiar flush of humiliation, and she ground her fingernails into her palms. "As it happens," she continued stiffly, "his lordship's absence is quite convenient. I daresay we shall be able to complete the first phase of my project prior to his return."

"What project is that, Lady Sheridan?" the butler asked idly.

"We are going to refurbish Twin Oaks from top to bottom, Crawford. From the attic to the cellar and everything between."

"Refurbish." He moistened his lips.

"Yes, and we shall also make a number of changes in the operation of the household. Let us, for example, consider the breakfast parlor." She turned and drew him into the room. "I collect that the table was laid on"—she performed a rapid mental calculation—"on Saturday. I further collect that as I am presently here alone, it would normally be relaid after I had used the final setting. On Thursday afternoon or Friday morning."

"That is the way we have always done it, ma'am."

"Well, that is *not* the way we shall do it in the future," Marietta said firmly. "The table will be covered with a fresh cloth every morning, and there will be only as many places laid as there are guests for breakfast. But I digress, for the breakfast procedure is but a minor problem. Our first task will be to clean the public rooms. Every one of them, and they must be finished by Friday."

"Begging your pardon, ma'am." Crawford's brow was glistening with moisture, and he withdrew a handkerchief from the pocket of his frock coat and discreetly mopped it. "Begging your pardon, but I must point out that the staff is wholly inadequate for the . . . er . . . *project* you propose."

"I quite agree," Marietta said. "I therefore charge you with the engagement of supplemental employees. I have selected April to be my abigail, so I fancy we shall initially require two chambermaids, an additional parlormaid, a scullery maid, and a footboy. For the grounds, let us begin with two additional gardners."

"Yes, ma'am." The butler swabbed his forehead again, this time with no discretion whatever. "It will require some time, of course—"

"It should require no time at all," Marietta interrupted crisply. "Unemployment is rampant, Crawford. If you travel to Chelmsford yet this morning and ask about, I daresay you can complete the hiring by nightfall. Those who prove unsatisfactory can later be dismissed."

"This morning." The butler's handkerchief had grown quite limp by now, and he attempted to replace it in his pocket. He missed, and it fluttered to the floor. "The fact is, ma'am, that I am a trifle indisposed today."

"The fact is, Crawford, that you are a trifle indisposed *every* day. I well know why, and it is a matter I wish to clarify at once. If, during your hours off, you elect to imbibe spirits—*your* spirits, and in moderation—I shall not object. However, I shall not tolerate a rumpot in my service. If I ever again suspect that you have been drinking while on duty, if your revels ever again render you 'indisposed,' I shall immediately discharge you. Have I made myself understood?"

"Yes, ma'am." The butler licked a veritable mustache of perspiration from his upper lip and gazed longingly down at his fallen handkerchief.

"Very well. While you are in town, I should also like you to order suitable clothing for the staff. I have observed that everyone looks quite disreputable." Crawford nervously caressed his shirt-points, which had wilted most dramatically. "With the notable exception of yourself," Marietta said wryly. "We shall proceed to the kitchen now. While I am speaking with Mrs. Sampson, you will consume as much coffee as you can, and I fancy you will be sufficiently recovered to leave for Chelmsford within the hour."

Mrs. Sampson, comfortably ensconced at the scarred oak table, reacted very irritably indeed when Marietta requested a pot of coffee for Mr. Crawford.

"The staff ate two hours since," she snapped. "Mr. Crawford had his share of coffee."

"Perhaps so," Marietta said lightly, "but Mr. Crawford will shortly be departing for Chelmsford, and he desires *more* coffee. I shall have a cup as well. And please do brew it a trifle stronger than normal; I have noticed that your coffee is decidedly weak."

The enormous cook lumbered out of her chair, slammed a pot upon the range, and marched indignantly to the scullery. Marietta beckoned Crawford to a position at the table and sat beside him. Mrs. Sampson panted out of the scullery, crashed cups and saucers down in front of them, and stalked again to the stove. When the coffee was ready, she smashed the pot on the table—forcing a brief brown geyser from the spout—and collapsed back in her own chair. Marietta calmly poured, delicately sipped.

"Yes, this is much better, Mrs. Sampson," she said. "Quite good, in fact."

"Humph," the cook snorted.

"You will be happy to learn," Marietta added, "that Mr. Crawford is going to town to engage new staff. I have specifically instructed him to hire a scullery maid."

Mrs. Sampson's expression moderated from furious scowl to severe frown. "And about time," she grumbled. "I cannot possibly perform all the cleaning"—her wave encompassed the blackened utensils arrayed about the room—"and the cooking as well."

"Of course you can't," Marietta agreed soothingly. "Indeed, I have been wondering whether Mr. Crawford should engage another cook as well."

"That is very kind of you, Lady Sheridan." Mrs. Sampson preened a bit, straightening the straps of her soiled apron. "However, I daresay that with the assistance of a scullery maid, I can manage without a second cook."

"I fear you misunderstood, Mrs. Sampson." Which was precisely what Marietta had intended. "I am not contemplating a *second* cook; I am pondering a replacement."

"A replacement?" Mrs. Sampson snapped one apron strap neatly in half.

"Believe me when I say that I bear you no personal ill will." Marietta essayed a sorrowful smile. "I am sure you were directed, nay, *mis*directed, into the wrong trade; you were no doubt very young. Be that as it may, it is apparent that you have never learned properly to cook—"

"*Never learned properly to cook?*" Mrs. Sampson drew herself up, and the second strap gave way. The bib of her apron tumbled to her waist, exposing a bosom fairly quivering beneath her black bombazine dress. "Never learned to cook? I wish you to know, Lady Sheridan, that I was once employed by His Royal Highness himself. In Brighton, no less, and I returned to Essex only after the death of my dear husband." She dabbed her eyes, unconvincingly, with a fragment of her ruined apron. "And a sorry day it was, if I may so say, when Lord Sheridan employed me; he has never cared what was put upon his plate."

"Well, I *do* care," Marietta said, "and I shall henceforth expect you to cook for his lordship and myself quite as conscientiously as you did for the Regent."

"I can but *try*," Mrs. Sampson sniffed. "The foodstuffs hereabouts are most inadequate—"

"Lady Cadbury's cook manages exceedingly well with the local foodstuffs," Marietta interrupted. Mrs. Sampson colored and toyed with her tattered apron straps. "Permit me to suggest, Mrs. Sampson, that you accompany Crawford to town. You can consult with the butcher and the greengrocer and the other purveyors; indeed, you may select new ones if you prefer. I shall leave the method to you, but I anticipate, beginning with this evening's dinner, that everything you serve will be faultless."

Marietta drained her coffee and rose. "Until the dining room has been cleared, I shall dine in my bed-chamber promptly at seven; I believe you will find, Mrs. Sampson, that April will be pleased to deliver my dinner. I shall breakfast each morning precisely at nine. During tomorrow's breakfast, Crawford, I wish to meet with you so as to discuss our progress and our immediate course of action. Good morning."

Marietta nodded to each of them in turn and left the kitchen, expecting to hear a furious whisper of conversation in her wake. But she had apparently stunned them to silence: the only sound she detected as she hurried up the steps was the nervous rattle of Crawford's cup against his saucer.

When Marietta reached the breakfast parlor the next morning, she found the butler stationed just outside the door. His posture was so rigid as to resemble that of military attention, his dress was immaculate, and he was utterly, unquestionably sober. Marietta returned his greeting with an approving nod, and Crawford seated her at the table.

Her instructions in regard to the breakfast procedure had been followed as well, Marietta observed: the linen cloth was positively pristine, and one sparkling setting had been laid. The clock in the morning room began to chime the hour, and the first footman raced through the entry and crashed the silver tray upon the table.

"That will not do at all, Patterson," the butler snapped. "Place the tray on the sideboard and serve her ladyship's plate from there."

"Yes, sir. Yes, ma'am."

Patterson retrieved the tray with trembling hands and removed it to the sideboard with a fearful clatter; evidently word of the terrible new Lady Sheridan had filtered through the household. At length, the footman presented a plate of eggs, bacon, and muffins and started to bow out.

"You will remain in the room while her ladyship is eating," Crawford said sternly. "And you have neglected to pour her coffee; please do so at once."

"Yes, sir."

Patterson hastily filled Marietta's cup, then hovered behind her chair, and Marietta was hard put to repress a smile. She sampled each of the courses and judged the eggs and bacon excellent, the muffin only fair. She recognized a similarity to last night's dinner: the turtle soup and mutton casserole had been extremely tasty, but the crust of the lemon tart had been a trifle soggy.

"Mrs. Sampson is exceedingly anxious to know your opinion of the food, Lady Sheridan." Crawford sounded rather anxious himself.

"On the whole, quite commendable," Marietta replied. "I do believe that Mrs. Sampson needs to sharpen her baking skills a bit, but I am prepared to be patient. For a *reasonable* period of time. Now sit down, Crawford; I have composed a list of household regulations which I should like you to review."

Marietta extracted a sheet of paper from the pocket of her skirt and, as the butler took the chair across the table, passed it to him.

"Someone to be on duty at all times," Crawford said sonorously, paraphrasing the first point. "Yes, that is essential, Lady Sheridan. Servants not to enter bedchambers without knocking and not to depart without specific dismissal. I could not have phrased it better myself, ma'am. Guest rooms to be kept clean at all times and clocks wound . . ." He continued through the list, pronouncing his unqualified agreement with each item, and laid the paper on the linen cloth.

"You do concur then?" Marietta pushed her empty plate aside. "You were able to engage an adequate staff?"

"I should hardly term them 'adequate,' ma'am; most are sorely lacking in experience. But I daresay *I* can provide the necessary training."

"I daresay you can." Marietta stifled another grin. "Insofar as the cleaning is concerned, I believe the dining room will prove our foremost challenge. If you will have the books removed to the library, I shall take responsibility for arranging them on the shelves. The papers must go to the attic."

"Yes, ma'am."

"Before we can begin, however, we shall have to expel the dogs. I presume there is an outdoor kennel; if not, I fancy the grooms or gardeners can readily construct one."

"Yes, ma'am."

"Please see to the dogs then, Crawford; have all of them taken out. In the interim, I shall explore the ground story so as to determine where to relocate his lordship's card room."

"Relocate his lordship's card room." Crawford tugged at his snowy neckcloth. "Begging your pardon, ma'am, but I am not at all certain that Lord Sheridan would consent to any such endeavor—"

"Lord Sheridan is not here," Marietta interposed crisply, "and in his absence I am entirely in charge. Tend the dogs, Crawford, and I shall meet you in the foyer in half an hour's time." She tossed her napkin on the table, and Crawford leaped up, Patterson bounded forward, to vie for the honor of assisting her out of her chair.

Marietta had no notion of the ground-floor layout beyond the center wing, so when she reached the entry hall, she proceeded arbitrarily to her left, past the drawing room and along the corridor toward Christopher's study. The door to the latter was open, and Marietta paused a moment, shaking her head at the overflowing desk and the books and ledgers piled on the floor. But she dared not invade his lordship's private domain, she decided, and with a despairing sigh she continued down the hall.

The corridor eventually widened, and Marietta calculated that she had found the wing directly below the family bedchambers. She initially fancied that it had once been used as servants' quarters, for the first two rooms she inspected were bedchambers as well—small and furnished with plain iron bedsteads and simple wooden accessories. However, the succeeding rooms

made it clear that this had been the nursery wing:
there were four additional bedchambers, all furnished
with miniature pieces, and, at the end of the hall, a
large schoolroom. It seemed unlikely, she reflected
grimly, that she and Christopher would need this portion of the house, would require quarters for a nanny
and a governess. But she supposed his lordship would
be exceedingly annoyed if his card room were placed in
such childish surroundings, and she turned and hurried
back the way she had come.

The foyer was fairly alive with dogs: Crawford was
supervising as two grooms and the new footboy drove
Juno and Merlin and perhaps a dozen others through
the entry hall and out the front door.

"Ah, Lady Sheridan," he said. "As it happens, there
is a kennel near the stable, and I daresay the dogs will
be quite comfortable." He frowned. "I have looked all
about, ma'am, but I have been unable to locate
Poppy."

"I shall worry about Poppy," Marietta said briskly.
She glanced into the dining room and observed that
two maids and both of the footmen were stacking the
debris into neat piles. "Lord Sheridan's card room cannot be moved to the west wing," she continued. "Come
with me, Crawford, and we shall investigate the other."

They walked along the corridor on the eastern side
of the house, past the stairs leading to the understory,
and at once discovered the perfect location. It had
originally been a music room, Marietta collected, but
all that remained was a single sagging stand and an ancient velvet couch—threadbare and missing a leg.

"This will serve very well indeed," Marietta declared. "When the staff has finished in the dining room,
Crawford, have them remove the music stand and the
couch to the attic and arrange the card table and chairs
in here."

"Yes, ma'am," the butler agreed dubiously.

Marietta stepped out of the erstwhile music room
and gazed around. There was but one other door in the

east wing, a great double door actually, situated at the end of the hall. She proceeded curiously ahead, threw the doors open, and sucked in her breath. It was a ballroom, quite as large and grand as that at Cadbury Hall. Marietta stood in the entry, seeing through the dusty floor and the grimy chandeliers and the sheeted furniture, seeing the ballroom gleaming and glowing, with a horde of glittering dancers whirling about the floor.

"A ballroom," Crawford sniffed, peering over her shoulder. "Well, ma'am, I shall return to the main wing now—"

"When everything else is completed, Crawford, please set the staff to cleaning the ballroom."

"Oh, I hardly think that will be necessary, ma'am; Lord Sheridan never entertains."

"Lord Sheridan never *has* entertained, but he and I shall have an assembly." She had formulated the idea only a few seconds since, but it had already become an absolute certainty in her mind. "Yes, I fancy we shall have an assembly within the next week or two. Please see to it. Crawford."

She closed the double doors, and the butler trailed her back to the center of the house.

By Thursday noon, the dining room and drawing room had been cleared, and as the servants began to scrub and dust, to wax and polish, Marietta turned her attention to the library. She had intended to arrange the books by subject, then alphabetically by author, but she soon realized that this program would require weeks rather than hours of her time. She consequently compromised by merely placing the A's together, then the B's, and she exhausted all the shelf space midway through the T's. She withdrew a sheet of paper from her pocket. jerked the pencil from behind her ear, and under the heading "New Furniture/Accessories," jotted "book cabinet for library." She scanned the list; she had previously noted that the library sofa, chair, and carpet would have to be replaced. She stacked the excess volumes neatly round the perimeter of the room, and, as it was nearing seven, retired to her bedchamber for dinner.

Everything was ready for final inspection early Friday afternoon, and as Crawford led her proudly about, Marietta was compelled to own herself pleasantly surprised. The drawing room was virtually flawless; with the dreadful table and chairs removed, the rest of the furniture properly arrayed, it quite rivaled Aunt Charlotte's main saloon. Marietta did observe that the Grecian couch needed new upholstery, and she scrawled a reminder on her list.

The dining room looked exceedingly handsome as well; the mahogany table and chairs, the matching sideboard, were in excellent condition. Indeed, she could identify only one hopeless casualty: the pale China rug, which was irreparably snagged and spotted from its service as bedding to several generations of hunting dogs. She added "dining-room carpet" to her roster and followed Crawford to the library. Despite its wretched complement of furniture, it, too, had been substantially improved by Marietta's rearrangement of the books and the subsequent thorough cleaning.

"I am extremely pleased, Crawford," she said. She flashed the butler a warm smile, and to her astonishment he blushed a bit. "Now I should like to place some flowers around, so if you could gather up half a dozen vases . . ."

It was nearing four when Marietta tucked the last rose into the last crystal vase, and as she stood away to evaluate the effect, she heard the rapid tattoo of hoofbeats in the drive. She rushed to the great oval mirror opposite the drawing-room hearth and anxiously studied her reflection. She was wearing the new yellow walking ensemble—a round dress of primrose jaconet topped by a saffron-colored spencer—and she thought it made her skin look darker, her hair fairer. She fussed with the curls upon her neck but admitted that her pulling and puffing were quite gratuitous: April had done a truly commendable job. Yes, she immodestly decided, she, like the house itself, looked as well as she could.

She detected the sound of the front door opening, closing, and she drew herself up, eagerly awaiting Christopher's reaction.

9

"Marietta!"

His lordship's bellow resembled nothing so much as the roar of a wounded bull, and Marietta dashed across the drawing room. The Viscount was standing just outside the dining-room door, his stature suggesting that he had been struck by some sort of paralysis. However, as she stepped into the foyer, he managed to turn his head and fix her with a frigid glare.

"Marietta!" he hissed. "What the *deuce* have you done? Where are my papers? I warn you that if you have destroyed my papers—"

"I cannot suppose it would signify in the least if I *had* destroyed your papers." He was not responding at all as she had imagined, and her initial disappointment turned at once to anger. "I could not but observe that many of your precious papers are nearly as old as I. Be that as it may, they were removed to the attic; the books are in the library."

"That attic!" he fumed, glowering back at the dining room. "The library. Am I to conclude that I dare not risk a day from home? That as soon as I depart, you will . . . will . . ." Words apparently failed him; he waved a furious hand in the general direction of the mahogany table.

"You were gone far more than a day," Marietta

snapped. "And under most peculiar circumstances, I might add: you profess an intense dislike for the city, and we had been married but a few hours—"

"Never mind," Christopher interrupted quickly. "Actually the room looks quite well. I daresay it was time to store the papers, though they are, of course, exceedingly important." He coughed, frowned. "Where are the dogs?"

"They have been taken to the kennel," Marietta replied. Her own mood was moderating a bit. "But too late to save the carpet, I fear; I'm sure you will agree that it must be replaced."

"Replaced?" The Viscount's frown briefly deepened; then his face cleared. "Replaced. Yes."

He turned away from the dining room and walked toward her. He looked quite resplendent, Marietta noted: he was clad in rust-colored pantaloons, a biscuit waistcoat, and a frock coat of copper-hued superfine. He reached her side and smiled down at her, and Marietta felt a familiar tremor and, with it, a keen twinge of regret that he had chosen to make a hollow mockery of their marriage.

"The dining room looks very well indeed," he repeated. His gray eyes drifted aimlessly over her shoulder. "I fancy I was a trifle hasty . . ." He stopped, and his eyes widened. "My table!" he croaked. "My chairs! Good God, Marietta . . ." His voice trailed off into something approximating a moan.

"Your table and chairs are quite safe," Marietta said soothingly. "I had them moved to the music room, which I believe will serve extremely well as a card room."

"*You* believe?" His eyes had gone as pale and cold as winter frost. "*You* believe? Did it not occur to you to seek my permission?"

"It would have occurred to me had you been available," Marietta retorted warmly. "However, as I have previously pointed out, you had . . . had *abandoned* me without a word of explanation and gone traipsing off to London. I had inferred from our conversation that you regretted the condition of Twin Oaks; evidently I was mistaken. I shall have everything put back as it was, and we can continue to live in a . . . a sty. Good afternoon."

She started to stalk past him, but his long fingers snaked around her arm and caught her up. "I am sorry, Marietta," he said stiffly. "Now that I think on it, the music room will no doubt prove an excellent location for cards. I was startled, and I spoke prematurely."

"You do that a great deal," Marietta muttered.

"So I do." His lordship's smile was extraordinarily wry, as though he were recalling a private and rather bitter jest. "I shall have a glass of brandy now; pray join me."

Marietta was much inclined to refuse, but he gave her no option; his fingers remained firmly wound about her arm as he propelled her to the library. He opened the door and glanced about, and Marietta detected a distinct twitch of the muscles at his jaw.

"I note that you have been at this room as well." His tone was commendably moderate. "I wonder if I shall be able to locate any of my books."

"You will if you know your alphabet," Marietta said crisply, "for they are arranged by letter. Unfortunately, I did run short of space." She indicated the volumes stacked around the edge of the threadbare carpet. "I plan to purchase a new book cabinet for the overflow."

"A new book cabinet," Christopher echoed noncommittally.

He led her on into the room, dropped her arm, and crossed to the liquor chest. He picked up one of the decanters and frowned at it suspiciously.

"Has my brandy been replaced with some other substance?" he asked.

"No, it has not. All the decanters were washed, and your brandy now looks like brandy rather than mud."

"I see." He cleared his throat. "What will you have?"

"A sherry, thank you."

The Viscount withdrew two glasses from the lower portion of the cabinet and filled them both. He dribbled a few drops of brandy on the mahogany top of the chest, and Marietta was pleased to observe that he extracted a handkerchief from the pocket of his frock coat and speedily mopped up the spill. He strode back to the center of the library, handed Marietta one of the glasses, and raised his own.

"To your efforts, my dear. I am compelled to own that my earlier remarks were most ill-considered; the house looks very handsome indeed." He sipped from his glass and peered about again. "Your accomplishment is particularly remarkable in view of the small staff with which you had to work."

"The staff . . ." Marietta gazed into her sherry. "As it happens, Christopher, the staff is no longer so small; I found it necessary to engage additional personnel."

"Did you? Well, I daresay we required a further maid or two."

"Four maids, a footboy, and two gardeners, to be exact," Marietta said. His lordship's glass clattered against his teeth, and he licked a wayward trickle of brandy from the corner of his mouth. "And I am not yet certain that they will suffice."

"They will *have* to suffice." The Viscount was still choking a bit. "I do not possess unlimited resources, Marietta, and I believe you have already mentioned that you desire new furniture. A carpet for the dining room, as I recollect, and a book cabinet here."

"And a rug as well, and a sofa and a chair, and the couch in the drawing room must be recovered . . . But I have made a list; perhaps you would like to review it."

She removed the now-tattered sheet of paper from her pocket, and Christopher snatched it out of her hand. His silver eyes rapidly scanned the front side, and he flipped the paper over; prior to the afternoon inspection, Marietta had conducted a preliminary tour of the guest bedchambers and had noted any number of cabinets and washstands, chests and wardrobes that required replacement. His lordship looked up and passed the list back.

"Very well," he said tersely. "I must agree that Twin Oaks has been shamelessly neglected over the years." His tone implied that said neglect was due to mysterious forces quite beyond his control. "You may proceed with the procurement of the furniture."

"Thank you." Marietta spoke with studied meekness. "I only wish that the furniture could be here in time for the assembly, but I fear that will prove impossible. We shall simply have to confine the guests to the vicinity of the ballroom."

"Ballroom?" Christopher barked. "What ballroom? What assembly?"

"The ballroom in the east wing," Marietta replied innocently. "Just beyond the music room."

"I know where the ballroom is," the Viscount snapped. "But insofar as an assembly is concerned—"

"I should like to hold it as soon as possible," Marietta interposed smoothly. "It will serve as my introduction to the neighborhood."

"I was given to understand that Aunt Charlotte's ball had introduced you to the neighborhood."

"But that was different," Marietta said. "Our own assembly will demonstrate that Twin Oaks is now open to company." She recalled his lordship's interminable macao games. "*Proper* company," she amended. "I perceive no advantage in delay, so I should like to hold the ball next Friday if that is satisfactory."

"It is *not* satisfactory." Christopher drained his snifter and marched back to the liquor cabinet. "You seem to be laboring under a very serious misapprehension, Marietta; you apparently entertain a notion that I am altogether made of money. I am not." He unstopped the brandy decanter with a dramatic clang. "You have engaged a great army of new servants." Seven hardly seemed an "army," but Marietta bit back a rejoinder. "You wish to purchase thousands of pounds' worth of new furniture." Marietta would have estimated a figure in the low hundreds. "You now desire to conduct an assembly." The Viscount emitted a martyred sigh and replenished his glass. "I simply cannot afford to finance all your whims."

"Very well," Marietta said obediently. "Perhaps we might discuss just what you *can* afford then. I realize that you have heavy gambling debts, to say nothing of certain other . . . er . . . payments. I am specifically aware of recompense to a gentleman in Norfolk, although, I collect, he was but one of many—"

"That is quite enough, Marietta!" Christopher whirled around, his dignity somewhat impaired by the veritable river of brandy he sloshed upon his highly polished hessians. "After careful consideration, I calculate that we can hold a ball after all."

"Splendid." Marietta set her glass on the occasional table beside the chair, observed a deep scratch she had not previously noticed, and made a mental note that the table would be refinished. "If you will excuse me, then, I fancy I had best be making plans." She crossed to the door, opened it, and Poppy bounded into the library, greeting both Marietta and his lordship with damp, doggy passion.

"Is that Poppy?" the Viscount asked gratuitously. "How did she escape banishment to the kennel?"

"I kept Poppy inside because I wish a companion in my bedchamber," Marietta said coolly. "If you, too, desire *something* to sleep with, do feel free to select a dog of your own."

She stepped on into the corridor, Poppy scampering behind her, and heard an angry ring as Christopher recapped the decanter. She felt that, for once, she had played his lordship to a draw or better, and she wondered why the victory—like their marriage itself— seemed so very empty.

By Saturday morning, Marietta had filled another sheet of paper with requirements for the assembly, and she studied the list with a sinking sensation. Six days was dangerously little time in which to complete the arrangements, but she had made such an issue of the matter that she dared not retreat. And though she knew Aunt Charlotte would be delighted to assist, she frankly feared to risk the scrutiny of her ladyship's shrewd blue eyes. Marietta consequently dispatched Crawford to Cadbury Hall to borrow Aunt Charlotte's roster of names and addresses while she herself hurried to Chelmsford to purchase cards of invitation.

Marietta appropriated the *bonheur-du-jour* desk in the morning room and set to work immediately upon Crawford's return. She penned invitations to all the Essex folk on Lady Cadbury's list as well as those from other shires whom she personally remembered from Aunt Charlotte's ball. The task took far longer than she had anticipated: it was late Sunday afternoon when she laid her pen aside and sat back in the chair, her neck so stiff that she could scarcely move it.

"Are you tired, Marietta?"

She had not heard Christopher's approach, and she started, tried to look around at him, winced.

"No, don't move; relax."

She did so, and he placed his hands on her shoulders and began to knead them, his thumbs on her shoulder blades, his long fingers near her collarbones. Marietta closed her eyes, and her head fell back until it came to rest against his chest. She opened her eyes and found him staring down into her face, his own eyes oddly dark. He abruptly ceased his ministrations and strode around to the side of the desk.

"Is there any way in which I may help you?"

The Viscount's voice sounded a trifle hoarse, but to Marietta's considerable surprise his inquiry seemed sincere.

"In point of fact, there is." Her own words emerged a bit breathlessly, and she was keenly aware of the spots he had touched, as though he had left small, warm dents in her shoulders. "I used Aunt Charlotte's invitation list; I have checked off the cards I wrote. But I may have omitted some you would like to have, and I fancy there are others, friends of yours whom Aunt Charlotte did not include."

"Let me have it."

Marietta passed him the list, and he pulled the arc-backed chair next to the desk and sat down. He picked up a pencil and ran it down the several sheets of paper, making an occasional mark.

"Yes, there are others," he said when he had finished. "Mr. Archer, Mr. Lloyd . . ." He tugged a blank sheet across the desk and began jotting names. Marietta had not realized he was left-handed though she thought she should have guessed it from the back-slanted script on his papers. "There."

He dropped the pencil, sat back, and extended Lady Cadbury's list and his own addendum. Marietta rapidly perused them and estimated that some three dozen further invitations would be required. Her neck had started to throb again, and she wearily retrieved the pen.

"I shall write them if you like," Christopher said.

It was an astonishing offer, and Marietta felt her mouth drop open. But he once more appeared entirely sincere, and she nodded. "I should be very grateful indeed if you wouldn't mind."

"I don't mind in the least." The Viscount rose and assisted her out of her chair. "I suggest you rest for an interval prior to dinner." He frowned. "Speaking of which, I have intended to comment that the food has been quite excellent. I collect that you discharged Mrs. Sampson and engaged a replacement."

"That did not prove necessary," Marietta said. "I was able to . . . to *encourage* Mrs. Sampson to unleash her culinary artistry."

"I see." A smile tickled the corners of his lordship's mouth. "Just as you were able to '*encourage*' Crawford to forgo his brandy?"

"You noticed then."

"Of course I noticed. And I wish to say, Marietta, that I appreciate your efforts. You have wrought a most remarkable improvement." His eyes had darkened again, and Marietta's cheeks grew warm. "Well, off with you now," he added gruffly. "If I continue to dally, I shall never complete these damned invitations."

He took Marietta's vacated chair, plucked up one of the cards, and seized the pen. Marietta proceeded to her bedchamber, reflecting for perhaps the hundredth time that he was surely the most incomprehensible person she had ever encountered.

On Monday morning, Marietta assigned a pair of grooms to deliver the invitation cards, exhorted Crawford to greater speed in the cleaning of the ballroom, and ordered out the barouche to bear her again to Chelmsford. She stopped first at Mr. Taylor's home, located on the edge of town, and the orchestra leader pronounced himself delighted to accept a commission at Twin Oaks.

"We played there often in Lady Sheridan's time," he reminisced. "The *previous* Lady Sheridan's time, that is. I well recollect a particular occasion, around the New Year, I believe it was. The Regent was there—he was not the Regent then, of course—and one of his brothers. Was it Clarence or York? Well, in any event . . ."

As soon as Mr. Taylor paused for breath, Marietta solicited his promise to appear promptly at half-past eight on Friday evening, excused herself, and hurried on to Mr. Mead's. The caterer recorded her order, calculated the price, then announced that as the assembly was to take place just four days hence, he would be compelled to charge a substantial premium.

"How unfortunate," Marietta sighed. "Lady Cadbury recommended that I employ a London caterer, but I had hoped to avail myself of the local merchants. However, if the cost is to be the same, I daresay I should engage a city firm after all. Good day, Mr. Mead."

The caterer hastily reviewed his figures and discovered that he had made an error: he had forgotten to include the discount he normally provided the Thornings, a discount which *quite* compensated for the premium. He was still apologizing for his oversight as

Marietta backed out of the shop. She reached the door, gave Mr. Mead a final nod of forgiveness, retreated blindly into the street, and collided with a passerby.

"Oh, I am sorry." Marietta whirled around and met Elinor Winship's cool, dark, amused eyes. "Lady Winship," she murmured.

"Lady Sheridan. And what brings you to town so bright and early on a Monday morning? Since you have been visiting Mr. Mead, I collect you are planning some sort of entertainment."

"Yes, a ball." Marietta had briefly thought to exclude her ladyship from the festivities but had soon recognized that any such cut would prove far more embarrassing to herself than to Lady Winship. "On Friday evening. I daresay your invitation has been delivered by now."

"What a remarkable concidence," Lady Winship cooed. "I myself am planning an assembly for *Saturday* evening. I was just on my way to confer with dear Mr. Mead about the refreshments."

Marietta would have wagered her last groat that Lady Winship had not considered a ball until that very instant; that she sought only to detract from Marietta's assembly; that if it were in any way possible, she would schedule her impulsive gathering for Thursday, for tomorrow, for tonight. But she managed a pleasant nod.

"It *is* a remarkable coincidence," she agreed, "and I fancy the neighbors will be quite overwhelmed. I fear you must pardon me now, Lady Winship; I have a great deal to do."

Marietta inclined her head again and started to cross the street, but Lady Winship moved smoothly to bar her way.

"I hope you will not exhaust yourself," her ladyship said kindly. "If I may be permitted a personal observation, you look exceedingly pale. I seem to recollect an ancient adage on the subject of blushing brides; perhaps it does not invariably hold true. Or perhaps blushing brides require blushing grooms."

Marietta felt the blood surging into her face, creeping from the base of her throat to the roots of her hair, and she dismally suspected she was blushing quite as much as Lady Winship might have wished.

"Be that as it may, I shall see you later in the week." Her ladyship toyed with the bow of her great French bonnet. "I suppose I shall have to *beg* Mr. Mead to fit me into his busy schedule, but that is my problem, eh, Lady Sheridan? You clearly have problems of your own."

Lady Winship turned and sailed into the caterer's establishment, and Marietta proceeded unsteadily across the street to consult with Mr. Pierce. She thought she conducted herself with considerable aplomb; she was halfway back to Twin Oaks when she began to entertain the terrible notion that she had requested the florist to supply two hundred—rather than two dozen—potted palms on the night of the ball.

10

Bᴜᴛ ᴡʜᴇɴ Mʀ. Pierce's assistants arrived late on Friday afternoon, they bore in exactly twenty-four palms and the dozen arrangements of roses and daisies Marietta had ordered in addition. She supervised the placement of pots and vases alike, trailing the florist's men about and utilizing the opportunity to conduct a final inspection of the ballroom. Crawford appeared just as Mr. Pierce's employees finished, and the butler anxiously inquired as to whether Lady Sheridan judged the premises satisfactory.

"Almost entirely so, Crawford," she replied warmly. "However, I could not but observe that the rear win-

dows, those to the left of the door, require further
cleaning."

"So they do, ma'am." The butler snapped his fingers. "Indeed, I noticed them myself earlier in the
afternoon, but the maids were occupied in Lord Sheridan's study."

"His lordship's study?" Marietta felt her eyes widen
with horror. "Surely, Crawford, you did not take it
upon yourself—"

"Certainly not, ma'am," the butler interrupted indignantly. "Lord Sheridan summoned me around midday
and requested some assistance in . . . well, he termed
it 'tidying up.' He said that as the rest of the house
looked so well, he did not wish his study to suffer by
comparison. I must confess, ma'am, that a great deal
more than 'tidying up' was needed."

Marietta did not doubt this; she herself had privately
likened Christopher's study to the legendary Augean
stable. She was briefly astonished that the Viscount
should have authorized its cleaning, but the fact that he
had done so reminded her of another circumstance.

"Be sure to 'tidy up' his lordship's card room as
well, Crawford," she instructed. "The guests will be
compelled to pass it by en route to the ballroom."

"I have already done so, ma'am," the butler said.
"Though, in that case, very little effort was required:
Lord Sheridan has not used the card room since his re-
turn from London."

Marietta had been far too busy to follow the Viscount's activities, but it now occurred to her that she
had not glimpsed a single one of the familiar carriages
during the course of the preceding week. She could
only conclude that Christopher did not find the new
card facility suitable after all. But she hadn't the time
to dwell on it: it was half-past six, and Mr. Mead was
scheduled to come at eight.

"Very well, Crawford," she said. "Pray see to the
windows while I am dressing then."

The butler nodded, and Marietta hurried to the center wing and on up to her bedchamber. Anticipating a

last-minute crush of preparations, she had bathed and washed her hair earlier in the day, and she was gratified to discover April waiting in her room, smoothing imaginary creases from the apple-green ball gown, which had already been pressed to a fare-thee-well.

April seemed determined to rig her mistress out to utter perfection, and it was a quarter to eight when the abigail at last pronounced herself satisfied. Marietta rose, stood away from the mirror, and owned herself tolerably pleased as well. The dress was an exquisite creation of lace over a satin slip, with a bodice of slightly darker green and great white satin roses round the bottom of the skirt. Marietta thought the white satin *toque* a bit too high, but it was the only one of her headdresses that matched the gown; it would have to suffice. Nevertheless there was something missing, and Marietta eventually perceived that the low bodice of the gown left her neck unattractively bare. Aunt Charlotte's amethysts would not do at all, and the only other jewelry Marietta possessed was a string of pearls and matching earrings left her by her mother. She put them on and frowned; they were entirely too simple for the elegant dress.

But the pearls, too, would have to suffice. Marietta sighed and reached for her gloves, and at that moment there was a knock at the door. April rushed to open it, and from the corner of her eye Marietta glimpsed Andrews, the Viscount's youthful valet. Andrews was to serve as a footman during the ball, and Marietta happily noted that he looked quite resplendent in his livery, which had been delivered—along with boxes and boxes of other servants' attire—the previous morning. The valet chatted with April a moment; then the maid closed the door and bore a large, flat velvet case to the dressing table.

"Jack said his lordship had sent this over, thinking you might be in need of it."

April had turned noticeably pink, and Marietta suspected she had developed a bit of a *tendre* for "Jack." But there was no time to explore that subject either, and rather impatiently Marietta opened the case. She sucked in her breath, for it obviously contained the rest of the first Lady Sheridan's jewels. Christopher's mother had not owned an abundance of jewelry, Marietta saw, but every item was in faultless taste. She stared into the case and immediately spotted the pieces that would perfectly complement her ensemble—an emerald-and-diamond choker and long matching earrings. She fished them out, but for some reason her hands were trembling, and she was forced to solicit April's aid in changing from the pearls to the emeralds.

The morning-room clock was chiming eight as Marietta dashed through and pounded down the stairs. Mr. Mead was awaiting her at the entrance to the ballroom, pointedly examining his watch and irritably tapping his foot.

"Ah, *here* you are, Lady Sheridan." The caterer's tone suggested that she was two hours, rather than two minutes, tardy. "I have searched all about, but I cannot seem to locate the refreshment parlor."

"That is because there *is* no refreshment parlor," Marietta said pleasantly. "However, I have screened off a portion of the ballroom."

She led him to the rear-right-hand corner, where, indeed, she had directed that half a dozen potted palms be arrayed so as to suggest a wall. Mr. Mead peered through the opening and frowned.

"The table is quite small, Lady Sheridan," he said with keen displeasure. "My trays are . . . ahem . . . rather large."

"Well, you may certainly borrow some of *our* trays," Marietta said. "I fancy my cook, Mrs. Sampson, will be delighted to help you." She gave him directions to the kitchen, nodded, and walked away, leaving the caterer to sputter amongst the palms.

By a quarter to nine, everything seemed well in hand. Mr. Mead's minions were carrying trays—Twin Oaks's *small* trays—into the refreshment area, and in the gallery the orchestra was tuning their instruments. Marietta circled the ballroom one last time and could find almost nothing to criticize: the chandeliers were sparkling, the floor was gleaming, the furniture was spotless. She did detect a tiny patch of grime on one of the panes of the rear corner window, and she extracted a handkerchief from her reticule, spat indelicately upon it, and swabbed the spot away. As she moved back to inspect her handiwork, she felt a finger in her ribs and whirled around.

"Christopher!" she gasped.

"Must the lady of the manor be washing windows a scant few minutes before the ball?"

"It was but one pane," she said stiffly. "One pane which was a trifle soiled . . ." She belatedly realized that he was jesting and lowered her eyes. "I am sorry," she murmured. "I daresay I'm a trifle overset."

"You've no cause to be overset, Marietta. The house looks very handsome. Almost as handsome, I fancy, as you yourself."

His silver eyes swept over her in frank appreciation, and Marietta felt a familiar flush. *He* certainly looked handsome, she reflected: he was wearing his small clothes and wasp-waisted coat and, tonight, striped stockings below his breeches. And his dark face was uncharacteristically animated, almost as if he were now anticipating the assembly to which he had so strenuously objected.

"Permit me to repeat, Marietta, that you have wrought a most remarkable improvement—"

"Christopher?" Aunt Charlotte's shrill voice assailed them from the entry. "Marietta?" Lady Cadbury bounded across the ballroom, the Marquis in tow. "It is splendid, my dears, simply *splendid*." Aunt Charlotte screeched to a halt beside them, the ostrich plume on her *toque* fairly quivering with enthusiasm. "I had initially thought to offer my assistance in the planning of the ball, but Ralph assured me you could manage quite well on your own. And how right he was! I could scarcely credit the testimony of my own eyes; indeed, as I told Ralph, I at first supposed that we had stumbled upon the wrong house . . ."

Lady Cadbury continued to rattle her backward compliments, and Marietta nodded at appropriate intervals. It was fortunate, she thought, that Aunt Charlotte's appraisal of Twin Oaks had altogether distracted her ladyship from an inspection of the bride. The *blushing* bride, as Lady Winship would have phrased it. Marietta bit her lip and solemnly agreed with Aunt Charlotte that Captain Robert Thorning *should* have had the foresight to construct a terrace off the ballroom.

Lady Cadbury was still chattering when Crawford announced the first arrivals, and Marietta and Christopher excused themselves to attend their guests. The group included Sir Hugh, who at once unnerved Marietta by raising his glass and scrutinizing her most intently.

"I am now persuaded, Lady Sheridan, that I did *not* encounter you at Lady Weatherley's assembly," the baronet said firmly.

"No?" Marietta's heart pounded painfully against her ribs.

"No. I am *quite* certain that I saw you at Hampton Court; were you not there?"

"Indeed I was, Sir Hugh."

Marietta saw no reason to add that she had visited this attraction at the age of eleven, when Sir Henry had first taken her to town. Sir Hugh nodded triumphantly and bowed away.

Marietta was pleased to note that she recollected the names of most of the guests she had met at Aunt Charlotte's, and the Viscount smoothly reminded her of those few that had escaped her memory. She reflected at one juncture that she and Christopher made an excellent team, and she wondered the reaction of the company, now filling the ballroom, if they knew the true, peculiar nature of Lord and Lady Sheridan's marriage.

By a quarter to ten, it appeared that the great majority of those invited had arrived, and Christopher suggested that Marietta mingle with the guests while he awaited the latecomers. Marietta proceeded toward the refreshment corner, thinking to ensure that Mr. Mead was not stacking great mountains of food on the small trays he'd been compelled to use, but Sir Mark accosted her halfway and asked her to stand up with him.

"I should like that very much, Sir Mark, but I was just on my way to check the refreshments."

"I assure you that the refreshments require no attention. I have already consumed several oysters and a lobster patty, and they were excellent. Come, Lady Sheridan, you must permit yourself to enjoy your own assembly."

"Perhaps you might call me Marietta?" she said as the baronet took her in his arms. "I know that Christopher regards you quite as a member of the family."

"I should be delighted, but only if you will return the favor." He smiled down at her and guided her expertly amongst the whirling couples on the floor. "May I add, Marietta, that the excellence of the evening is by no means confined to the refreshments? I hope you will not take it amiss if I own myself astonished. I do not believe I should have recognized Twin Oaks. No, that is not true at all," he amended. "In fact, I recognized it at once, for it looks much as it did in Lady Sheridan's time."

"It is very kind of you to say so," Marietta murmured. She hesitated a moment. "I . . . I think Christopher is pleased as well," she added at last.

"Chris is exceedingly pleased," the baronet confirmed. He, too, paused for the space of a few bars. "Indeed, I daresay Chris is far more pleased than he himself yet knows."

Marietta judged this a rather odd comment, but there was no chance to pursue it; the music ended, and Mr. Lloyd scurried up to claim her hand for the ensuing set. The plump, balding man of business was several inches shorter than Marietta, but this circumstance did not seem to trouble him in the least: he beamed up at her through his glittering spectacles and enthusiastically welcomed her to Essex.

"I fancy you will be undertaking a number of improvements to the property, Lady Sheridan," he continued. "I wholeheartedly approve, of course, but naturally you must be constantly on guard against unnecessary expense. I am frequently forced to remind his lordship of that very thing." Mr. Lloyd briefly frowned. "I asked Lord Sheridan if you had brought any property to the marriage which would require my attention, but he indicated that you had not. Not that it signifies; his lordship's estates fairly span the British Isles and several of the colonies as well. To say nothing of his other interests . . ."

By the end of the set, Mr. Lloyd had described these "estates" and "interests" in excruciating detail, including, in several cases, the precise annual income which they produced. Though Marietta was pleased to have her curiosity satisfied, the little man's discourse served to remind her that Mr. Lloyd was far too free in discussing the affairs of his clients. Perhaps, if the right opportunity presented itself, she would mention the matter to Christopher.

Despite his diminutive stature, Mr. Lloyd was an extremely energetic dancer, and when he at last released her, Marietta found herself quite overheated. She glanced about and spotted the Viscount chatting with Lady Winship, who had evidently just arrived. Marietta thought the latter peered in her direction, and having no wish to converse with her ladyship, she decided to slip outside for a breath of air.

As Aunt Charlotte had pointed out, Twin Oaks possessed no terrace; beyond the ballroom door, three shallow steps led directly to the garden. Marietta descended the stairs and stopped at the bottom, deeply inhaling the fresh, fragrant air. The day had been cloudy, the night was dark, and she could see but a few feet along the main gravel path. She knew, however, from her earlier inspections that the garden had been substantially improved as well. There remained a great deal to do, but the scene, in daylight, was vastly differ-

ent from the weed-choked jungle which had existed a
scant ten days since.

The ballroom door opened, and a river of light
splashed down the steps to Marietta's feet.

"Ah, here you are," Christopher said. The door
closed again, leaving only the squares of light which radiated through the panes, and the Viscount walked
down the steps and stopped beside her. "Are you tired,
Marietta?"

She searched his face for some sign of criticism but
perceived only concern, and she shook her head. "Not
tired; I got very warm. And I fancied things were progressing sufficiently well that I could dare a moment or
two away."

"Things are proceeding very well indeed," his lordship agreed. "It is fortunate you are *not* tired, for I fear
some of our guests will linger nearly till dawn."

"What a shame that would be," Marietta snapped.
"Then *they* will be too tired to do justice to Lady Winship's assembly tomorrow evening."

She had not intended to say it, and she bit her lip,
but Christopher merely chuckled. "Yes, Elinor bitterly
mislikes to be outdone. I daresay that on this occasion,
however, she will be compelled to accept second
place." He paused and looked down at her, and in the
darkness his eyes were altogether silver. "What I had
begun to say, Marietta, when Aunt Charlotte burst into
the ballroom"—he flashed a wry smile—"is that your
transformation of Twin Oaks is truly remarkable. I
wished you to know that I am extremely pleased."

Marietta recalled Sir Mark's comment and sensed
that the Viscount was no longer referring entirely to
the house, the ball. No, he was speaking of her, of
them, and much as she had longed for the moment, she
could not quell a familiar shiver of terror. He had
taken her unawares, and, in defense, she chose deliberately to misconstrue his remark.

"You cannot be *wholly* pleased," she said. "For example, you do not appear to care for your card room
at all; I observe that you haven't used it once."

"I have no objection to the card room," Christopher said; "I have merely lost my fascination for cards. Perhaps, as Uncle Ralph would no doubt elect to believe, I have recognized that it is the time to 'settle myself down.'"

His silver eyes had never left her face, and Marietta was seemingly powerless to escape them. Her hand flew nervously up to her throat and came to rest on the emerald-and-diamond choker.

"I . . . I wanted to thank you for the . . . the jewelry," she stammered.

"No thanks are necessary." His lordship's voice sounded rather rough. "The jewels are yours by right; you *are* Lady Sheridan."

Marietta tore her eyes away at last and looked down. She realized that he was standing very close to her; his shoes were scarcely an inch from her white satin-slippers.

"Look at me, Marietta," he commanded.

But she could not, and she eventually felt his fingers under her chin. She distantly noted that at some point he had removed his gloves: his hand was terribly, uncomfortably warm. He tilted up her face, and his pale eyes again met hers.

"I have always found it exceedingly difficult to talk to you," Christopher said. "From the very beginning, you have managed to confuse me."

Marietta started to protest, but he moved his thumb to cover her lips. It was a casual gesture but, for some reason, a disturbingly sensual one.

"Permit me to finish," he said. "I do not hold you responsible for my failing, but as you yourself recently pointed out, every word I attempt to speak to you seems to emerge quite wrong." He sketched another rueful smile, and his teeth gleamed briefly in the darkness. "So I fancy I viewed Mama's jewelry as a message, but I now recognize that it was a clumsy one indeed. The fact is, Marietta, that I propose to . . . to normalize our relationship. I cannot suppose you wish to live a lie any more than I."

It was happening with dizzying speed, so quickly that even when he moved his thumb away, Marietta could not conceive a single word of response.

"I shall not rush you," his lordship continued; "I did rashly promise that I should not take advantage of the situation." His teeth flashed again. "But my immodest hope is that you do not judge me altogether odious, which leads me further to hope that you will consider my proposition."

He released her chin, and Marietta momentarily thought he would let her go entirely. Then his arms encircled her, and he drew her toward him and lowered his head. At the last instant, when she could see nothing but his eyes, Marietta closed her own eyes, and his mouth captured hers. Her lips parted—quite independently, it seemed—and her arms crept round his neck. His muscles hardened, and he pulled her against his chest until she could feel his coat buttons digging into her flesh. His mouth went to her throat, to the hollow just below the choker, and she heard a moan; whether it issued from him, herself, the both of them, she could not determine. But as if it were a signal, Christopher lifted his head, stepped slightly away, and transferred his hands to her shoulders.

"Before you reach a decision, Marietta, I should like to say one other thing."

She wanted him to say nothing at all; she wanted him to kiss her again, wanted to lose herself in his mouth, his hands, his tall, lean body. But the Viscount pressed stubbornly ahead.

"I fear I did you a grave injustice. I trust, when I explain the matter, that you will understand why I leaped to conclusions that seemed very obvious at the time—"

"Lady Sheridan!" The ballroom door crashed open, and Crawford blinked down at them from the threshold. "I should not have disturbed you, ma'am, but there is a *dreadful* crisis. It is Mrs. Sampson: she has packed her things and is threatening to leave at once. Indeed, she demanded that I order out a carriage to take her to Chelmsford, but I *knew* you would wish to speak with her."

In fact, Marietta would cheerfully have murdered Mrs. Sampson, Crawford, and the several hundred guests cavorting about the ballroom. But she could not, of course, and she reluctantly dislodged Christopher's fingers and walked up the stairs. Her knees were alarmingly weak, but she succeeded in trailing the butler through the ballroom, along the corridor, and down the steps to the kitchen.

Mrs. Sampson was in a "dreadful" state indeed: the enormous cook was seated at the oak table, sobbing into the formerly crisp skirt of one of her new aprons.

"They have destroyed my kitchen, Lady Sheridan," she wept.

Even as she spoke, "they"—in the form of one of Mr. Mead's assistants—dropped half a tray of oysters and hastily scooped them up. It was fortunate, Marietta thought, that the floor had been thoroughly scrubbed that very morning.

"They will depart when the ball is over, and I shall be left to mop up. Katie will be no help," Mrs. Sampson added bitterly. Katie was the new scullery maid. "*She* has been dallying all evening with one of *them*; I should not be in the least surprised if they ran off together before the night is done. Well, I shall not have it, Lady Sheridan. As I told Mr. Crawford, I—who once cooked for the Regent—will not be reduced to cleaning in the wake of a mob of . . . of *oafs*."

Another of the caterer's employees selected this inauspicious moment to dribble curried crab all over the top of the range. Mrs. Sampson broke into a fresh torrent of tears and, her apron quite soggy, dabbed at her eyes with the hem of her new black bombazine dress.

Eventually Marietta was able to assure the cook that she would have ample assistance as she "mopped up" after the "oafs"; if necessary, Lady Sheridan herself would wash her share of trays and pots and chafing dishes. She further suggested that Mrs. Sampson might like a glass of champagne to see her through the remainder of the difficult evening, a proposal which cheered the cook sufficiently that she canceled her order for a carriage and moved her battered valise well out of sight beneath the table. Marietta led Crawford back up the kitchen stairs, dispatched him to the ballroom for Mrs. Sampson's champagne, and, as the butler rushed away, collapsed against the corridor wall.

She wondered what Christopher had been at the point of saying when Crawford had opened the ballroom door. On second thought, the Viscount's interrupted words did not appear to signify: it was clear that their situation, for whatever reason, had altered most dramatically. Marietta closed her eyes and felt the warm touch of his lordship's lips, and her eyes flew open again. She had only to tell Christopher that she, too, wished to "normalize" their marriage, and after the last guest had departed, they would proceed to the Viscount's bedchamber . . .

But hours remained before the departure of the final guest, and if she dwelt upon the bedchamber—which she had never seen and, in the present context, could not imagine—she would not make it through the assembly. She stood away from the wall, squared her shoulders, and started toward the ballroom, but she had progressed only a few feet when she heard a sound at the front door.

Marietta frowned. It was half-past eleven, she surmised—a trifle late for even the most fashionably tardy of arrivals. And she had extinguished the lights at the main door, illuminated those at the east entrance, specifically to avoid just this sort of error. Nevertheless, if there *were* guests at the front door, she did not wish to leave them fumbling about in the night, and she hurried up the hall.

The foyer, again by design, was dim, and Marietta paused to light the lamp on the bow-fronted commode. The wick caught, creating a bright, warm glow, and at that moment the door opened, and Roger Thorning stepped into the entry hall.

11

"GOOD EVENING," ROGER said politely.

Marietta distantly, incredulously awarded him points for his astonishing aplomb, then collected that the younger Thorning had not yet recognized her. He closed the door and proceeded across the foyer, and she observed that he looked considerably the worse for wear: he was noticeably limping, favoring his left leg, and his left arm was bound up in a sling.

"Good evening," he repeated. "I hope I did not startle you, but the fact is, I live here. Though I must own that I should scarcely have known the place . . ." He stopped, and his mouth fell open. "Marietta?" he gasped. "*Marietta?*"

"Yes, it is I," she snapped.

"But what the devil are you doing here? I supposed you had returned to Suffolk long since—"

"And I supposed you were long since abroad," she interrupted frigidly. "I believe your note stated an intention to leave the country at once."

"My note." He coughed. "Yes, I did intend to go abroad. However, as I am sure you can see for yourself, I met with an accident. A most serious accident, I might add." He assumed a martyred expression. "I am fortunate to have escaped with my life, so I shan't complain of having been invalided for nearly a month." He emitted a deep sigh. "I still find it exceedingly difficult to get about, of course: both my ankle and my arm were broken."

Marietta glanced from said ankle, now suspended dramatically above the floor, to his sling and could not generate the smallest flicker of sympathy. Evidently her emotions, or lack thereof, were clearly written on her face, for Roger coughed again and essayed a winning smile.

"I am happy to see that *you*, on the other hand, look extremely handsome, Marietta."

She continued to study him with detached curiosity she might have afforded an exotic circus animal. He had lost perhaps half a stone in weight, she calculated, but on the whole he had changed very little in the preceding six weeks. He was still a trifle stocky for his height, and his chestnut hair was in the perpetual disarray she remembered. There was one difference, but she counted that a modification of her own perception. She had fancied that his hazel eyes sparkled and danced; she now realized that they darted—ceaselessly and furtively—about.

"Do not think to turn me up sweet," she said at last. "A glib compliment or two will hardly compensate for your disgraceful behavior."

"I am sorry you harbor bitter feelings." Roger sighed again. "Though I am forced to concede that there is some justification for your hostility."

Some justification! Marietta fumed.

"Be that as it may, you have not told me why it is you are here. And what is afoot? There are carriages all up and down the drive, and the east wing is alight like a victory illumination."

"There is a ball in progress, Roger. And if you will pardon me, I really must return—"

"A ball?" Roger interposed. "That is impossible; Chris never entertains."

"Well, he *is* entertaining this evening, and as I indicated, I should like to rejoin the festivities. I regret that there is no servant to escort you to your bedchamber, but they are all quite occupied."

"A ball." Roger shook his head. "And you traveled down from Suffolk for the assembly, did you? That is why you are here?"

The events of the evening had rendered Marietta's

mind a trifle foggy: she had entirely forgotten that Roger did not know of her marriage. She wondered if she retained sufficient wit to relate the story and, if so, how she could possibly begin.

"Ah, here you are, Lady Sheridan." Crawford strode into the entry hall. "I took the liberty, ma'am, of delivering an entire *bottle* of champagne to Mrs. Sampson, and I daresay she will soon be altogether cheered." The butler stopped and peered at Roger. "Mr. Thorning?" he said dubiously.

"Lady Sheridan?" Roger had turned a shade considerably whiter than his sling, and his hazel eyes had widened to great saucers. "Lady Sheridan?"

"Mr. Thorning?" Crawford repeated. "Whatever has happened to you, sir? Never mind. It is clear that your injuries have affected your entire constitution; you are deathly pale. Begging your pardon, sir, but I must suggest that you retire at once."

"Lady Sheridan," Roger mumbled. "Lady Sheridan."

"I fear he is delirious, ma'am," Crawford whispered. "He could grow violent; I shall fetch his lordship." Before Marietta could protest, the butler whirled around and retreated, at a dead run, back down the corridor.

"Lady Sheridan."

Roger looked about the foyer, apparently seeking a place to collapse, but Marietta had removed the ancient carved chair from beside the plant stand. Roger staggered to the library door, threw it open, stumbled inside, and promptly tripped over a stack of books just beyond the door. He hit the floor with an alarming crash, and Marietta decided that Christian charity compelled her to go to his assistance. She rushed into the library, tugged him up from the threadbare rug, and helped him to the chair.

"Brandy," he croaked. "Brandy."

Marietta lit the library lamps, proceeded to the liquor chest, and poured a generous snifter. Roger swallowed half the contents in one gulp, and a trace of color crept back into his cheeks.

"Lady Sheridan." He took another sip of brandy and choked a bit. "You and Chris are *married*?"

"I perceive no other way in which I could be Lady Sheridan, do you?"

"No, of course not. But . . . but . . . but . . ."

"I fail to comprehend your surprise, Roger," Marietta said coldly. "As I recollect it, your note—the note by which you so abruptly abandoned me—stated your confidence that Christopher would attend my needs."

"Yes, and I *was* confident. But I never dreamed . . ." His voice trailed off, and he drained his brandy. "If you would not mind, Marietta . . ."

He extended the snifter, and Marietta snatched it irritably out of his hand. "Just what *did* you dream?" she demanded, stalking to the liquor cabinet. She unstopped the decanter with a clang and refilled the glass. "I have wondered that," she continued, marching back across the room. She passed him the snifter and remained beside the chair. "I suppose you thought Christopher would pack me back to Suffolk with a few pounds for my trouble, and everything would be satisfactorily settled."

"Hardly 'a few pounds,' Marietta." The brandy had evidently restored Roger in spirit as well as body, for his tone was one of patient, wounded indignation. "I assumed Chris would provide for you quite handsomely; he is, after all, a very wealthy fellow."

"What an exceedingly cozy scene," the Viscount drawled. "I trust you will not object if I join you?"

Marietta spun around, and Roger briefly attempted to struggle to his feet.

"Pray do not strain yourself, Roger; Crawford advises me that you are at death's very door." Christopher strode into the room, brushed past Marietta as though she were quite invisible, and gazed down at his brother. "Well, perhaps not at death's door, but I must own that I have seen you in better force. What the deuce happened?"

"An accident, Chris."

The Viscount continued to the liquor cabinet and

splashed brandy into another snifter; though Marietta could not be sure, she fancied his hands were a trifle unsteady.

"As I mentioned to Marietta earlier, it was a most serious accident; I have been largely abed since it occurred. The carriage altogether rolled over."

"Did it indeed?" Christopher turned, his black brows slightly inclined, and sipped his brandy. "And where did the accident take place?"

"Near Brentwood."

"Brentwood," the Viscount mused, staring into his glass. "You were en route to Dover at the time, of course."

Roger appeared to flush though, again, Marietta could not be certain. "Of course."

"And having recovered sufficiently to resume your travels, you elected to return to Essex. I wonder that you did not proceed abroad."

"I am scarcely *recovered*, Chris," Roger protested. "Indeed, I am able to hobble about only with the greatest difficulty." He rotated his injured ankle and winced most convincingly. "It was quite out of the question for me to follow my original plan."

"I daresay it was." Christopher seemed to be talking as much to himself as to his brother. "I daresay it was. And did Marietta neglect to inform you that an event of considerable magnitude has transpired in your absence?" The Viscount's eyes rested on her a moment; they were hard and pale as ice.

"Yes. No. That is to say, Marietta did advise me of your . . . your marriage."

"I fancy you were extremely surprised," Christopher suggested dryly.

"I was indeed; so much so that the matter briefly slipped my mind. Naturally I wish to offer my most sincere congratulations."

"Naturally. Did Marietta also advise you that we are conducting a ball this evening in celebration of our happy marriage? Perhaps not, for it appears that she has entirely forgotten it."

"Christopher, please—"

"Do not tease yourself about it, my dear; I can well conceive that you and Roger have a great deal to discuss. Since I have confirmed that my dear brother is unlikely, after all, to expire within the next few hours, I shall rejoin our guests. I trust that you, too, will return to the ballroom at your earliest convenience? When you and Roger have *quite* finished your conversation?"

The Viscount drained his snifter and smashed it down upon the chest, shattering it into a dozen fragments. Shards of glass tinkled to the floor, and Marietta saw a bright trickle of blood on his lordship's forefinger.

"You have cut yourself, Christopher—"

"It is the merest trifle, my love; nothing in comparison to *Roger's* injuries. Good evening." He stalked past them and out of the room and slammed the door with a force that momentarily shook the floor.

"Chris seems a bit overset," Roger observed in historic understatement. "But, as I believe I once told you, Marietta, we have never got on. I well remember our first quarrel; I fancy Chris was ten and I only three . . ."

Roger related the tale—something to do with a toy soldier—but Marietta hardly heard him. Overset? she thought, staring miserably at the door. It appeared, in fact, that Roger's arrival had utterly destroyed her and Christopher's budding intimacy, had totally erased that magical interlude in the garden. She could perceive but one reason for the Viscount's fury: he must suppose that she still cared for his brother. And she could see only one way to disabuse Christopher of his absurd notion: despite her exhaustion, her own distress, she would agree to "normalize" their marriage at once. Roger had set his snifter on the table beside the chair, and Marietta surreptitiously picked it up and took a long, deep sip of brandy.

"I fear you will have to pardon me, Roger." She interrupted him in mid-word; she was not sure whether he was still narrating his original story or had launched into another. "If necessary, I shall send back a foot-man to help you to your bedchamber."

Roger assumed his martyred expression and said that "somehow" he would manage to negotiate the stairs without assistance. "However, you might pour me just a *drop* of brandy, Marietta . . ."

She refilled his snifter to the rim and, leaving him to sigh contentedly in the chair, rushed back down the corridor to the east wing. There was a quadrille under-way in the ballroom, and she eventually spotted Christo-pher leading Mrs. Sutton through the steps. When the set had ended, Marietta sped across the floor, and the Major's wife, evidently recalling their horrifying en-counter at Aunt Charlotte's, blushed quite scarlet and scurried away.

"Ah, here you are," the Viscount said coolly. "Am I to collect that you have seen my invalid brother safely to bed?"

In view of the message she had determined to con-vey, his choice of words was most provocative, and Marietta felt her own cheeks redden. "I left Roger in the library drinking brandy," she replied rather stiffly.

"Yes, drinking brandy is an activity of which Roger is exceedingly fond. But then I daresay you are well aware of that." The orchestra experimented with the first bars of a waltz. "Now if you will excuse me, my dear . . ."

He bowed and started to walk away, and Marietta grabbed the sleeve of his wasp-waisted coat. "Christo-pher, please; there is something I wish to say." The or-chestra burst into full song, and couples began to circle around them. Sir Mark and Lady Winship whirled by, and her ladyship cast them a sharp, curious look. "Dance with me," Marietta hissed.

The Viscount took her in his arms with unmistak-able reluctance, and Marietta noted that he had donned his gloves again. "How . . . how is your hand?" she asked.

"If you accosted me merely to inquire about my

hand, you could have spared yourself a great deal of trouble. My injury, as I believe I pointed out in the library, pales to insignificance when compared to those sustained by my dear brother."

"*Please*, Christopher." Lady Winship floated past again, and Marietta tried, and failed, to smile. "I did not intend to inquire about her hand, nor do I want to discuss Roger." Her heart was pounding painfully against her ribs, and she drew a deep, ragged breath. "I wished to resume our earlier conversation."

"What conversation is that?"

"In . . . in the garden. You indicated that you would like to . . . to change the basis of our relationship—"

"Pray permit me to put you at ease, Marietta," his lordship interposed. "I now recognize that my proposal was extremely foolish, and I assure you that I shall not pursue it."

"Foolish?" she echoed dumbly. "Not pursue it?"

"Your relief is manifest, and I apologize for having alarmed you. I suspect I was seduced by a summer night and an excess of champagne; I am, after all, a man. But I realized at once that it wouldn't do at all. To the contrary, it would be most hazardous to risk the injection of emotion into an already difficult situation."

"Risk?" Marietta's voice was shaking. "I doubt there was any risk whatever, milord; I doubt you have suffered a single moment of emotion in the whole of your life."

"Then I fancy we make an excellent pair," the Viscount snapped. "And now that you have enjoyed your little burst of dramatics, allow me to suggest that you conduct yourself, publicly at least, with discretion. I should hope we can project an image of harmony until the situation is resolved."

It was the second time he had used the word "situation" to describe their marriage. As though it were an unpleasant, but fortunately temporary, circumstance which, as he had phrased it, could be "resolved." Marietta stumbled, and Christopher jerked her arm so sharply that she was hard put not to cry out.

When the set was over, the Viscount led her to Major Sutton, who, his lordship said, had demanded a dance with Lady Sheridan in exchange for Christopher's quadrille with Mrs. Sutton. Sir Hugh claimed Marietta's hand as soon as the Major had released her, then Cousin Mortimer, and after that she lost track of her partners. She did recall a waltz, late in the evening, with Uncle Ralph, for the Marquis, well lubricated with champagne, seized the opportunity to boom forth his fervent approval of his new niece.

"Naturally I take some credit for having encouraged the boy to wed," Lord Cadbury bellowed. "However, the selection of a bride was his alone, and an excellent choice it was, my dear."

Marietta wondered Christopher's reaction to this roar of praise, but the Viscount was far across the floor, dancing with Lady Winship. "Thank you, Uncle Ralph," she murmured wearily.

The Marquis and Aunt Charlotte, first to arrive, were also last to leave the assembly, and as Marietta watched their carriage roll from sight, she detected pale streaks of gray in the eastern sky. She returned to the ballroom and glanced desultorily about, but to her utter lack of surprise Christopher had disappeared. She watched for a further moment as the servants began to extinguish the lamps and chandeliers, then toiled down the corridor and up the stairs to her bedchamber.

In view of the hour, she had excused April from attendance, and she undressed herself, donned her nightgown, and crawled into the bed. Poppy greeted her with a groggy kiss, and Marietta threw her arm about the dog, briefly, bitterly reflecting how differently the night might have ended.

But the interminable hours of dancing and smiling and inane chatter had done their work: Marietta closed her eyes and fell at once to sleep.

12

THE MANTEL CLOCK was chiming noon when Marietta woke, and as so often happened, she discovered that sleep had entirely changed her outlook. She recalled, ringing for April, that she had never informed Christopher of her lack of affection for his brother; pride had compelled her, on the occasion of their first meeting, to dissemble. So it was quite natural for the Viscount to assume that she had harbored a great *tendre* for Roger and had not overcome this mythical passion in the space of a few short weeks. The initial misunderstanding had led to further confusion: when Marietta had broached the subject of his lordship's proposal to "normalize" their marriage, he had clearly inferred that she intended to *reject* rather than *accept* his suggestion. His own pride had come into play, and he had made his unpleasant remarks merely to salve his wounded dignity.

It seemed, in short, clear that once she had spoken to Christopher in a calm, rational manner, they could forget the nasty interlude in the library, the unfortunate scene in the ballroom, and proceed unimpeded from the moment in the garden. Marietta's heart danced unevenly against her ribs, and she hurried to the wardrobe to select her costume for the day.

Though Marietta rushed April mercilessly through her toilette, nearly three-quarters of an hour had elapsed before she reached the breakfast parlor. To her dismay, she found Roger alone, fairly wolfing down an enormous serving of eggs and three large kidneys.

"Good day," he said cheerfully. "May I say that you look exceedingly handsome again this afternoon?"

Marietta, clad in a new walking dress of gray Circassian cloth, had immodestly judged herself rather handsome as well. However, she was in no frame of mind to entertain Roger's compliments, and she coolly inclined her head and took her place. Patterson bounded forward and set a plate on the table before her.

"I should like to add," Roger bubbled on, "that the food has improved most astonishingly. I can scarcely credit the testimony of my own mouth." He reinforced this observation by demolishing half a kidney in one great bite.

Marietta nodded again, tasted her eggs, and frowned. Though the fare was no doubt "astonishing" to Roger, Marietta herself detected a sharp deterioration from yesterday morning's offering.

"Mrs. Sampson is a trifle unwell," Patterson whispered, apparently reading Lady Sheridan's displeasure. "She claims to have a fearful headache, and I myself observed, ma'am, that her hands are trembling most violently."

Marietta recollected the "entire *bottle*" of champagne Crawford had provided the portly cook and bit back a smile. "Very well," she said as sternly as she could. "Thank you, Patterson."

Marietta glanced about the table and noted that Christopher's place had already been cleared; only his lordship's ubiquitous *Times* betrayed the fact that he had taken his breakfast earlier. She pulled the paper toward her and absently scanned the front page. The authorities, she saw, had achieved a rare victory over the nation's innumerable smugglers. Excise officers had intercepted a wagon of "ordnance stores," purportedly being returned from France, and had discovered—instead of shot, shell, and rockets—a load of claret and champagne. Marietta shook her head and turned to the second page.

"Not only the food is different," Roger said. Though Marietta had studiedly sought to ignore him, she could not but observe, from the corner of her eye, that he had cleaned his plate and was signaling Patterson for a refill. "As I believe I mentioned last night, Twin Oaks as a whole has been transformed almost beyond recognition. For which you are certainly to be commended."

"Thank you, Roger."

Her tone was one of cool, firm finality, but she realized, even as she spoke, that she could not continue to pretend that Roger did not exist. No, it was entirely possible that Christopher's brother would remain under their roof for months, for years, forever; and they must reach some sort of accommodation.

"Thank you, Roger," she repeated. "I trust you will be comfortable at Twin Oaks for as long as you choose to stay."

"I trust I shall." Roger punctuated his remark with a huge mouthful of egg and another half a kidney. "For my part, I believe I have adjusted to the notion that you are now my sister-in-law. Though I must own to a good deal of puzzlement as to how you could possibly have married old Chris."

"Christopher is not in the least 'old,'" Marietta snapped. "Insofar as our marriage is concerned, I must point out that you left me very little choice. As I believe *I* mentioned last night, you abandoned me most abruptly, and your desertion placed me in an utterly untenable position."

She paused, toying with her fork, but she was no longer hungry, and she pushed her plate away. "That is another circumstance I have wondered about, Roger. Why did you permit me to travel to Essex? Why did you not dispatch a letter to Rosefields to advise me of your desire to terminate our engagement?"

"A letter." Roger coughed but nevertheless managed to consume the remainder of his kidney. "I am truly sorry for that, but the fact is, I did not reach a decision until the very last instant."

"But you did," Marietta protested. "You departed at least two days prior to my arrival, perhaps three. Suffolk is only six hours distant; you could have sent a message even on the Sunday."

"Yes, I daresay I could have." Roger heaved one of his dramatic sighs. "I fear that my personal turmoil drove the matter quite out of my mind."

"The same '*turmoil*,' I presume, which prompted you not to inform anyone in the neighborhood of our impending marriage."

"I have never been one to chatter of my private affairs, Marietta."

Though he spoke with considerable dignity, Marietta would have wagered her last groat that he was lying. But this particular subject was one about which she could ill afford to berate him.

"As it happens, Roger, your . . . ahem . . . desire for privacy has proved most fortunate. I was forced to admit to Sir Hugh that I had met you in London, so it is no secret that we were previously acquainted. However, no one is aware of the precise conditions of Christopher's and my marriage, and I should appreciate it if you would continue to guard your tongue."

"Of course I shall," Roger said kindly. He devoured a final speck of egg and sat back with a satisfied belch. "I have no wish to create further problems for you, Marietta, for I am sure you have problems enough as it is. Marriage to Chris cannot be easy, especially as he no doubt fancies he was forced into the parson's mousetrap." Roger shook his chestnut head. "I cannot imagine what impelled him to such a step. Why would he *wed* you?"

Marietta quelled an insane urge to laugh. As she had the evening before, she was seeing Roger through new, objective eyes, and she suddenly perceived why it was that he judged Christopher "old." Roger himself was a perennial child, possessing not a single shred of responsibility, of honor, of simple tact. She decided it was far beneath her dignity to engage in further argument.

"I cannot imagine it either, Roger," she said dryly.

"Well, I daresay Uncle Ralph is pleased. He was

forever threatening to disown Chris if he did not settle himself down."

"Forever?" Marietta echoed sharply.

"Once a month at least for the past half-dozen years. Yes, Uncle Ralph would ride over to Twin Oaks—he has latterly taken to driving his curricle— and call Chris out from his macao game and rip him up. But what am I saying?" Roger flashed an apologetic smile. "I promised just a few minutes since to create no further problems, and here I am babbling of Chris's . . . Chris's . . ."

His voice trailed off provocatively, and Marietta suspected he was testing her. "Rakeshame habits," she supplied levelly. "Yes, I am given to understand that Christopher has a rather unsavory reputation. I collect that Mr. Lloyd frequently complains of the various expenses he is required to meet."

Roger colored a bit; Marietta would not have thought he would be so discomfited by her frankness. "Well, do not tease yourself about it," he mumbled.

"I do not intend to," she said briskly.

In fact, her heart was skipping against her ribs again. Apparently Christopher had *not* married her to appease his uncle, not if Lord Cadbury had "forever" roared out his dire threats of disinheritance. Roger's information had given her further reason to hope that she and the Viscount could speedily reach a reconciliation, could "normalize" their marriage in every sense of the word. She wanted to seek Christopher out at once, and she tossed her napkin on the table and rose.

"If you will excuse me, Roger—"

"Lady Sheridan!"

Crawford had called from halfway across the morning room, and when Marietta looked up, she found him hurrying toward the breakfast parlor in apparent agitation.

"Pardon me, ma'am, but there are people below asking for you. Rather . . . rather peculiar people, I must add."

"Peculiar in what respect, Crawford?" Marietta inquired idly.

"Well, I say they asked for you, but, in fact, they asked for 'Mrs. Thorning.' I assured them there was no such person in residence." The butler stared suspiciously at Roger—as though pondering the notion that the younger Thorning had somehow smuggled in a bride—but eventually shook his head. "As I stated, I advised them that there *was* no Mrs. Thorning, but they were most insistent about it. Consequently, I asked Mr. and Mrs. Hewitt to wait in the entry hall—"

"Mr. and Mrs. Hewitt!" Marietta sank back into her chair, her knees literally weak with dismay. She could not face her stepmother, not until she had had an opportunity to devise a smooth explanation of her dramatically altered circumstances. "You must send them away, Crawford."

"You do know them, then, ma'am? I wonder how they came to confuse your proper title?"

"I . . . I cannot imagine," Marietta said. "In any event, pray advise them that I am indisposed and that they may return tomorrow—"

"There she is! Yoo-hoo! Marietta, dear!"

Even had Marietta not had a clear view of the short, thin, blond figure rushing through the morning room, she would readily have recognized Agnes' shrill, grating voice. She leaped to her feet, and the chair crashed over behind her.

"You see, I told you, Ambrose, that I had made no error."

Agnes screeched to a halt at the breakfast-parlor door and glowered a bit at the man beside her. He was but a few inches taller than Agnes—a plump little man with shrewd blue eyes and the merest fringe of white hair bordering his bald pate.

"As for *you*"—Agnes scowled at Crawford—"I am unaccustomed to such devious machinations from a servant. No Mrs. Thorning indeed!" She peered into the room, and her own rather faded blue eyes fell on Roger. "And there is *Mr.* Thorning!" she squealed.

Roger belatedly rose as well, and Agnes gasped.

"But whatever has happened to you? Oh, my poor, dear boy! Did you sustain your injuries before or after the wedding?"

"You are excused, Crawford," Marietta said hastily.

"Well, if you are certain, ma'am . . ." The butler was obviously reluctant to leave the scene of such a fascinating interchange.

"I am quite certain," Marietta snapped. "Please go."

Crawford started across the morning room, pausing to flick invisible specks of dust from each and every item of furniture, and Marietta hurried round the table.

"Agnes," she hissed, "before you continue, I must draw your attention to some rather . . . rather unusual events which have transpired—"

"Pray resume your seat, Mr. Thorning," Agnes interposed. "Though perhaps, in light of our relationship, you would not object if I were to call you Roger?"

"I should not object at all," Roger said gravely. He lowered himself into his chair again, and Marietta shot him a furious glare. "Not in the least, Lady Chase. Forgive me; Mrs. Hewitt."

"But *you* must call *me* Agnes," she beamed.

"Agnes, please." Marietta glanced into the morning room and discovered, to her relief, that Crawford had disappeared. "There is a matter I really must explain—"

"And this," Agnes rattled on, "is my dear husband, Ambrose."

"Delighted, I am sure," the little man intoned.

"Mr. Hewitt," Marietta murmured. "I was at the point of describing the . . . the curious situation which has developed—"

"We shall have none of that," Mr. Hewitt interjected jovially. "No, indeed; you must refer to me as Ambrose, for I could not regard you more fondly if you were my natural daughter."

His attitude had undergone a remarkable change, Marietta reflected wryly: not three months since, he had informed Agnes that he would not have Marietta under his roof "for a single day."

"Very well, Ambrose," she said politely. "If I may proceed then—"

"The injunction applies to you as well, my boy." Ambrose beamed at Roger, and Marietta noted that Mr. and the new Mrs. Hewitt looked astonishingly alike. "I should like to think of you as my son. Indeed, I should like to think of us all as one happy family—"

"*Please!*" Marietta was fairly shrieking. "I have been attempting for some minutes to advise you that you are laboring under a very serious misapprehension. Roger and I are not married."

"Not . . . married?" Agnes' pale blue eyes widened with horror. "Not married?" She clutched the bosom of her brown bombazine carriage dress, staggered on into the breakfast parlor, and collapsed into the nearest chair. "I am totally at a loss to comprehend your behavior, Marietta." She emitted a strangled moan. "After all my years of careful training—"

"*Please*, Agnes. I am not married to Roger, but I *am* married to his brother. To Christopher Thorning, Viscount Sheridan."

"Viscount Sheridan?" Agnes jumped out of the chair, miraculously restored. "The one who will one day be Marquis of Cadbury? But that is *wonderful*, my dear. Did you hear that, Ambrose? Marietta is *Lady Sheridan.*"

"I did hear." Ambrose's bright blue eyes darted from Marietta to Roger. "And though I naturally wish to tender my congratulations, I must own that I judge the situation most irregular. I cannot but question the circumstances which led to such an astonishing modification of plans—"

"Oh, hush, Ambrose," Agnes said irritably. "When, Marietta, can we meet the dear Viscount?"

"Not today, I fear." Marietta essayed a sigh. "Christopher and I conducted an assembly last evening, and he is quite occupied with tidying up." She realized she had conveyed the impression that the Viscount might well be scrubbing platters in the scullery, but Agnes merely nodded. "Perhaps you might come back tomorrow."

"Tomorrow." Ambrose cleared his throat. "As it happens, Marietta—"

He was cut short by a tattoo of footsteps on the stairs, and a moment later Christopher strode into the morning room. He had evidently postponed his morning ride to afternoon, Marietta surmised: he was wearing his buckskin breeches, his riding coat, his hunting tops. He reached the breakfast parlor and greeted them all with a cool, impartial nod.

"But apparently he has completed his endeavors!" Marietta said brightly. "Christopher, I should like to present my stepmother and her husband, whom I believe I told you of. Mr. and Mrs. Hewitt."

"Mr. and Mrs. Hewitt." The Viscount's second nod was no warmer than his first. "Yes, Crawford advised me that you had arrived. What an exceedingly pleasant surprise."

"You can scarcely be as surprised as we, Lord Sheridan." Ambrose drew himself to his full height, a posture which placed his gleaming crown at the approximate level of Christopher's shoulder. "Marietta has just informed us of your marriage, and my reaction far surpasses 'surprise.' 'Shock' would be much the better word. I journeyed to Essex expecting to find my dear daughter wed to Mr. Thorning. I discovered, instead, that poor Marietta has been traded about, rather like a head of livestock, and is married to *you*."

"I am sure there is a perfectly logical explanation," Agnes said nervously.

"I do not share your confidence, my dear," Ambrose snapped. "I do, of course, *hope* that these *gentlemen*"—he glowered equally at both Thorning brothers—"can offer some reason for their very peculiar behavior. I should hate to think that dear Marietta has been compromised."

"I assure you that she has not, Mr. Hewitt," the Viscount said coolly. "Indeed, 'dear Marietta' has not been compromised *in any way*."

Marietta blushed, and Ambrose attempted, without success, to draw himself up yet further.

"That remains to be seen, Lord Sheridan," he said loftily. "I am certain you will understand, now that this *dismaying* situation has come to my attention, that I cannot simply abandon my daughter to who-knows-what additional humiliation. No, I shall remain here at Twin Oaks until I am *quite* persuaded of her proper treatment."

"I had rather fancied that you intended to stay on in any event, Mr. Hewitt," Christopher said politely. "I observed a great deal of luggage in the entry hall."

Ambrose colored a bit and cleared his throat again. "It is true that Agnes and I did plan a brief visit with our daughter and son-in-law. Our *presumed* son-in-law, I should say. As it is, I fear the visit may have to be a lengthy one."

"You are welcome to stay as long as you like." The Viscount's tone was infinitely courteous, and Marietta wondered if she was the only person present who saw the hard, dangerous light in his silver eyes. "Though I am somewhat surprised, Mr. Hewitt, that you are able to leave your business for extended periods of time."

Ambrose's flush deepened. "Fortunately, my business is one that requires a minimum of personal attention," he said stiffly.

"Yes, you are an importer, are you not? Specializing in wines and spirits, I believe." Ambrose turned a most alarming shade of scarlet, but Christopher did not appear to notice. "Be that as it may, you have come at a most opportune time. You missed Marietta's and my own assembly, which took place last night, but I am happy to say that one of our neighbors is conducting a ball this evening. I am sure Lady Winship will welcome your participation."

"How *lovely*," Agnes cooed. "And how very kind of you to include us, Lord Sheridan."

"Do not give it another thought, Mrs. Hewitt. I

daresay you would like to rest in preparation for the festivities, so I shall have your bags sent up at once."

Christopher tugged the bell rope, and Roger rose.

"I fancy I should rest as well; strength permitting, I, too, shall attend the assembly." He flashed a martyred smile. "Until tonight then. Agnes? Ambrose?"

Roger bowed and limped out of the breakfast parlor, nearly colliding with Bailey, who had arrived in response to his lordship's summons. Christopher instructed the footman to fetch Mr. and Mrs. Hewitt's luggage from the foyer.

"And which chamber do you wish it taken to, my love?" he asked Marietta.

"The . . . the yellow one, I suppose," she mumbled.

"The yellow one," the Viscount repeated. "Good day, Mr. Hewitt. Mrs. Hewitt. Please arrange to be dressed by a quarter before nine, and we shall see you then."

His exaggerated civility, in combination with the utter flintiness of his silver eyes, struck Marietta with an emotion very close to fear. She recognized, at any rate, that Christopher was in no humor to undertake the conversation she'd had in mind, and she moved to follow Bailey and the Hewitts.

"Perhaps I should just see them down to the room, ensure their comfort—"

"No, you will not, my dear." His lordship's long fingers snaked painfully round her elbow, and she suppressed a wince. "Not just now, for I cannot contain my curiosity a moment more. The plot has thickened so very quickly that I am quite at a loss to keep abreast of the action. I shall therefore begin by inquiring whether the cast is now complete. Or am I to anticipate the entrance of additional dramatis personae?"

She had expected him to upbraid her about Ambrose's dreadful remarks, and his actual words took her so entirely unawares that she felt her mouth drop open. "I do not have the faintest notion what you are talking about," she said with total honesty.

"I am talking about your cohorts. Roger arrived last

evening, shortly followed by the Hewitts. A *charming* couple, by the by." His smile much resembled that of a skull. "I now wish to know if there are other characters involved. Your American cousins, perhaps?"

He was hurting her arm, making it difficult for her to think, but she eventually perceived his meaning. "Are you suggesting that I *invited* them?" she gasped. "If so, I assure you that you are altogether mistaken. I daresay Roger's appearance stunned me rather more than yourself."

"Then permit me to stun you again." The Viscount dropped her arm so abruptly that she staggered. "I actually believed that for a moment or two last night. When Crawford came to the ballroom, bleating that Roger had come, mortally ill, I actually believed you were not responsible. I believed it until I reached the foyer. At that point, I recalled that earlier in the evening the entry hall had been dark; and when I touched the lamp, I found it barely warm. A very grave oversight, my dear: after you had signaled Roger, you really should have extinguished the lamp."

"I did not *signal* Roger," Marietta protested desperately. "I lit the lamp when I heard him at the door . . ." But his lordship's eyes had the hue and the glitter of frost, and she adopted another tack. "Be reasonable, Christopher. Even if I *had* expected Roger—which I did not—Roger has no connection with Agnes and Ambrose. He met Agnes, of course, when he was . . . was courting me, but he had never encountered Ambrose until this very afternoon—"

"Indeed?" The Viscount's voice caught her up almost as sharply as had his hand. "Then I collect they formed an instant and astonishingly warm friendship. I could not but note that Roger addressed both your stepparents by their Christian names."

"Oh, that." Marietta waved her own hand. "That occurred before you came, when Agnes and Ambrose fancied I was married to Roger—"

"Almost as immediate, as intimate a relationship as *you* formed with Mr. Hewitt." His lordship continued as though he had not heard her. "I was under the impression that *you* had not previously encountered him either."

"Well, I had not," Marietta said, somewhat puzzled.

"Yet within the space of ten minutes, he became 'Ambrose,' and you grew to be his 'dear daughter.' His dear daughter whom, he fears, has been irreparably compromised by the wicked Thornings."

He always managed to put her on the defensive, Marietta reflected. Always, and always unjustifiably; and she felt the first stir of anger.

"You obviously feel there is some sort of . . . of scheme afoot," she said coldly. "Of all your ridiculous notions, this is by far the most absurd, but I am tired of listening to your incessant insinuations. I do not care to discuss the subject any further."

"Nor do I wish you to, my dear. I have never bought a seat at Drury Lane when I knew the end of the play. Now, if you will pardon me, I myself should like to rest. I want to be *quite* refreshed for Elinor's ball."

"The ball! Good God." Marietta had scarcely attended Christopher's invitation to the Hewitts, but she suddenly perceived the horrible ramifications. "If Agnes and Ambrose go to Lady Winship's, they will surely inform someone of Roger's and my engagement."

"I should have thought such a circumstance would be all to the good. It would immeasurably strengthen Mr. Hewitt's contention that you have been shamefully mistreated."

"Please, Christopher." It pained her, almost physically, to plead with him, but she saw no alternative. "They cannot go. You must tell them you have reconsidered, that Lady Winship would not welcome extra guests—"

"But that would be a lie, my dear, and I—unlike some of my acquaintance—do not engage in premeditated deception. Elinor is, in fact, exceedingly hospitable, and I fancy she will be delighted to have the Hewitts at her assembly."

He was determined to embarrass her, Marietta thought, to torment her as though she were a helpless insect. Her anger turned to hot, blinding fury, and she lashed out with the first words that came to mind.

"Well, I daresay you know Lady Winship better than I," she hissed.

"And what is that supposed to signify?" the Viscount inquired mildly.

"I am well aware of your . . . your friendship. Your long, *long* friendship. You no doubt regret that you did not wed Lady Winship after all."

"Not half so much as you must regret your marriage to me. Surely you could have devised a less extreme solution to your problems."

"Had I realized how odiously you intended to behave, I certainly should have tried," Marietta snapped.

"It is not too late, my love," Christopher said soothingly. "But Mr. Hewitt has surely advised you of that. Yes, Ambrose the smuggler appears to have the situation well in hand."

"*Smuggler?*" Marietta echoed.

"Spare me your horror, my sweet; conserve your thespian talents for a more appreciative audience. As I stated, I should like to rest, and you really must excuse me. Until tonight?"

The Viscount tendered an elaborate bow and strode through the morning room, and a long moment elapsed before Marietta turned and walked away in the opposite direction.

13

THOUGH SHE HAD had adequate hours of rest, Marietta suddenly found herself quite exhausted, and when she reached her bedchamber, she decided she would nap as well. She stripped off the gray dress and crawled beneath the bedclothes, but her mind was fairly spinning, and she could not relax.

The events of the day had been so confusing that she could hardly begin to sort them out. She closed her eyes, and one certainty emerged from amongst her jumbled thoughts: as she had suspected, Ambrose Hewitt was a smuggler. Marietta recalled the newspaper article she had read that morning and painted in another portion of the picture. While the paragraphs in *The Times* might not have referred specifically to Ambrose, her step-stepfather had no doubt suffered a similar confrontation with the excise officers. He had lost one of his shipments, had discovered himself financially embarrassed, and had rushed to Essex to "visit" his "dear daughter" and her husband. He had planned an indefinite stay from the start and had cleverly seized upon Marietta's situation to justify an extended sojourn at Twin Oaks.

Ambrose was a smuggler, and—another certainty—Christopher had somehow learned of his occupation. Marietta's surprise, the surprise the Viscount had so derided, had not been for the fact of Ambrose's "business" but for Christopher's knowledge of it. It now seemed clear that the Viscount had inquired at length into Ambrose's circumstances, which could only mean that he had set out to investigate Marietta's own background.

And that brought her to the matter of the Plot. It was obvious, as she had stated to Christopher, that his lordship believed there was a conspiracy afoot. Far less obvious—indeed, entirely murky—was what sort of scheme the Viscount could possibly envision. Surely he did not suppose Marietta had wed him with the sole intention of providing a home for her relatives. In the unlikely event he *did* suppose such a thing, what did he imagine Roger's role to be? True, Christopher had erroneously inferred that Roger and the Hewitts were fast friends, but a relationship between the three of them did not appear to signify at all. Roger lived at Twin Oaks on Christopher's sufferance, not hers.

Marietta burrowed fretfully into the pillow, attempting to blank her mind, and recollected one of the Viscount's final comments. He had implied that it was not too late to undo their marriage, an echo of the vague hints he had uttered the night before. Marietta's eyes flew open, and she gazed sightlessly at the ceiling. He was alluding to annulment, of course; there was no other explanation. And he must have considered this avenue of escape from the very beginning, when he had declined to consummate their union. He had wavered briefly in the garden, "seduced" by a combination of extraneous factors, but Roger had appeared before he could pursue his impulsive intentions. His lordship must view the intervention as most fortunate: since their marriage remained a union in name only, it could be dissolved with relative ease.

Marietta felt a sudden chill, and she raised her head. But the windows were closed, as was the door, and she could not conceive why the room seemed so very cold. She turned over, buried her face in Poppy's warm fur, and eventually tumbled into sleep.

The clock was striking seven when Marietta woke, but several hours of fitful dozing had not refreshed her in the least. To the contrary: he head throbbed, her limbs were aching, and her brow, when she checked it, felt quite feverish. She had clearly fallen ill, and her condition provided a perfect excuse to avoid Lady Winship's ball. Marietta was formulating the precise message she would send to Christopher—debating between "exceedingly" and "extremely" to describe the magnitude of her distress—when she remembered the Viscount's perverse invitation to the Hewitts. She could not permit Agnes and Ambrose to attend the assembly unchaperoned, and she sighed and jerked the bell rope.

As luck would have it, April was exceedingly *and* extremely enthusiastic about the upcoming festivities.

"*Our* ball was a stunning success, ma'am," she said smugly, filling the tub with steaming water. "My sister June works for Major Sutton, and she had the afternoon free, and she came by for a little chat. I saw no harm in it, ma'am," the abigail added defensively; "you were sleeping. At any rate, June said our assembly was the talk of the entire neighborhood."

Or of Major Sutton's household at least, Marietta thought dryly. "How many sisters do you have, April?" she asked aloud.

"Five, ma'am."

"Are any of them named January? Or July perhaps?"

"Certainly not, ma'am," April replied indignantly. "Those would be very odd names indeed. Why would you think such a thing?"

"Never mind." Marietta suppressed a giggle and feared she might be succumbing to a fit of hysteria. She scrubbed her arms till they turned quite crimson.

"As I was saying, ma'am, our ball was a grand success, and we must not permit Lady Winship's to surpass it. So you must make it a point to look your very best."

Marietta found the abigail's logic a trifle confusing. But her momentary giddiness had passed, leaving her abysmally depressed again, and she did not care how she looked.

"An excellent idea, April," she said as brightly as

she could. "I shall leave it to you to select the proper gown."

It was, perhaps, a further mark of heavenly displeasure that April chose Marietta's least favorite ensemble: a black crepe dress over a black sarcenet slip, with a bodice far too narrow and sleeves much too full. The white *toque*, which matched the *rouleau* round the skirt, was overornamented with great crepe roses, spilling, on the right side, nearly to Marietta's chin. The general effect, she decided grimly, was that of a small girl masquerading in her mother's clothes.

"I do fancy it needs a touch of color, ma'am," April said dubiously. She dug through the jewel case and triumphantly produced a necklace and a pair of earrings. "Yes, these will be *perfect*."

The abigail fastened the various pieces of jewelry and stood back to admire her handiwork, and Marietta started. The necklace and earrings were composed of rubies and sapphires and diamonds, exactly matching Marietta's rings. Her meaningless rings . . . She shook her head.

"They are *not* perfect?" April said. "We shall find something else then—"

"No, they are fine, April; the jewelry is fine. If you will just assist me with my gloves, I shall be off."

April tugged the black *chamois* gloves over Marietta's hands, fussed with the black velvet Vandykes at the bottom of her skirt, minutely adjusted one of her back curls.

"You look simply ravenous, ma'am," the abigail declared at last.

Marietta supposed she meant "ravishing," though she herself thought she looked quite wretched. But the clock was chiming three-quarters past the hour, and she merely nodded and picked up her reticule. She left the bedchamber and started along the corridor, but she was assailed by a familiar voice behind her.

"Marietta! Do wait, dear; Ambrose is nearly ready."

Marietta reluctantly turned and was hard put to quell a burst of laughter. Ambrose, just emerging from the yellow bedchamber, was properly clad in knee breeches and evening coat. However, his legs, protruding from below his small clothes, were incongruously, painfully thin, and in combination with his plump little torso, lent him a distinctly Elizabethan aspect: he might well have been wearing a padded doublet and thigh breeches and long, clinging hose. Agnes, for her part, wore a gown of scarlet silk which would surely have been the envy of an expensive London Cyprian. They walked toward her, arm in arm, and Marietta sternly bit her lip.

"I hardly thought to encounter you here, dear," Agnes said as they proceeded together down the hall. "I had assumed this was a guest wing."

"It is," Marietta confirmed.

"Then whyever are you residing here? On the opposite side of the house from the dear Viscount?"

"Why?" Marietta gulped. "Er . . . as it happens, the family wing has been in a state of disrepair for some years. Yes, a *fearful* state of disrepair, and I am in the process of renovating Christopher's mother's bedchamber."

"Well, I hope the work will soon be done, dear," Agnes said soothingly. "I am sure the present arrangement proves *most* inconvenient."

Marietta gulped again, quickened her pace, and was fairly galloping as she descended the stairs to the foyer.

Crawford and Roger were standing in the entry hall, and the butler at once announced that his lordship had traveled ahead to Lady Winship's.

"He recollected, ma'am, that it would be extremely uncomfortable if all five of you were to attempt to fit into the barouche. He consequently decided to drive himself to Winrose, and he departed a quarter-hour since."

"I see," Marietta murmured. "If the carriage is ready then, Crawford, we shall be under way ourselves."

The journey to Winrose was, fortunately, a short one, for the conversation was exceedingly strained. The barouche had scarcely clattered to a start when Ambrose inquired about Roger's injuries: when, where, and under what circumstances had the accident occurred?

"It happened just under a month ago," Roger replied. "I was en route to Dover, planning to proceed abroad, when my carriage overturned. A hired chaise, and I certainly intend, when I am able, to bring suit for damages."

Roger issued one of his plaintive sighs, but Ambrose did not appear in the least impressed.

"Going abroad, were you?" he growled. "How very peculiar."

Roger colored and hurriedly changed the subject to that of Ambrose's business. "I do not believe I know your precise occupation, sir."

This was, of course, a topic Ambrose did not wish to discuss at all, and *he* shifted the conversation to the matter of the weather. Everyone in the barouche agreed that it was a lovely summer night, though perhaps a trifle warm, and—the subject rapidly exhausted—they continued to Lady Winship's in awkward silence.

Had she been in better humor, Marietta might have taken some petty satisfaction in the discovery that Winrose possessed no ballroom. The butler admitted them at the front door, and a footman escorted them to the first-floor drawing room. This, Marietta grudgingly conceded, had been converted to quite a passable *semblance* of a ballroom: the furniture had been removed or shoved against the walls; Mr. Pierce had strewn his ubiquitous potted palms tastefully about; and Mr. Taylor and his minions, seated in one corner, were tuning their instruments. The Thorning/Hewitt party paused in the doorway, and Marietta glimpsed the Viscount on the far side of the room, deep in conversation with Sir Mark. She had just torn her eyes away when Lady Winship scurried forward to greet them.

"Good evening, Lady Sheridan." She nodded coolly. "And Roger, you careless boy! Christopher informed me of your *terrible* accident, and I shall be eager to obtain details later in the evening. And this must be Mr. and Mrs. Hewitt. How delighted I am that your visit to Essex coincides with my assembly."

"We are delighted as well, Lady Winship." Agnes was frowning a bit, and Marietta wondered if she had noted her ladyship's casual use of the Viscount's Christian name.

"You were no doubt quite surprised when you reached Twin Oaks," Lady Winship continued.

"*Quite* surprised," Ambrose agreed, scowling at Roger. "The situation was altogether different from what we had expected—"

"Lady Winship was referring to the physical condition of the house," Marietta hastily interposed. "My stepparents have not previously visited Twin Oaks, Lady Winship, so they were *not* surprised." She belatedly registered the full import of Ambrose's words. "That is to say, they *were* surprised, but only insofar as I had written them that the property required a good deal of attention, and they were expecting the worst."

"How could you have written us, dear?" Agnes said. "You did not know—"

"I daresay Ambrose read the letter and neglected to pass it on," Marietta hissed.

"Perhaps so." Agnes, who was not endowed with an abundance of sense, nodded and frowned again at Lady Winship. "I do believe your gown and Marietta's are the same," she said. "The colors are different, of course, but is the design not identical?"

Marietta and her ladyship frowned for a moment at one another, and Marietta realized that Agnes, with her unerring eye for the trivial, was entirely right. Elinor Winship's dress was done in shades of blue rather than black and white, but the style was, indeed, identical to that of Marietta's gown. And Marietta could not but observe that Lady Winship, with her voluptuous figure, did not remotely resemble a child.

"I fancy you are correct, Mrs. Hewitt," Lady Win-

ship said. "The dress is the same, but fortunately Lady
Sheridan and I do not look at all the same *in* it, do we?
If you will excuse me now, I see that the Suttons have
just arrived."

She inclined her head and stepped past them, and
Roger, stating that he desired a "drop" of champagne,
bowed away in the opposite direction. Agnes seemed
impatient to move on into the drawing room as well,
but Ambrose was regarding Marietta with narrowed,
speculative, bright blue eyes.

"I . . . I should have cautioned you," Marietta said.
"No one in the neighborhood knows of Roger's and my
engagement, and I should naturally prefer that it not
be mentioned." She wondered, even as she spoke, why
she was abasing herself before this reptilian little man:
if Christopher *did* seek to annul their marriage, the local gossips would be sated for years to come.

But Ambrose was sorrowfully, kindly nodding his
bald head. "I quite understand, my dear, and we shall
not breathe a word of it. Nor, may I add, shall I question you as to the circumstances which led to such a
shocking situation. I am certain you find the matter far
too painful to discuss. I wish to assure you, however,
that when you *are* prepared to discuss it, you will discover mine to be a most sympathetic ear. Yes, Marietta, I shall welcome your confidence at whatever time
you choose to extend it . . ."

Ambrose rattled on, and Marietta glanced around
the drawing room again. Christopher had disappeared,
and Sir Mark, looking rather bemused, was standing
alone in the center of the dance floor. She recalled the
conversation which had been in progress when she arrived and glimpsed a ray of hope.

"Please pardon me," she said, interrupting Ambrose
in mid-word. "I should like to speak with someone for
a moment. Perhaps you might have a glass of champagne, and I shall join you later."

She slipped away before either of her stepparents
could object and hurried across the room. "Good evening, Mark," she said, reaching his side.

He had been gazing in the opposite direction, and he started and peered down at her. "Good evening, Lady Sheridan," he rejoined coolly.

Marietta noted that he had reverted to formality, and she wondered whether his use of her title had been deliberate or an oversight. He continued to regard her, his expression one of impassive courtesy, and she perceived that his slight had been intentional.

"Evidently you are annoyed with me, Sir Mark," she blurted out.

She should not have said it, and she waited for him to issue a polite demurral. But he pondered her words at some length before he shook his head.

"I am not so much annoyed with *you*, Lady Sheridan, as I am annoyed with myself. I fear I gave Chris some very bad advice."

"Advice?" she echoed. "What advice?"

His eyes narrowed a bit, but he eventually shook his head again. "Never mind, Lady Sheridan. If you will excuse me, I believe I fancy a glass of champagne."

He bowed and started to walk away, and Marietta seized his sleeve. *"Please,"* she begged. "I daresay you find this discussion quite improper, but you are the only person who can assist me. I realize that Christopher is exceedingly overset, and I believe he has told you why. And I must know, Sir Mark; I simply must."

He stared down at her for a moment, and she thought she detected a brief flash of puzzlement before his face once more closed. "You are extremely clever, Lady Sheridan, but I shan't be deceived again. You must ask Chris how much he knows; I shall not tell you." The orchestra struck up a quadrille, and he disengaged his sleeve from her grasp. "If you absolutely insist, I shall stand up with you, but on the whole I'd rather not. So if you will pardon me . . ."

He bowed once more and strode off, and Marietta gazed miserably after him. How much Christopher knew about *what?* she wondered desperately. She spotted the Viscount near the entry and tentatively raised her hand, but he averted his head and led Lady

Winship onto the floor. Marietta entertained an eerie notion that she had somehow been rendered invisible, that she would be quite trampled by a horde of happy dancers. Her eyes flew frantically about, and she glimpsed the Cadburys and Roger chatting in a corner of the room. She rushed toward them, dodging several gay, chattering couples, and literally collided with Aunt Charlotte.

"My dear child, whatever is the matter?" Lady Cadbury demanded. "You must exercise some care, for we should not wish to have *two* invalids at hand." She turned back to Roger. "Dear Roger was just relating his *harrowing* adventures. He did not go abroad after all, Marietta; he was nearly *killed* on the road to Dover."

"So he has advised me," Marietta said dryly.

"I was at the point of telling Roger how very thankful we are that he was spared, for he has always been our *favorite* nephew. As it is, I trust that with proper rest the darling boy will be entirely restored within a week or two." Aunt Charlotte tapped him fondly under the chin with her silver-embroidered fan.

"I do trust so." Roger sighed. "At the moment, however, I discover myself with an empty glass, and I believe I shall repair to the refreshment parlor for a refill. Will you accompany me, Uncle Ralph?"

Though it was doubtful that Lord Cadbury had heard his nephew's question, the Marquis certainly comprehended the significance of an empty glass. He drained his own champagne and nodded, and the two men bowed and strolled toward the entry. Marietta peered surreptitiously at the dance floor. The orchestra was now playing a waltz, and Christopher and Lady Winship were whirling, laughing . . .

"I collect that you and Christopher are in the throes of your first quarrel," Aunt Charlotte said.

Marietta tugged her eyes from the handsome couple on the floor and essayed a brilliant smile, but Lady Cadbury merely sniffed.

"Do not attempt to deny it, my dear, for the symptoms are readily apparent. Christopher arrived alone, he has not directed a single word to you since your own arrival, and he is fairly falling over himself so as to shower attention upon his former *amie*. Do not tease yourself about it; it is typical male behavior. Ralph conducted himself in similar fashion more than once during the early years of our marriage."

Marietta was tempted to ask whether Lord Cadbury had imagined a vague, perfidious Plot, had subtly, but darkly, threatened an annulment of their union. But she bit her lip and bobbed her head.

"I must advise you that he will *never* apologize," Aunt Charlotte continued. "No, when he has overcome his little miff, he will pretend that nothing untoward has occurred. And you, my dear, must simply swallow your pride and forget his horrid, inexcusable behavior. I well recollect a particular incident; Ralph and I could not have been wed above a month . . ."

Aunt Charlotte had just begun to describe the Other Woman—an earl's daughter romantically named Lady Aphrodite—when Agnes and Ambrose bounded up. Marietta performed the introductions with considerable reluctance, but she was forced to own that the Hewitts conducted themselves quite acceptably. Agnes did inquire about the health of the "dear Marquis" and—when Lady Cadbury replied that his lordship was in splendid health indeed—could not suppress a moue of disappointment. However, Aunt Charlotte did not seem to notice this small lapse of courtesy, and in general the presentation went remarkably well.

After the initial amenities had been exchanged, the four of them compared notes of mutual acquaintances in Suffolk and discovered that they had none, at which point the conversation started to wane. As Marietta desperately groped for some topic with which to fill the increasingly lengthy intervals of silence, Mr. Lloyd approached. He had "wonderful news" for Lady Cadbury, he announced, and if her ladyship would be so kind as to stand up with him, he would impart his tidings forthwith. Aunt Charlotte nodded—rather gratefully, Marietta thought—and the little man of business escorted her to the floor.

Mr. Lloyd was somewhat shorter than Lady Cadbury as well, and he was compelled to rest his temple approximately upon her cheekbone in order to whisper into her ear. Marietta watched their cumbersome progress for a moment, wondering how she might again escape her stepparents.

"Shameful." Ambrose clicked his tongue resoundingly against his teeth. "Simply shameful."

"It does not signify in the least," Marietta said. "Mr. Lloyd is our man of business—"

"I was not referring to Mr. Lloyd and Lady Cadbury," Ambrose interposed. "I was referring to the conduct of your husband."

He raised his thick white brows, and as if on cue, Christopher and Lady Winship sailed past them. As usual, her ladyship was not wearing a headdress, and Marietta calculated that her high-piled hair—tied up with blue bows—was almost touching the Viscount's jaw. No, she amended upon closer inspection, Lady Winship's hair was *definitely* brushing his lordship's face.

"I cannot but observe, Marietta, that Lord Sheridan has dallied with our hostess virtually every instant since our arrival. *Before* our arrival, too, I daresay." Ambrose's tone implied that Christopher and her ladyship might well have visited one of the bedchambers, satisfied their lust, and dressed again within the space of fifteen minutes. "Naturally I should like to assume that Lord Sheridan's attentions are merely those of a courteous guest, but your husband's behavior has rendered any such assumption quite impossible. He is fairly staring down the bosom of her gown—"

"Ambrose!" Agnes admonished.

"Hush, Agnes!" Ambrose turned back to Marietta with a gentle, woeful smile. "The fact is, my dear, that your mother is thrilled by the splendid marriage you have made." Marietta distantly noted that Agnes had now become her mother. "However, as I have attempted to explain to her, no title, no riches, can compensate for the abject misery of an unsatisfactory union."

Marietta opened her mouth, not sure precisely what she intended to say, but Ambrose waved her to silence.

"I promised not to question you, my dear, and I shan't. I wish only to assure you that you need not endure the shocking mistreatment to which your husband has chosen to subject you. There are means of rectifying the situation, and when the time is right, I shall assist you. Fortunately, Lord Sheridan is a wealthy man, and I should not suppose you will suffer any financial hardship. To the contrary."

Ambrose gazed intently at *her* bosom, and Marietta's hand flew instinctively up to shield the low bodice of her dress. But she soon perceived that the little smuggler was not interested in the flesh exposed by her low-cut gown.

"The jewels he has given you are very handsome indeed," he said. "Do not allow them out of your sight, for they may become an item of negotiation."

Marietta felt another onslaught of hysterical amusement. Christopher and Ambrose both wanted the marriage terminated though, of course, with entirely different consequences to her. She envisioned them as two boxers, warily circling one another, awaiting an advantageous opportunity to land the first blow. She choked back a giggle but detected, as she did so, a swelling lump in her throat.

"Excuse me," she muttered.

She whirled around and fled toward the entry. Her head and limbs were aching again, her face was once more feverish, and she thought she might well be dying. The Viscount would welcome her demise, of course: it would spare him a great deal of trouble, and he could peer down Lady Winship's scanty dresses to his heart's content. She looked back to see if Ambrose was pursuing her and promptly crashed into a tall, hard body.

"Are you all right, Marietta?" Christopher asked sharply.

The sheer momentum of their collision had forced his arms around her, and for a fleeting moment his expression seemed one of genuine concern. Then he stood her away, and his gray eyes turned hard, metallic, silver.

"Are you all right?" he repeated coldly.

"No, I am not." Marietta swallowed her infuriating threat of tears. "In fact, I fancy I have taken ill, and I wish to leave."

"Leave?" the Viscount drawled. "But you have hardly arrived."

"I should not have supposed you noticed *when* I arrived," Marietta snapped. "Be that as it may, I now desire to go."

"You may certainly do so, my dear, but do not expect me to accompany you."

"I do not expect it," Marietta hissed. "Indeed, I expect nothing from you, now or in the future."

"That is cheering news indeed." Christopher flashed a frigid smile. "Good night, then, my love. Please request Grayson, after he has delivered you safely home, to return for the rest."

He swept her a mocking bow, and Marietta stalked past him, down the stairs, and into the foyer. A party of latecomers cast her a curious glance, but she stared stonily away and instructed Lady Winship's butler to summon Lord Sheridan's carriage. Grayson, the coachman, was unmistakably curious as well, but he handed her into the barouche without comment, remounted the box, and clucked the horses to a start.

Marietta rested her head against the seat, and only after they had turned into the road, only after the bright lights of Winrose had faded from view, did she allow herself to burst into hot, uncontrollable tears.

14

AMONG MANY OTHER unproven theories, Marietta subscribed to a notion that emotional distress often led to physical disability. She was consequently unsurprised when she woke on Sunday morning and discovered that she was truly, wretchedly ill: she *was* feverish, and she ached in every limb and organ of her body. She got out of bed and tottered to the window, drew the drapes and beheld an exceedingly bleak scene. The weather had changed overnight; the sky was low and gray, and rain was spattering against the glass and drenching the drive below. She interpreted this as a sign from heaven and decided to remain in bed until her condition—self-imposed or otherwise—improved. She scrawled a list of books sufficient to see her through her convalescence, rang for April, and dispatched the abigail to the library for the designated reading material.

"Do you wish nothing to eat, ma'am?" April inquired anxiously.

"No, thank you; I am not hungry. Just the books please."

April nodded, and Marietta collapsed back into the bed and listened to the dismal tattoo of raindrops on the windowpanes.

In fact, Marietta consumed very little food during the ensuing three days. On Monday, she did manage to force down a few spoonfuls of broth, and on Tuesday April delivered a hearty chowder, which, she insisted, she would, if necessary, "pour down" Lady Sheridan's throat.

"Mrs. Sampson made it *especially* for you, ma'am,"
the abigail continued. "She has only just recovered herself, and she is most concerned about you."

Marietta wryly reflected that the cook's illness and
her own were rather different in nature, but under
April's worried supervision she ate the better part of
the soup before sending the tray back to the kitchen.

Mostly, however, Marietta slept and read, read and
slept. She sometimes fantasized that her problems
would miraculously resolve themselves while she lurked
in her bedchamber: when, at last, she emerged, Roger,
Ambrose, and Agnes would be gone, and Christopher
would abjectly apologize for his odious behavior. Or
the Viscount, fairly mad with anxiety, would storm to
her bedside and abjectly apologize for his odious behavior.

At other times, Marietta thought (another theory)
that if she erased her difficulties from her mind, she
would devise the perfect solution in a blind, uncon-
scious flash of genius. She would suddenly perceive a
way to eject Roger and the Hewitts from Twin Oaks,
at which point Christopher would abjectly apologize
for his odious behavior . . .

But no resolution presented itself, and on Wednesday morning Marietta realized—with mixed reaction—that she was considerably better. Indeed, she
woke quite ravenous and gave the bell rope a sharp,
eager tug. To her intense annoyance, the mantel clock
ticked off nearly half an hour before April answered
her summons.

"My indisposition is no excuse for idleness," she admonished as the abigail closed the door. "I have been
waiting upwards of twenty minutes—"

"I am sorry, ma'am." April's interruption was an
unmistakable mark of her own poor humor. "As it
happens, I was with Mrs. Hewitt, and I could not seem
to get her hair right. Or so she said."

Marietta recollected that no one had ever been able
to dress Agnes' hair "right," and she essayed a forgiv-

ing smile. "Very well, April. I should like some breakfast now—"

"If I may make a suggestion, ma'am," the abigail
flew unheedingly on, "I do feel that Mrs. Hewitt needs
her own maid. She requires a great deal of attention,
and I doubt I can continue to serve her and yourself as
well."

Marietta searched April's face for some sign of cun-
ning, some hint of intimidation, but the abigail appeared very close to tears.

"The situation will *not* continue, April," she said
soothingly. "Mr. and Mrs. Hewitt will be here but a
short time—"

"That is not the impression *I* got, ma'am." April
emitted a great, indelicate sniffle. "Indeed, just this
morning, while I was rigging Mrs. Hewitt out—*trying*
to rig her out—she asked about larger quarters. She
said she and Mr. Hewitt would like a sitting room as
well as a bedchamber. She even mentioned the possibility of bringing some furniture down from Suffolk.
'The furniture here is quite inadequate,' she said—begging your pardon, ma'am, but those were her exact
words—'and Rosefields is not being used.' When I left,
she and Mr. Hewitt were discussing the hiring of a
moving wagon."

Apparently Ambrose was attempting to maintain
both his options, Marietta reflected: if her marriage
could not be terminated to his advantage, he and
Agnes would live permanently, royally, in Essex.

"Do not tease yourself about it, April," she said
aloud. "Whatever they were discussing, they will not be
at Twin Oaks for long." Her brave pronouncement
notwithstanding, she had no idea how she might evict
her stepparents; perhaps she would receive another supernatural signal.

"Yes, ma'am." April swabbed her eyes with the cuff
of one sleeve. "I should add that your mother did ask
after you and indicated she would like to visit."

"She is not my mother," Marietta snapped. "And I
am not yet well enough to see her." This was only par-

tially untrue; the conversation was rendering her distinctly queasy, and her appetite had begun to wane.

"Isn't it a pity, ma'am?" April shook her head. "How people in families sometimes don't get on, I mean. Take me and my sisters: I get on splendidly with June, but May and I lead a cat-and-dog life. I often wish *June* worked here, and *May* was at Major Sutton's. Or take Lord Sheridan and Mr. Thorning. Jack says his lordship's been cross as crabs ever since his brother came back. They had a terrible quarrel just yesterday, and right before Jack's eyes."

"A quarrel about what?" Marietta asked.

"Well, it was a silly thing, ma'am; it was about brandy. Lord Sheridan said Mr. Thorning had consumed every drop of brandy in the house—though, his lordship said, Mr. Thorning had had a good deal of help from Mr. Hewitt. Begging your pardon, ma'am. Lord Sheridan said he fancied the *least* Mr. Hewitt could do, in view of his business, was to replace the brandy, and then, says Jack, *Mr. Hewitt* got very huffy. In the end, his lordship sent Jack to Chelmsford for more brandy, and Jack says Mr. Thorning and Mr. Hewitt have already drunk half of *that*. But it's neither here nor there, is it, ma'am? I'll fetch your breakfast now."

The abigail curtsied out, and Marietta sank back amongst the pillows. Evidently, she thought grimly, Roger and the Hewitts had quite appropriated Twin Oaks, and Christopher's mood, if possible, had deteriorated even further. By the time April returned, Marietta truly had lost her appetite, and she ate only one slice of toast and a single rasher of bacon.

On Thursday morning, Marietta was compelled to own herself entirely recovered, and when she went to the window, she found that the weather again reflected her condition. The sun had reappeared, and after four days of rain the trees along the drive looked brilliantly, astonishingly green. She recognized that if she remained in her bedchamber, she would be malingering, merely playing the invalid, and she sighed and rang for

April. She then went to the dressing table, glanced idly into the mirror, and recoiled with shock.

She had supposed that her failure to eat would cause some slight loss of weight, but it seemed that all the decrease had occurred in her face: her cheekbones had grown exceedingly prominent, and there were great hollows beneath them. To add to this deathbed aspect, her skin had gone waxen, there were dark smudges under her eyes, and her hair was in filthy, tangled disarray. She was still staring, openmouthed, at the pathetic creature in the glass when April arrived.

"Yes, it will take considerable work, ma'am," the abigail said, peering over Marietta's shoulder, "but fortunately we've plenty of time. Mrs. Hewitt rose very early, and she and Mr. Hewitt and Mr. Thorning have gone for a long drive. They asked Mrs. Sampson to pack them a picnic—it required *three* hampers—and borrowed Lord Sheridan's barouche, and I doubt they'll be back before evening."

"And his lordship?" Marietta asked.

"Oh, no; *he* didn't go, ma'am." April had clearly misinterpreted the question. "No, indeed; Jack says he fairly flew into the boughs when he heard about it. Lord Sheridan saddled his horse—he was in such a hurry he did it himself—and went tearing off, and Jack says he may *never* come back. So, as I said, ma'am, we've plenty of time."

The task needed "plenty of time": it was well after noon before Marietta was bathed and dressed, her hair washed and dried and coiffed. She looked somewhat better, she judged, studying her finished image in the mirror; she was clean, and the smudges beneath her eyes had faded to pale bluish circles. But the peach walking ensemble had proved a poor choice of garb—it seemed to emphasize her pallor—and Marietta decided she could effect the most dramatic improvement by sitting for a time in the sun. She accompanied April to the foyer, and as the abigail returned her mistress' breakfast tray to the kitchen, Marietta proceeded through the drawing room and out the rear doors to the garden.

The gardeners were availing themselves of the fine day as well—planting and pruning and weeding—and they murmured their "Good afternoons" to Lady Sheridan as she wandered along the gravel pathways. She eventually retraced her steps and seated herself on a stone bench near the house, tilted her face to the sun and closed her eyes. It occurred to her that she had arrived at Twin Oaks precisely one month since; in the space of thirty-one days, she had been jilted, engaged, wed, and threatened with annulment of her brief marriage.

Despite the warmth of the sun, Marietta felt a chill and briefly wondered if she might be suffering a relapse. She then realized that she had glimpsed the solution to her "situation," the solution which had eluded her throughout her illness. If Christopher was determined to dissolve their union, she would not wait timidly about until the Viscount elected to broach the subject. No, she would salvage, if nothing else, a few shreds of pride: *she* would request an annulment. Ambrose would no doubt counsel her to demand enormous financial recompense, but she did not intend to consult the plump little smuggler. She would ask Christopher to lend her passage to Virginia, for this seemed, after all, her best solution; and a modest sum to see her through her first days in America. And if his lordship insisted on tendering a gift rather than a loan, she would not decline. In view of the circumstances, twenty, fifty, even a hundred pounds could hardly be construed as charity.

Marietta heaved a ragged sigh of relief, but her face remained cold, and when she reached up to touch her sunken cheeks, she discovered them wet. It was a meaningless reaction, of course: the dissolution of any marriage—no matter how artificial, how abbreviated, how unhappy—was a painful matter. The tears began trickling off her chin, dampening the collar of her spencer; and following April's example she mopped her face with her sleeve.

"Lady Sheridan?" Marietta's eyes flew open, and she beheld Sir Mark gazing curiously down at her. "Oh, I say; I believe you really *have* been ill."

"Yes, I have." She had intended to snap out her response quite smartly, but her regal tone was vastly impaired by the necessity to gulp back a new freshet of tears. "So if you came to check on me, Sir Mark, you have done so, and you may now issue a full report to Christopher. Tell him that though I am most inconveniently alive, I shall not trouble him any further."

"I beg your pardon?" Sir Mark belatedly removed his beaver hat. "I *came* to see Chris, but Crawford was unable to locate him and thought he might be in the garden."

"Oh, no; he is not in the garden." Marietta dabbed her face, as discreetly as possible, with the opposite sleeve. "No, Christopher has gone riding. Or so I am told; you will understand that I have not personally communicated with him for some days. He has gone riding, and my abigail, who knows far more of his activities than I, advises me that he may *never* return . . ."

To her utter horror, Marietta at last succumbed to a fit of sobbing, an inexplicable onslaught of despair that set her shoulders to heaving and literally stole her breath away.

"Good God, Lady Sheridan! Have you no handkerchief?"

"No," she wailed.

"Good God." Though Marietta couldn't see him, she thought Sir Mark *sounded* pale. "Use this then."

Marietta extended one hand, and the baronet placed a square of linen in her palm. When she considered the horrid cake she was making of herself, her weeping intensified, and she fairly howled into the handkerchief, soon soaking it quite through. Several minutes passed before her sobs waned once more to sniffles, and she reluctantly forced her eyes open. Sir Mark had had the grace to turn his back, and Marietta struggled to her feet.

"Thank you," she said stiffly. The baronet turned back round, and she thrust the limp, soggy handkerchief into his hand. "Pray forgive my unseemly conduct; I collect my illness has rendered me a trifle unstable. If you will pardon me—"

"Good God, Lady Sheridan," he said again. He *was* pale, and he spoke as though he had not heard her. "I fear we have done you a terrible injustice after all."

She had started to walk past him, but his choice of words drew her up quite as effectively as if he had physically moved to stop her.

"Injustice?" she echoed sharply. "That is exactly what Christopher said on the night of our ball, just before Roger came. It was in this very garden . . ."

Her mouth started to quiver again, and Sir Mark hastily took her elbow. "*Please*, Lady Sheridan," he begged, "do not cry again, for I've no other handkerchief. Come now; sit down."

He guided her back to the bench, and Marietta collapsed upon it. Sir Mark perched next to her, on the very edge of the bench, and began to twist his hat round and round in his fingers. They were short and thick, not at all like Christopher's long, lean fingers, strong, warm fingers . . . She drew a deep, unsteady breath, and Sir Mark looked at her with considerable alarm.

"*Please,*" he repeated. "Oh, God, Marietta, what a hobble you've put me in. Anything I tell you will be a betrayal of Chris's confidence, but perhaps it would be a greater mark of friendship if I *did* tell you—"

"Tell me what?" Marietta snapped. She was sufficiently recovered that she was starting to grow impatient.

"I hardly know where to begin." Sir Mark dropped his hat, plucked it off the gravel, and painstakingly dusted it off—brushing the fur, examining the results, brushing again. "Very well," he sighed at last. He set his hat on the bench between them. "I shall start by asking you a question. How did you fancy Roger Thorning proposed to support you?"

It was the last thing she had expected him to say, and she studied him warily for a moment, wondering if his inquiry was in the way of a trick. But his rather homely face, though pained, was unmistakably open, and Marietta gazed at her hands.

"Roger advised my stepmother that he had an independent income," she replied. "He said the principal consisted of a settlement he'd received at the time of his father's death."

"Roger *did* receive such a settlement." Sir Mark nodded. "It was maintained in trust until he was one-and-twenty, at which time control passed directly to Roger. He frittered away every last farthing before he was *two*-and-twenty, and from that point since, Roger's 'independent income' has been whatever he could wheedle from Chris."

Marietta was unsurprised; Sir Mark's information precisely fit her new comprehension of Roger. But he had deceived her just two months ago, and her gullibility now seemed a further embarrassment.

"I see," she said with as much dignity as she could muster. "However, I do not perceive that Roger's financial circumstances have any bearing on the current situation."

"They have *every* bearing, Marietta." The baronet rose, paced the gravel for a moment, looked down at her. "I believe Chris would have supported Roger forever if Roger had demanded nothing more than a comfortable country life. He could have remained at Twin Oaks, eaten well, dressed well; Chris even told him he could have a *wife*."

Marietta flushed, but fortunately Mark was staring at the rocky path beneath his feet, the dust on his hessians.

"But Roger fancied himself a pink of the *ton* and behaved accordingly." The baronet kicked at the gravel and looked up. "I infer that Lady Cadbury informed you of Chris's gambling debts? His payments of . . . of conscience?"

He had apparently changed the subject, and even as she nodded, Marietta felt her brows knit with puzzlement.

"It wasn't Chris; it was never Chris; it was always Roger. I do not mean to suggest that Chris is a saint; he is not. But he always gambles with cash, and he has never, to my knowledge, compromised a lady. The checks of which Mr. Lloyd complains so loudly and bitterly were written in Roger's behalf."

"But why?" Marietta blurted out. "Why would Christopher accept the blame?"

"Because he does not wish to destroy Lord and Lady Cadbury's illusions. Roger was only thirteen when Lord and Lady Sheridan died, and Chris was rather wild for a time, quite unable to supervise an adolescent brother. Consequently, Roger lived with Lord and Lady Cadbury during his holidays from school, and they came to regard him as a son."

Or, at least, as their "favorite nephew," Marietta thought, recalling Aunt Charlotte's comment at Lady Winship's assembly.

"When Roger grew into a shameless rake," the baronet continued, "Chris couldn't bear to expose his character. Chris paid and paid, scarcely saying a word, until last year."

"What happened last year?" Marietta asked.

"Insofar as I can ascertain, nothing 'happened,' " Mark responded. "I daresay Chris simply exhausted his patience; he does have a temper, you know."

Marietta suppressed a familiar, somewhat hysterical inclination to laugh.

"At any rate, Chris told Roger there would be no more money. Roger would have his room and board, Chris said, and a reasonable allowance for clothing, but no more cash, no more payments. And at that juncture, Roger was compelled to rely on . . . on . . ."

"On schemes," Marietta supplied. It was as though he had lit a single lamp in a large room: the corners remained shadowy, but the walls, the outlines, were clearly visible.

"Schemes." Mark inclined his head. "As I recollect, Roger first claimed to have run down a child with his curricle, and he requested a thousand pounds for damages. Following that incident, Chris sold Roger's equipage, and he has since been reduced to hiring public transport. Roger next bilked an elderly widow of five thousand pounds, and when her son learned of the matter, Chris was forced to make restitution. I believe Chris advised Mr. Lloyd that that payment was a gambling debt. Roger's most recent plot revolved round a young woman he had purportedly seduced. He stated that the girl was . . . ahem . . . in a delicate condition." The baronet colored and peered intently at the gravel again.

"And Christopher dispatched a check to her father in Norfolk," Marietta said.

"Her 'father' proved to be, upon investigation, her middle-aged protector." Mark's blush deepened, but he managed to raise his eyes. "The girl herself is an actress. I daresay the two of them received a percentage of the proceeds, and Roger pocketed the rest. Be that as it may, you can surely imagine Chris's surmise when you arrived."

The Viscount had assumed that *she* was in league with Roger as well, Marietta thought. And, though unwittingly, she had been. Roger had expected Christopher to "attend" her "needs"; had expected, specifically, that the Viscount would compensate her for breach of promise. But then what? Marietta frowned. Roger had intended to go abroad . . .

No; no, he hadn't. Marietta shook her head as Roger's last scheme became clear. He had planned to lurk about the neighborhood, to accost her on the road back to Suffolk, to "wheedle" away his lordship's payment. But Roger had met with an accident, and before he could return to Twin Oaks, she had married his brother. It all made perfect sense. Except . . .

"Then why did Christopher offer for me?" she demanded. "Every circumstance could only have enhanced his suspicion; he even remarked upon the fact that the postboy had left my luggage in the drive. Why did he offer?"

"He was calling Roger's bluff."

It was a term Marietta had not heard before, and she frowned and shook her head again.

"There is a game of cards called brag." Mark resumed his seat, and his hat tumbled to the ground again, but he did not appear to notice. "A player may wager a great deal of money on a very poor hand in hopes of intimidating the other players to throw in; the technique is called a bluff. Roger had bluffed Chris out three times, and Chris finally decided to call his hand. Chris believed you would beat a hasty retreat, and Roger would come slinking back, properly chastened, and reconsider long and hard before he attempted another scheme."

And, Marietta reflected, her consent to remain at Twin Oaks, shockingly unchaperoned, had served as final confirmation of his lordship's suspicion. He had naturally presumed her to be some sort of demimondaine, with no reputation (if ever she had had one) left to guard.

"Christopher did not intend to marry me then," she said aloud. Her mouth had gone terribly dry, and she was compelled to lick her lips.

"No, but there was a small question in his mind." Mark smiled kindly, as though this were great consolation indeed. "He particularly felt that your statements about Mr. Hewitt—your ill treatment at the hands of Mr. Hewitt—carried the ring of truth. Chris consequently asked me to go to London to . . . to . . ."

"To play the spy," Marietta said.

"Yes." The baronet flushed again. "I was unable to learn anything of Mr. Hewitt, but I did discover that you were apparently a respectable gentlewoman. You can conceive how horrified I was. Of course you can; as I recall, we fairly collided in the entry hall upon my return. When I related my findings to Chris, he was more distressed than I, for he realized . . ."

Mark's voice expired in a cough, and he bent, retrieved his hat, and began busily to dust it off.

"That he was compelled to wed me," Marietta said grimly. "He *had* compromised a 'lady,' and he was honor-bound to proceed with the marriage." She hesitated a moment. "But he was not yet entirely persuaded of my good character," she added, half to herself. She remembered the Viscount's suspicious regard of her new wardrobe, his reluctance to introduce her into society, to give her his mother's engagement ring. "Even on the day of our wedding, he rather expected Roger to interrupt the ceremony."

"Yes." The baronet replaced his hat on the bench and nodded. "That was largely due to your insistence that the wedding be held on the fifteenth."

She had insisted on no such thing, of course, but there seemed little point in contradiction.

"At any rate," Mark continued, "after the wedding *did* proceed without incident, Chris decided to travel up to London himself so as to resolve his last lingering doubts. He learned that Mr. Hewitt was a smuggler, but your own reputation appeared quite impeccable. Furthermore, Chris was exceedingly pleased with you, with your transformation of Twin Oaks. He was, in short, prepared to own himself altogether wrong when Roger and your stepparents arrived. He now fancies that the failure of the original scheme prompted a new and far more elaborate plot."

"But what *sort* of plot?" Marietta asked desperately. "What does he imagine we are at?"

"He is not certain," the baronet said, to Marietta's dim satisfaction. "He briefly supposed you had married him so as to lay your hands on his mother's jewels: with the jewelry safely in your possession, you signaled Roger. But you and Roger did not abscond with the booty, and Mr. Hewitt appeared, muttering of your 'irregular' situation. Chris is not sure of the scheme," Mark reiterated, "but he suspects Mr. Hewitt will demand a termination of the marriage—with an appropriate financial settlement—and that the four of you think to depart Twin Oaks with money and jewels alike fairly falling from your pockets. Roger has, by the by, already extracted fifty pounds by threatening to divulge the circumstances of your and Chris's marriage."

Marietta swirled one foot in the gravel for a moment, watching the white kid toe of her shoe grow gray and gritty. "I should like to ask one more thing," she said, her voice unsteady. "Does Christopher wish our marriage to be terminated?"

Mark was silent for such a long time that she mentally braced herself, physically squared her shoulders. "No, he does not," the baronet replied at last.

Marietta's heart bounded into her throat, and her eyes flew to his craggy face. "Then I've only to talk to him!" she said. "To explain all the circumstances . . ."

But Sir Mark was shaking his head. "To begin with, you would necessarily be forced to betray *my* confidence in you; and had I thought you would do so, I should never have revealed my knowledge. In the second place, Chris would not believe you." He essayed another compassionate smile, but it did not mitigate the harshness of his words. "He no longer trusts you; you will have to prove yourself with actions rather than explanations."

What actions? she wondered despairingly. She had been virtually banned from the Viscount's sight, to say nothing of his bed. "Then why did you tell me?" she burst out.

The baronet snatched up his now-battered hat, studied it with understandable displeasure; and Marietta fancied he would decline to answer. But eventually he rose, and his eyes met hers.

"I told you because, as I stated earlier, I judged it the greater mark of friendship. Because, as I mentioned at your assembly, Chris was more pleased than he knew." He gazed back at his hat and bit his lip, as though he had said enough, but at length he raised his eyes again. "If Chris were not so stubborn, he would have confessed long since that he has fallen in love with you. But perhaps he has a motive on that account; we laid a wager years ago."

Marietta's pulses were racing—pounding in her wrists, crashing in her neck—and she scarcely heard his final sentence.

"And I told you," Mark continued, "because when I saw you this afternoon, I collected that you love Chris as well. I couldn't permit you to leave him, to toss it all away, from sheer ignorance. My conscience is now clear; if you allow Roger and your stepparents to destroy what you and Chris could have, the burden is yours. Good day, Marietta."

He replaced his hat, and she noticed a great patch of dust high on one side. "And good luck."

He bowed and strode down the gravel path, round the corner of the house, and out of sight.

15

MARIETTA CONTINUED TO sit as though she, like the bench, had turned to stone. She did love Christopher, of course; Sir Mark was correct on that account. She loved him, and since she could not identify a moment when her feelings had changed, she could only collect that she had loved him from the start, from the moment he had glanced up from his cards and directed his silver eyes to the drawing-room door. If she had wished it, she could somehow have escaped him; she had wed him because she wanted to be his wife.

And if Mark was right about her emotions, could he possibly be right about Christopher's as well? She remembered the early days of their acquaintance, the

brief flashes of warmth his lordship had so quickly sub-
merged. She had thought at the time that he found her
at least slightly handsome, somewhat interesting. So
perhaps, believing her to be a demirep, he had refused
to own to his attraction. Refused until the night of
their assembly, and then Roger had appeared and
destroyed their tenuous relationship.

But that was precisely what Sir Mark had said she
must *not* permit: she must not allow Roger and the
Hewitts to destroy them. She still could not conceive
the "actions" that might prove her feelings to Christopher, but if he loved her . . . Her heart skipped
against her ribs. If he loved her, anything was possible.

A shadow fell across the bench, and Marietta idly
turned, expecting to see one of the gardeners. But it
was the Viscount who stood in the pathway, his cheeks
ruddy, his black-and-silver hair tousled from his ride.

"Christopher!" She leaped to her feet. "Good . . .
good afternoon."

"What a pleasant surprise," he drawled. "I fancied
you had gone off to picnic with your guests."

"They are not . . ."

She had started to snap a reply, but she bit her lip.
Until such time as she could devise a suitably dramatic
"action," she would be utterly civil, altogether pleasant.
"That is to say, they did not invite me to accompany
them." It sounded quite wrong. "Not that I *should*
have accompanied them if they *had* invited me," she
added.

His lordship's gray eyes narrowed. "You look like
hell," he growled.

"I have been ill," Marietta said. "Which you would
have known had you seen fit to visit me . . ." She bit
her lip again. "But I realize you have no doubt been
too busy to entertain any concern for my health."
Wrong again. "That is to say, I am sure you were *concerned*, but I daresay you have been occupied with
other matters."

"Indeed I have been," Christopher said coolly. "Roger and your stepparents are fairly eating me from

house and home. No, let me be accurate: Roger and Mr. Hewitt are *drinking* me from house and home. To say nothing of the fact that they apparently feel free to appropriate my carriages and go cavorting about the countryside. Furthermore, I assumed that Roger was capable of seeing you through your travail. And vice versa: who better to comfort an invalid than another equally afflicted?"

Marietta's lip was growing raw, so she clenched her hands instead. "I have not spoken with Roger since the night of Lady Winship's ball," she said. She was exceedingly pleased with the mild timbre of her voice.

"No? I am sorry to hear that, but then Roger has never been notably dependable. Now, if you will excuse me, my dear . . ." He tendered an almost imaginary bow and started to walk away.

"Shall I see you at dinner this evening?" Marietta blurted out.

"I fear not." The Viscount turned back and sighed. "I have been invited to dine with Major and Mrs. Sutton. I should naturally suggest that you go as well, but I have already informed Mrs. Sutton that you are far too ill to attend."

He sighed again, bowed again, and proceeded up the path. A full half-minute elapsed before Marietta unclenched her hands and discovered little red crescents where her nails had bitten into her palms.

In view of his lordship's absence, Marietta ordered dinner in her bedchamber, where, to April's joy, she cleaned her plate and dispatched the abigail to the kitchen for a second serving. Evidently Mrs. Sampson was equally thrilled: she sent back *two* additional slices of blueberry pie, one of which—after April had left—Marietta fed to an ecstatic Poppy.

Marietta tossed and turned through most of the night, pondering her dilemma, but by morning she had glimpsed no solution. She was inclined to breakfast in her room as well, but she recognized that a confrontation with her adversaries might trigger some idea. She consequently instructed April to assist her into her last

new walking ensemble—a round dress of pale blue
mull surmounted by a spencer of dark blue silk—and
ventured with considerable reluctance to the breakfast
parlor. She found Roger and the Hewitts finishing a
hearty meal, which, despite the earliness of the hour,
Ambrose and Roger were washing down with generous
snifters of brandy.

"Marietta!" Agnes gasped. "How perfectly dreadful
you look! Come in, my dear; perhaps a bit of breakfast
will help."

"A bit" of food was all that remained: Patterson
was able to present two scant spoonfuls of eggs, a
single rasher of bacon, and half a cold muffin. "If you
wish more, ma'am," he said apologetically, "I'll speak
to Mrs. Sampson."

"No, thank you, Patterson." Marietta had again begun to lose her appetite.

"My poor, dear child," Agnes clucked, as Patterson
returned to the sideboard. "Had I had any notion how
ill you were, I should have *insisted* on seeing you. Even
though April advised me that you were far too ill to receive visitors."

Agnes did not appear to detect anything contradic-
tory in these remarks, and Marietta merely nodded.

"It is hardly surprising that Marietta has been ill,"
Ambrose sniffed. He drained his brandy, signaled Patterson for a refill, and transferred his bright blue eyes
to Marietta. "Roger and I have become quite well acquainted in the past few days, and he has given me a
good deal of information concerning Lord Sheridan's
character. Information which, I must say, I judge most
distressing."

Marietta wondered whether Roger had also informed the little smuggler of his jilting. Apparently not,
for Ambrose was beaming across the table at his new
friend.

"Umm," she mumbled noncommittally.

"We shan't discuss it now, my dear," Ambrose said
soothingly; "we shall wait till you are stronger. However, I did want you to know that I feel we are in an

excellent position." He punctuated his words with a very large sip of brandy.

"But there are matters we *should* discuss now." Agnes cleared her throat. "As I mentioned to April, dear, Ambrose and I have discovered our quarters to be *most* confining. I took the liberty of exploring about—day before yesterday, I believe it was—and found two *connecting* rooms just adjacent to ours. It occurred to me that we could convert one of the bed-chambers to a sitting room and make a lovely little suite. I had thought to bring some of the furniture down from Suffolk—the rosewood writing table and the green couch and chair. You may not recollect the chair, Marietta; it is in my bedchamber—"

Ambrose cleared *his* throat.

"As I say," Agnes flew on, "I had *thought* to transport the furniture, but Ambrose reminded me that we might not be at Twin Oaks long after all. So I fancy that if we can move some of the furniture from the morning room, Ambrose and I shall be quite comfortable. I should like the desk and the arc-backed chair, but I am debating between the yellow sofa and the blue . . ."

Agnes continued to prattle, and Marietta ground her fingernails once more into her palms. She would have adored to order them all from her home at once, before Ambrose had even finished his brandy. But she could not command Roger to leave, and his departure was essential to any "action" she might contrive. She laid her napkin on the table and rose.

"I shall consider it, Agnes," she said politely. She thought her stepmother had decided on the blue couch, but she wasn't sure. "In the interim, I fear I must ask to be excused; I have a great deal to do."

"Well, you must *do* it, then, dear," Agnes said firmly, "for tomorrow we plan to take a picnic to the shore, and we were in hopes you could join us. Our outing yesterday was so amusing . . ."

Agnes was still chattering as Marietta left the break-fast parlor. Not only had she failed to formulate an

idea, she thought grimly, she would now be compelled
to spend another day in her bedchamber, lest Agnes
perceive she had *nothing* to do. The sun was streaming
through the morning-room windows, and Marietta impulsively decided to drive into Chelmsford. She had no
mission in town either, but she would, at least, be out
of doors and away from her unwelcome houseguests.
She hurried to her bedchamber, dispatched April to
order out the barouche, and hastily tied the ribbons of
her new French bonnet.

Marietta sat in the open portion of the carriage and
instructed Grayson to drive very slowly, as a result of
which the journey required nearly an hour. She had always found the sun a splendid restorative, and this day
was no exception; by the time they passed Mr. Taylor's
home at the edge of town, she felt enormously better.
She was inclined to ask Grayson to turn around at once
and proceed back to Twin Oaks, but she feared the
coachman might judge such behavior a trifle odd. She
consequently desired him to wait in the innyard while
she performed her mythical errands.

Marietta wandered along the left-hand side of the
main street, gazing into the shop windows. When she
reached the draper's establishment, she recalled that
she had not yet considered the new upholstery for the
Grecian couch in the drawing room, and she stepped
inside and studied the fabrics for a time. However, she
reminded herself, she must salvage her marriage before
returning her attention to the redecoration of Twin
Oaks; and to the draper's keen disappointment she departed the shop without making a purchase.

Marietta started back up the opposite side of the
street and paused outside Miss Bridger's, briefly
tempted to march in and berate the mantua-maker for
the embarrassing similarity of her and Lady Winship's
ball gowns. But, she conceded, the identical dresses had
been but a minor circumstance on that wretched evening, and she sighed and walked on. The clock in the
church tower struck noon, and she calculated that she
had departed the inn almost an hour since. She quick-

ened her pace, still glancing into the shop windows as she passed, and literally stumbled into Mr. Lloyd.

"Lady Sheridan!" His diminutive stature created the impression that a rabbit had bounded into her path and tripped her up. "What a great pleasure it is to see you." He whipped off his beaver hat and swept an extremely courtly bow. "What brings you to town on such a fine day?"

He straightened and gazed up at her, and Marietta waited for the inevitable reference to her shocking appearance. But perhaps the sun had done its work, perhaps his spectacles did not entirely correct his shortsightedness; in any case, he merely smiled.

"I was just on my way to the Crown and Rose for lunch." The little man of business tossed his head toward the door of the inn, now but a few yards distant. "Would you join me?"

"That is very kind of you, Mr. Lloyd," she murmured, "but as it happens, I am *quite* busy today, and I must return to Twin Oaks at once."

She glanced idly over his balding head and, to her horror, beheld Lady Winship bearing down upon them. There was no one, including Satan himself, she less wished to encounter, and she seized Mr. Lloyd's arm.

"But I daresay I have time for a cup of tea," she said shrilly. "Yes, I shall have some tea while you eat."

She fairly dragged him on to the inn and through the door, slammed the door behind them, and sagged against it. Mr. Lloyd, whose short legs had matched her stride only with the greatest difficulty, peered up at her with considerable confusion, gasping for breath. Fortunately the landlord scurried forward to meet them, escorted them to a prime table in the dining room, and asked for their order.

"The roast beef and vegetables for me," Mr. Lloyd responded, still wheezing a bit, "and tea for Lady Sheridan."

Marietta looked out the window and observed Lady Winship disappearing into the innyard. "No, I haven't the time for tea after all," she said. "Thank you, Mr. Lloyd, but I shall simply sit a moment."

Mr. Lloyd frowned with understandable puzzlement, but he eventually waved the innkeeper away and propped his plump, black-clad arms on the table. "Well, Lady Sheridan, do you plan to journey to Australia?"

"Australia?" she echoed distantly.

She had continued to watch the innyard, and she saw Lady Winship, at the reins of a high-flier phaeton, stop at the entry to the street. Her ladyship glanced to left and right and, to Marietta's relief, clattered on out of the yard and in the direction of the country.

"Australia?" Marietta repeated sharply, at last registering Mr. Lloyd's question. Perhaps Christopher had determined that this would be an even better place of exile than Virginia. "Why Australia?"

"You do not know then?" Mr. Lloyd wriggled about in his chair, clearly delighted to have uncovered a morsel of news to relate. "As I advised Lady Cadbury on Saturday night, Lord Cadbury and Lord Sheridan have co-purchased an extensive piece of property on the Dark Continent."

Marietta believed that Africa was the "Dark Continent," but she said nothing.

"Their lordships hope to raise sheep," Mr. Lloyd added, "though I personally feel any such venture is premature. Be that as it may, I counseled them to proceed with the purchase, for I was able to negotiate an excellent price for the land." He preened a bit and named a figure whose "excellence" Marietta could not begin to evaluate. "So perhaps you *will* travel to Australia one day, Lady Sheridan."

"Perhaps so," Marietta murmured.

With Lady Winship safely removed from the scene, she was eager to be under way herself. However, a buxom waitress delivered Mr. Lloyd's meal, and Marietta fancied it would be quite rude to desert him before he had even started to eat. She sat, shuffling her feet impatiently beneath the table, as the little man of business attacked his beef, his potatoes, his green beans, with astonishing appetite.

"I am particularly delighted to have met up with you today," he said through a mouthful of food, "because I wished to inquire about your stepfather."

"My stepfather," Marietta echoed warily.

"Yes; we had a lengthy chat at Lady Winship's assembly."

"A lengthy chat." Marietta tried to swallow, but her throat had gone dry, and she wished she had ordered tea after all.

"Yes. Mr. Hewitt stated that he has numerous business enterprises both in Britain and abroad. As I recollect, he specifically mentioned France; I believe he has interests in France."

"Yes," Marietta confirmed wryly; "Ambrose *does* have interests in France."

"Umm." Mr. Lloyd wolfed down a heaping forkful of potatoes. "He also indicated that he might be in Essex for some time, and I assured him that *I* am entirely qualified to handle his affairs. If the subject arises, Lady Sheridan, I do trust you will give me a word of recommendation."

"I certainly shall," Marietta said solemnly. She eased her chair away from the table. "Now, if you will excuse me—"

"Mr. Hewitt inquired about Lord Sheridan's affairs as well." Mr. Lloyd had, incredibly, managed to clean his plate, and he sat back and patted his round little belly. "Naturally I advised him that Lord Sheridan is *quite* capable of supporting you. I informed Mr. Hewitt of his lordship's many investments though I did *not* mention the property in Australia, for the papers were signed only on Monday, two days *after* the ball—"

"You talk altogether too freely, Mr. Lloyd," Marietta snapped.

His eyes widened owlishly behind his spectacles, and he emitted a great belch of surprise. Marietta had not intended to chide him, but, having begun, she was compelled to continue.

"You have no right to discuss Christopher's affairs with *anyone*. Not with Lord Cadbury, not with my stepfather, not, I daresay, even with myself."

"But I intended no harm, Lady Sheridan—"

"I am sure you did not," she interrupted, her tone a bit more temperate. "I am sure you never *have* intended any harm, but the fact remains that you have chattered Christopher's private concerns to the very world. Please be advised, Mr. Lloyd, that I shall not tolerate it. If I ever again learn that you have been gossiping about Christopher's activities, I shall insist that he employ another man of business. Good day."

Marietta rose and elected, for emphasis, to fling her napkin upon the table. Unfortunately, as she had not removed her napkin *from* the table, she threw down her reticule instead. Cheeks burning, she retrieved it and stalked as regally as she could out of the dining room and out of the Crown and Rose. As she marched past the window, she peered inside and observed Mr. Lloyd mopping his face with his own napkin and tugging at his suddenly wilted shirt-points.

Grayson proceeded back to Twin Oaks at a somewhat brisker pace, and as they rounded the final curve in the drive, Marietta observed a phaeton drawn up before the hitching post. Even had she not recognized the vehicle, she would readily have identified the figure that emerged from the front door and turned to wave at an invisible party within. Lady Winship then walked to the carriage and untied her horses, mounted the ladder to the seat and smartly cracked her whip. The phaeton raced down the drive, the plumes on Lady Winship's bonnet waving merrily in the wind. Marietta quelled a stab of annoyance; she supposed she should be gratified to have avoided her ladyship twice in a single day.

Grayson assisted Marietta out of the barouche, and she ascended the front steps and paused in the foyer to adjust her eyes to the gloom. She had just begun to venture ahead to the stairs when Christopher's voice caught her up.

"May I have a word with you, Marietta?"

She whirled around and glimpsed the Viscount in the library doorway, his arms folded across his chest, one shoulder propped against the jamb. It was a casual pose, but Marietta could now see sufficiently well to detect a familiar, metallic glitter in his eyes.

"Y-yes," she stammered. "Yes, of course."

"A *private* word," Christopher said pleasantly. "In here, please."

Marietta traversed the entry hall, and at the last possible instant he straightened and beckoned her into the library. He was wearing his terrible, artificial, courteous smile, and Marietta stopped at the threshold.

"Perhaps it would be best if we were to speak later," she murmured.

"No, that would *not* be best, my dear." He took her elbow and pulled her through the door, dropped her arm, closed the door. "I should offer you something to drink, but I find myself rather short of spirits at the moment. I am given to understand that Roger and Mr. Hewitt consumed the last of the brandy at breakfast this morning, and I collect they subsequently requisitioned the claret and the sherry. But wait!" He dramatically snapped his fingers. "I do believe, through some incomprehensible oversight, that they left the Tokay."

Apparently he had called her in to complain, again, of Roger and Ambrose's drinking habits. Marietta, remembering her determination to behave with perfect civility, bit back a sharp rejoinder.

"I don't wish any Tokay, thank you," she said politely. "And I am sorry there is nothing else. Had I known earlier, I could have purchased additional spirits while I was in town."

"Ah, yes, you *were* in town, weren't you?" The Viscount leaned against the door, refolded his arms, crossed one ankle over the other. "You had errands, did you?"

"Not . . . not exactly," Marietta replied. "I wanted to get away for a bit."

"Oh? What *did* you do then? In Chelmsford, I mean."

"I went to the draper to check on fabrics for the drawing-room couch. Though I purchased nothing," she added hastily. "Apart from that, I simply strolled about, looking in the shop windows."

"Indeed," Christopher said coolly. "And was that before or after your meeting with Mr. Lloyd?"

Marietta had not yet decided whether to mention the encounter to his lordship, and she felt her mouth drop open.

"Don't deny it." The Viscount drew himself abruptly up, seeming even taller than he was. "Elinor saw you outside the Crown."

"I did not intend to deny it," Marietta protested. "I *did* meet up with Mr. Lloyd, entirely by accident—"

"By accident?" Christopher emitted a mirthless chuckle. "According to Elinor, you carried him almost bodily into the inn."

"Elinor!" Marietta's splendid intentions had been quite drowned in a sea of rage. "Elinor! Is she your latest spy, then? And what must you think of me, to imagine I would dally with Mr. Lloyd? If I wished to conduct a . . . an *affaire*—which would not be unlikely under the circumstances—I daresay I could locate someone far younger and considerably more attractive."

"I daresay you could," the Viscount snapped. "Roger comes immediately to mind."

"I shall not continue to entertain your lewd and ludicrous innuendos," Marietta said stiffly. "If you will pardon me . . ."

She spun away and opened the door, and his fingers clamped painfully round her wrist.

"Do not turn your back on me," he hissed. "Not ever again. I did not imagine you were tumbling Mr. Lloyd in bed"—Marietta flushed—"but I fancy you were wielding your undeniable charms nevertheless. Hoping to beg fifty or a hundred or a thousand pounds. Well, I shan't have it, Marietta; do you understand me? If you attempt to extract another shilling, I shall have our marriage annulled and pack you off without a groat. Do you understand me?" he repeated.

He cast her hand away, and she massaged her wrist, mutely nodding.

"Very well. You are excused then."

As though she were a servant, she reflected. A very minor servant; a scullery maid perhaps. She slipped through the door, closed it, collapsed against it. She thought she detected a shadow flitting beneath the darker shadow of the stairs, but she was too overset to be sure.

16

MARIETTE TRUDGED UP the stairs and along the corridor to her bedchamber, where she sank into the chair before the dressing table. She gazed at her image in the mirror and distantly noted that she looked much better, but she was too despondent to care.

Though she regretted her display of temper, she could not suppose it had effected any real harm. No, it was clear that Christopher's suspicion, his bitterness, had destroyed any slight affection he might have entertained. And perhaps, she reminded herself, there had been no affection to destroy; perhaps Sir Mark had been wrong. In any event, the Viscount had, for the first time, openly threatened to annul their marriage, and Marietta was compelled to own that this might be the best solution after all. She could not continue to live with a man who distrusted her every drive to town, her every conversation, her every thought. She was young, and she could, she must, somehow put Christopher Thorning behind her.

Marietta's reflection wavered a bit, and she felt telltale patches of dampness on her cheeks. She snatched a handkerchief from the top of the table and furiously dabbed her face; she would permit herself no more tears. There was a knock at the door, and she drew a deep, steadying breath.

"Come in, April," she called as brightly as she could.

But it was Ambrose who cracked the door, peered across the threshold, then rushed to her side, extracting his own handkerchief from the pocket of his frock coat.

"My poor dear child." he clucked; "it appears I've arrived not a moment too soon. Here, dry your eyes, and then we shall talk."

Actually Marietta's eyes were largely dry already, but she took the proffered handkerchief and pressed it once against either lid. She could scarcely conceive that her tiny sniffles had been audible in the hall, and, her imaginary drying concluded, she frowned up at her step-stepfather.

"What is it you wish to discuss, Ambrose?" she asked.

"Your future," he replied heavily. He glanced about the room. "May I?"

Without awaiting a response, he walked to the bed and perched upon the edge. Poppy regarded him with sleepy displeasure, issued a weak growl, and closed her eyes again. Ambrose laced his plump fingers over the rounded front of his waistcoat.

"Your future," he repeated sonorously. "I could not but overhear your and Lord Sheridan's recent conversation. I was not on the listen, of course; I had gone to the library to borrow his lordship's Tokay."

"Having exhausted the brandy, the claret, and the sherry," Marietta suggested.

"Yes; Lord Sheridan's supply of spirits is entirely

inadequate." Ambrose sniffed with annoyance. "Be that as it may, I did, as I have stated, chance to over-hear your husband's shocking threat to seek an annul-ment of your marriage. I am sorry to say that I was not in the least surprised; it is a typical example of his lordship's scandalous behavior. I daresay Roger en-visioned just such a circumstance as well; he has told me that he was extremely reluctant to consent to the marriage."

"Con-consent?" Marietta stammered disbelievingly.

"Do not dissemble, my dear," Ambrose said kindly. "Roger has related the whole sordid story. He ex-plained that when you arrived at Twin Oaks, Lord Sheridan found you most attractive and determined to wed you himself. I am sure you understand that Roger was forced to agree: Lord Sheridan had illegally seized his fortune and left poor Roger quite penniless. Never-theless, Roger feared his brother would soon tire of you, as he has of so many others—"

"Roger told you *that?*" Marietta gasped.

"Do not tease yourself about it, dear; he had only your interests at heart. Roger hoped I could remedy your appalling situation, and I fancy I can." Ambrose emitted a modest cough. "I do believe annulment is the best course though, naturally, we shall not allow his lordship to 'pack you off without a groat.' Those—I re-gret to say—were his exact words."

Marietta well recollected the Viscount's exact words, and she bit her lip.

"No," Ambrose continued, "we shall demand sub-stantial recompense. And we shall brook no objection, for I have learned from several sources that Lord Sheridan is exceedingly wealthy." From Roger and Mr. Lloyd, no doubt, Marietta surmised. "We shall first specify a London town house, suitably furnished and staffed, and an annual income sufficient for its oper-ation. We shall take your jewels as insurance, so to speak . . ."

Ambrose rattled on, and Marietta suppressed a mad,

and maddeningly familiar, inclination to laugh. She felt like the central character in a particularly outlandish comedy, and she eventually shook her head.

"No?" Ambrose barked. She thought he had cut short a description of the several carriages that were to grace their London coach house. "You will not assent to an annulment? Good God; Agnes was right, then." He unlaced his fingers and ran them across his bare scalp; in younger days, he might have uprooted his hair in an excess of agony.

"Right about what?" Marietta inquired politely.

"When Agnes learned of your illness, she at once presumed . . ." Ambrose's voice trailed off, and he coughed again. "She presumed you were . . . ahem . . . in a delicate condition."

"That is . . ." Marietta had started to say "absurd," but she suddenly had the glimmer of an idea, perhaps the supernatural signal she had long awaited. "That is possible," she murmured.

She hoped it would not occur to Ambrose that two and a half weeks was a rather brief interval in which to suspect even the *possibility* of a "delicate condition." Apparently it did not.

"Good God," he said again. "And Lord Sheridan, knowing this, is still prepared to terminate your marriage?"

"He does not yet know," Marietta replied. "And," she added hastily, "I should naturally prefer that you not inform him."

"No; no, I shall not." Ambrose massaged his scalp again.

"However, as you yourself pointed out, I can hardly, under the circumstances, consent to an annulment."

"No, I fancy not," Ambrose agreed glumly.

"It is too late for me." Marietta essayed a great sniffle and daintily swabbed her eyes with the little smuggler's handkerchief. "But I do most firmly concur in your opinion that we—as a family—are entitled to substantial recompense." She paused for dramatic emphasis and lowered her eyes. "You . . . you once said I could confide in you, Ambrose."

"And you *can*, my dear; yes, indeed. I wish to know all the details, however disgraceful and shameful they may be."

"They are certainly shameful." Marietta allowed her mouth to quiver a moment and once more patted her cheeks with his handkerchief. "The fact is, Ambrose, that Roger jilted me. But here; you may see for yourself."

She had absently, almost inadvertently, placed Roger's note in the center drawer of the dressing table, and she now withdrew it. She rose, crossed the room, and deposited the crumpled ball in Ambrose's eager palm. By the time she resumed her seat, Ambrose had smoothed the paper out, and she watched as he read it, his face going unmistakably pale.

"*Roger*!" he choked at last. "Roger *deceived* me!"

Marietta bit back another insane threat of laughter. "Yes, he did," she said mournfully. "The truth is that Christopher wed me because he judged that the only honorable alternative."

"Honorable?" Ambrose snapped. "To wed you and then mistreat you? You are saddled to a monster who has got you with child, only to continue disporting about the neighborhood . . ." Words evidently failed him; he stopped and shook his head.

"Perhaps we should not be so harsh with Christopher," Marietta said carefully. "He was, after all, forced into a marriage he did not wish. Whatever the case, I *am* bound to him; as I have said, it is too late for me." Another sniffle, another dab at the eyes. "But fortunately it is not too late for you, Ambrose."

"No?" His tragic expression moderated considerably, and he sat forward, clasping his plump hands between his knees.

"No," Marietta said. "It has come to my attention that Christopher and Lord Cadbury have purchased a splendid new estate; the papers were signed only on

Monday. They will surely require the services of a talented bailiff, and who, Ambrose, is more talented than
yourself?" She smiled, sobered. "But in light of your
vast business experience, you probably feel such a position beneath your dignity. I daresay they will provide
elegant quarters and a magnificent salary, but that is
not sufficient, is it? Put it out of your mind, Ambrose;
it was an exceedingly poor idea."

"Umm." Ambrose cleared his throat. "Actually it is
quite a *good* idea, my dear; my . . . er . . . business is
subject to . . . ahem . . . frequent, unpredictable re-
verses. It is a very good idea indeed, and I shall speak
to Lord Sheridan at once."

"I fear that would *not* be a good idea; as you know,
Christopher is in rather poor humor just now." Marietta blew her dry nose into his handkerchief. "No, I
believe you should go directly to Lord Cadbury. Explain the situation to him; better still, show him Roger's note. And if Uncle Ralph offers the slightest
objection, you might wish to add that Roger has been
bilking Christopher of funds for half a dozen years.
Mention that Christopher recently paid a five-thou-
sand-pound gambling debt in Roger's behalf and compensated a lady in Norfolk whom Roger had
compromised. In short, Ambrose, do not accept a negative answer; the Thornings *owe* us this."

"They certainly do." Ambrose stood, tugged his
waistcoat over his belly, fussed with his neckcloth.
"They certainly do." He strode to the door and threw
it open.

"One last thing." He was halfway into the hall when
Marietta caught him up. "Tell Lord Cadbury that I
specifically wish you to oversee the *new* property, the
one purchased on Monday. Tell him I shall settle for
nothing less."

"I *shall* tell him," Ambrose promised. "His lordship
will discover that the Chases and Hewitts are not to be
trifled with, eh, my dear?"

He left the room, slamming the door behind him,

and the candlestick on the dressing table rattled a bit as he marched down the corridor. Marietta giggled for a moment at her reflection, but her hilarity soon evaporated. She had gambled everything, she realized: if Lord Cadbury declined to believe Ambrose's tale, he would speedily advise Christopher of the conversation, and the Viscount would assume that Ambrose's demands were but the latest maneuver in the Plot. Marietta went to the bed, stretched out upon the counterpane, and attempted to read the last of the books she had ordered for her convalescence. But she could not concentrate, and she closed her eyes and eventually fell into a fitful sleep.

She was awakened by a confusing medley of sounds—the chiming of the mantel clock, Poppy's furious barking, and, loudest of all, a frantic pounding at the door. Marietta scrambled out of bed, rushed across the room, and—bracing herself for a horrible confrontation with his lordship—cautiously cracked the door. But it was April who stood in the corridor, wringing her hands.

"It is your mother, ma'am," the abigail reported breathlessly. "Mrs. Hewitt, that is. She is frightfully ill; in fact, she has altogether collapsed. She is begging to see you, and if you do not hurry, ma'am, I fear it could be too . . . too late."

April raced back down the hall, Marietta at her heels, and shoved open the door of the yellow bedchamber. Marietta beheld a pathetic sight indeed: Agnes was abed, propped against the pillows, her face quite as pale as the snowy linen cases. Ambrose stood beside the bed, looking almost as waxen as his wife, holding and patting her limp hand.

"Marietta!" Agnes moaned as April closed the door behind them. "You must assist us, dear. Lord Cadbury intends to dispatch us to *Australia*."

"Australia!" Marietta feigned a gasp.

"Yes," Ambrose confirmed grimly; "that is the location of the new estate. I was not aware of it until Lord Cadbury began discussing travel plans."

"Australia," Marietta repeated. "I naturally presumed the property was nearby—"

"We are to set out for Plymouth *tomorrow*," Agnes sobbed, "for a ship is leaving later in the week. You must *do* something, Marietta. I cannot bear it; I cannot live with convicts and kangaroos and . . . and *Indians*."

Marietta did not believe Australia could boast of a single Indian amongst its scanty population, but she elected not to issue a correction. "I am afraid there is nothing I *can* do, Agnes," she said dolefully. "Ambrose obviously bested Lord Cadbury, *forced* his lordship to give us our due." The little smuggler brightened a bit, preened a bit. "I am sure Ambrose understands that if you were now to refuse Lord Cadbury's offer, he and Christopher would probably send you off with no recompense at all." Apparently Ambrose had *not* considered this; he paled again. "I daresay Ambrose also realizes that there is a great deal of money to be made in Australia. For a man of *his* talents, at any rate."

"Indeed there is." Ambrose squared his shoulders and soothingly caressed Agnes' hand. "I fancy we shall get on quite well, my dear, and in a few years' time we shall no doubt be in a position to purchase an estate of our own."

"But *kangaroos*!" Agnes wailed. "And I shall not be here for the birth of your first child, Marietta—"

"Well, who knows?" Marietta interposed hastily. She had observed, from the corner of her eye, April's expression of keen, curious interest. "Who knows when *that* might occur?" Ambrose and Agnes frowned in puzzlement, and Marietta flew on. "In any event, I shall direct your dinner to be sent up, and I shall request a bottle of champagne so you may celebrate your good fortune." Ambrose appeared enormously cheered by the prospect of a bottle of champagne. "Then, after dinner, you must pack and rest in preparation for your journey tomorrow. Good evening, Agnes. Ambrose."

Marietta tugged April into the corridor and dispatched her to the kitchen to order dinner for herself as well as the Hewitts. The abigail scurried away, and Marietta entered her bedchamber, quelling a surge of triumph. She recognized that, in boxing parlance, she had won only the first round: she had disposed of Agnes and Ambrose, but she had yet to deal with Roger. Though perhaps, she thought, such dealing would prove unnecessary after all; perhaps she could now turn to Christopher. Yes, she decided with increasing optimism, she could kill several birds with a single stone: she could apologize for her earlier outburst, explain the nature of her meeting with Mr. Lloyd, reveal her clever manipulation of the Hewitts. The Viscount would be exceedingly pleased and might even permit Roger—now rendered harmless—to stay on at Twin Oaks.

Marietta, fairly brimming with confidence, was prepared to speak to Christopher at once, but April advised her that his lordship was from home.

"Mr. Crawford is in a terrible flame, ma'am," the abigail said, setting Marietta's tray on the dressing table. "And Mrs. Sampson is in the boughs as well. They had planned a lovely meal in the dining room, and there is no one to appreciate it: you and your parents are to eat in your rooms, and Lord Sheridan and Mr. Thorning are away. If you will pardon me for saying so, ma'am, I really feel it will be for the best when your parents depart. They are driving us all to distraction; for example, I know I have forgotten something important I was to do, but I cannot remember what it is."

With this rather redundant pronouncement, April clawed her hair out of her eyes and rushed down the hall with Agnes and Ambrose's dinner.

Marietta consumed every drop of mulligatawny, every morsel of haddock and cauliflower, of Stilton cheese and currant pie. After April had borne her ravaged tray away, she tried again to read, but her ears were attuned to the clock on the mantel and the drive outside. The clock had just struck half-past nine when she heard the clatter of wheels, the jingle of harness, and she dashed to the window and tweaked the drapes apart. But it was deep twilight, nearly dark, and she was able to discern only the vague shape of a carriage and an unidentifiable figure proceeding up the front steps. Before her courage could disintegrate, she strode to the mirror, adjusted her clothes and hair, pinched a little color into her cheeks, and hurried to the ground story.

The foyer was deserted, and Marietta paused until she detected a clink of glass emanating from the library. She continued cautiously to the door, hoping Christopher had procured a new supply of spirits; it would be a very bad sign indeed if he had stooped to swilling Tokay. She paused again at the threshold, peering into the room, and Roger whirled around to face her.

"Ma-ri-et-ta." He spoke very slowly and carefully, as though fearful that his tongue might otherwise become entangled in his teeth. He smashed the Tokay bottle down upon the liquor chest, where it rocked alarmingly for a moment, and lifted his brimming glass. "Come in; join me for a drink."

"No, thank you, Roger," she said politely. "And if I may say so, it appears you have had quite enough to drink already."

"I shan't deny it; I must own that I have just returned from a rather heavy wet at the Crown." He gulped down fully half the contents of his glass. "But I fancy I may be forgiven, for I am in the way of drowning my sorrows."

Marietta had started to retreat into the foyer, but his choice of words arrested her, and she stepped back into the room.

"Indeed?" she said. "And what sorrows are those, Roger?"

"Ah, you pretend not to know. You have won,

lovey, and I salute you." He raised his glass and drained it, seized the bottle and refilled the glass. "You have exacted your revenge, and I am man enough to admit defeat."

He began to hobble toward her, dribbling wine in his wake and stopping at frequent intervals to lean against the various items of furniture. He eventually reached her side and smiled down at her.

"You have won," he repeated. "And how cleverly you did it—casting Ambrose in the role of the wounded father. To say nothing of the tattle-box, eh?" Roger attempted another sip of Tokay, but the greater part of it trickled onto his untidy neckcloth. "As I am sure you expected, Uncle Ralph was *mosht* incensed. He summoned me to Cadbury Hall and ripped me up royally."

Actually Marietta had *not* expected the Marquis to react with such alacrity, and she was briefly at a loss for a suitable rejoinder. "Well, I daresay he will soon get over his miff," she murmured at last.

"But I shall not be here to witnesh the day." Roger shook his head and swayed a bit. "No, Uncle Ralph made it abundantly clear that I am no longer welcome in Esshex. He presented me fifty pounds with the explishit understanding that I am to remove myself from his sight and never darken his door again. I quote him precishly, Ma-retta." His speech was growing increasingly slurred. "He suggested I might wish to go to Australia with Agnes and Ambrose, and perhaps I shall. I fancy Ambrosh and I have a good deal in common, eh, Ma-retta? You tricked ush both, did you not?"

"*I* tricked *you*?" Marietta laughed. "Come now, Roger. I did not choose to inform Ambrose of your little scheme, but do not suppose I am unaware of it. You believed Christopher would compensate me for breach of promise, and you intended, somehow, to lay your hands on the money. Indeed, there is but one aspect I have not puzzled out: where were you bound when you met with your accident?"

"London," Roger responded airily. He did not seem in the least discomfited. "I planned to shtay a day and two nights in town before journeying back to Twin Oaks to await your arrival."

"And my abrupt departure," Marietta said dryly.

"Yes." Roger once more sipped at his Tokay and did somewhat better; only a few drops spilled upon his hessians. "And then the damnable carriage overturned. Really, if I had the time, I *should* shue for damages."

"But you do *not* have the time," Marietta said briskly. He was tilting his glass, threatening to douse *her* with wine, and she snatched it out of his hand and set it on the floor. "If you are to depart for Australia with Agnes and Ambrose, you must be ready tomorrow morning. I therefore suggest that you retire at once, for you have a long journey ahead. A *very* long journey," she could not resist adding; "Australia is an *exceedingly* distant place."

"So it is, and I fanshy I shall not see you again for some time to come. Indeed, I may *never* shee you again." He blinked his eyes, evidently suppressing a prickle of maudlin, alcoholic tears. "I do pray you bear me no ill will, Ma-Ma . . ." He swayed once more and grasped her shoulder for support.

"I do not bear you any ill will, Roger." In fact, she thought, she was perversely grateful to him: had it not been for Roger, she would never have met Christopher. "No ill will at all."

"Then I shall bid you farewell and be on my way."

He lowered his head and, before she realized what he was at, planted his mouth in the general vicinity of her right ear. She struggled for a moment, but he was sagging against her, threatening to bowl them both quite over, and she threw her arms around him in a desperate attempt to hold him up. At length, she managed to turn her head, but this action merely served to move his lips to the other side of her face, landing them firmly at the left-hand corner of her mouth. She tried to ease away, to push him carefully in the opposite direction; but she was jerked backward so abruptly that she stumbled.

"That will be quite enough," Christopher hissed.

The Viscount had fastened his fingers beneath the collar of her spencer, and he drew her sharply upright—half-choking her, compelling her to gasp for breath. Roger staggered back as well, collided with the chair, tumbled over the arm, and fell into the seat.

"There was no harm in it, Chris," Roger protested. His dignity was significantly impaired by the frantic waving of his feet as he strove—turtle fashion—to assume a proper position in the chair. "I was bidding Ma-retta good-bye; nothing elsh."

"That was most appropriate," the Viscount said frigidly, "for I wish you gone tomorrow, Roger."

"He *is* going tomorrow," Marietta said. "You do not understand, Christopher—"

"Hush!"

He shook her furiously, pulling her collar into her throat again, and she started to cough. His lordship turned back to Roger, fumbling in a pocket of his frock coat.

"I shall provide a bit of money to ease the agony of your departure." He extracted a wad of banknotes and tossed it on the floor. "Tomorrow," he reiterated, "and after that I shall not give you another farthing. You may seduce the Princess of Wales, and you will not receive a penny more."

Christopher transferred his fingers from Marietta's collar to her arm and dragged her out of the library and into the foyer. He strode toward the stairs, seeming not to notice that she was tripping, half-falling, behind him.

"*Please*, Christopher," she wheezed, vainly striving to regain her breath. "You do not understand at all. I have got rid of them: Agnes and Ambrose and Roger are leaving for Australia. I sent Ambrose to Uncle Ralph to report Roger's jilting and to demand a position at the new estate. Which Mr. Lloyd told me of this afternoon; that was the substance of our meeting. I fancied it was rather clever of me . . ."

They had reached the morning room, but the Viscount did not release her; indeed, he tugged her, perhaps more firmly, in the direction of the family wing.

"Where . . . where are we going?" Marietta panted.

"I believe it is time you learned to be a proper wife, my dear."

It was a moment before she collected his meaning; when she did, she stopped and tore her arm away. "No!" she gasped. "Not this way, Christopher."

"Not *what* way?" He spun around to face her. "I daresay I can maul and paw you quite as effectively as Roger."

His hands clamped upon her shoulders, and he yanked her forward and crushed his mouth on hers. Her teeth smashed painfully into the insides of her lips, and she struggled away.

"Please, Christopher . . ."

But he seized her arm once more and jerked her ahead, through the morning room and into the corridor. He halted at a doorway midway along the hall, threw it open, propelled her inside. He slammed the door behind them and leaned against it, his fingers still wound around her arm.

"Please, Christopher . . ." But she would not continue to plead. "Very well," she said stiffly. "If it is an assault you want—"

"It is *you* I want." His voice was hoarse, and his eyes had gone dark, had turned to charcoal. "You may make an assault of it if you will, but I shall wait no longer."

His arms went round her ribs, and he drew her to him, the buttons of his waistcoat biting through her spencer, through her dress. His mouth captured hers again, forced her lips apart, and she fought him for another instant; but then she felt the stirring of a strange, wild excitement, and she found her fingers in his hair. He moved his mouth to her ear, her neck, and she heard herself moan. She realized that she had melted into him, that she could seemingly detect his every bone, his every muscle.

The room was dark, so she could not remember exactly how it happened—how he removed first her spencer, then her dress, and left her trembling in her underthings. Nor how he himself stripped off his coat and waistcoat, his neckcloth, his shirt; she was merely suddenly aware that his chest was bare, that she was stroking the thick, soft mat of hair which covered his skin.

They went to the bed, but she did not remember that either, did not remember whether he carried her or they walked. They were simply there, and at some point no clothing remained between them; the whole length of him was bare against her own bare flesh. And his mouth, his tongue, his hands were all over her body, leaving her to gasp once more for breath.

She vaguely understood that, at the end, he could have hurt her very much. But he did not: he took her so gently, so smoothly, that she was initially disappointed. Then he began to move, to create sensations she had never imagined, and when it was over, she lay shuddering in his arms.

There were things she wanted to say, so many things she wanted to say. But she was tired—blissfully, wonderfully tired—and she buried her face in his shoulder and tumbled into sleep.

17

W HEN MARIETTA WOKE, she was momentarily disoriented; she heard the chiming of a clock, but it did not sound like *her* clock. She suddenly became aware that, beneath the sheets, she was quite naked, and with a furious blush of recollection she cautiously turned her head. But the other side of the bed, though still warm, was empty, and she sat up, modestly drawing the sheets to her neck.

"Christopher?" she called softly.

There was no response, and she gazed about, expecting to find their clothes strewn all across the Brussels carpet. But his, she observed, had disappeared, and hers were neatly piled on the back of an armchair near the door. She flushed again and glanced at the clock on his lordship's mantel. It was a few minutes past eight; evidently he had gone for his morning ride. Just after eight, and if she hurried, she could make it to her bedchamber before the servants began setting up for breakfast. She leaped out of bed and dressed as quickly as she could, opened the door and peered up and down the corridor. It, too, was empty, and she crept to the morning room, literally ran across it, and raced down the opposite hall to her own bedchamber.

Poppy greeted her with great, wounded eyes, and Marietta giggled. Ah, my dear companion, she thought, I fear your life will never be the same. Nor mine. She went to the mirror and discovered, with no surprise, that she looked quite awful; indeed, she looked as though she had been ravished. She giggled again and felt another wave of warmth. More than a flush—a flood of well-being which swept from the roots of her hair to the tips of her toes.

But she must be practical, Marietta advised herself sternly. She would don her dressing gown, attempt to create some order from the chaos of her hair, then ring for April. She would bathe and dress as though nothing had happened and bid Roger and her stepparents a suitably sad farewell. Later in the day, she would begin supervising the refurbishment of Christopher's mother's bedchamber; until the task could be completed, she would move a few things to the Viscount's room. She hugged herself and, electing to begin with her hair, sank into the chair in front of the dressing table.

Marietta reached for her brush and spotted an envelope just beside it, an envelope addressed to her in his lordship's bold, back-slanting hand. She had never fancied Christopher one to write love notes, and with a smile tickling the corners of her mouth, she tore it open.

Marietta [she read],

I have pondered our situation at considerable length and have reached the inescapable conclusion that, in view of our mutual unhappiness, separation offers the best solution. If you wish an annulment, I am confident that I can secure one; if not, I shall provide an independent household in whatever location you may choose. The matter is one of complete indifference to me as I have no desire to marry again.

I have enclosed a sum sufficient to see you to Virginia, should that prove your choice, or to any other destination. Upon your arrival, please advise me of your direction, and I shall arrange for a permanent settlement.

C.T.

Marietta reread the message once, twice, her hands shaking first with disbelief, then with humiliation. The

Viscount's consummation of their marriage had been an assault after all, an assault in every sense of the word: having, at last, conquered her body, he could pack her off and count himself the victor. She groped blindly in the envelope, drew out a sheaf of banknotes, counted them. Two hundred pounds; she must remember the figure in the event she someday decided to become a Cyprian.

She did not cry; she was too enraged to cry. She sprang out of the chair and, with no further thought for her appearance, furiously jerked the bell rope. By the time April knocked, Marietta had ripped off her spencer and dress and was pacing about in her underclothes.

"Oh, I say, ma'am." The abigail paused at the threshold, her eyes wide with shock. "You seem a bit . . . a bit—"

"Never mind!" Marietta snapped. "Have my stepparents and Mr. Thorning departed?"

"No, ma'am; they have not. Mrs. Hewitt indicated that the chaise was to come at half-past nine—"

"Splendid!" Marietta interrupted. "Please inform them that I shall join them and, if necessary, they are to wait. I shall have time only to sponge off; after you have spoken to my stepparents, bring hot water for the basin. Afterward we shall pack my things."

"Pack?" April echoed. "You are leaving as well, ma'am?"

"I thought I had made myself perfectly clear!" Marietta stamped her foot. "Now go; go at once!"

As it happened, the departing party was *not* compelled to wait; at twenty-five minutes after nine, April thrust the last of Marietta's gowns into her trunk. The trunk was filled to overflowing, and Marietta directed the abigail to sit upon it while she herself fastened the clasps. Bailey, who had been stationed in the corridor for several minutes, rushed in and bore away the trunk and the equally jammed valise. Marietta gazed around, trying to ascertain whether there was any item she'd forgotten.

Poppy gave her another mournful, reproachful look, and for the first time Marietta felt a lump in her throat. She would have liked to take the dog, but that, of course, was impossible. She had left Lady Sheridan's jewel case (it had never really been hers) in a prominent position on the dressing table, her engagement and wedding rings inside. She had stuffed his lordship's money into her reticule, but she regarded the wad of banknotes as a loan. She wanted him to know that, wanted to write *him* a note. But there wasn't time; she could only vow that somehow, someday, she would send it all back, perhaps with interest, and advise Viscount Sheridan, in no uncertain terms, that he could go to the devil.

She rushed down the corridor, April panting behind her, and down the stairs to the foyer. The front door was open, and Ambrose and Agnes were in the drive, shouting instructions to the postilion as he began hefting the luggage to the roof of the carriage. By some malignant stroke of fortune, it was the same postboy who had driven Marietta from Suffolk to Twin Oaks, and he ceased his labors long enough to flash her a triumphant gap-toothed smile. I knew ye weren't expected, he seemed to say; not expected, never welcome . . .

"Marietta!" Agnes bounded forward, her plump little husband hard on her heels, and seized Marietta's hands. "Are you going to Australia with us, dear?"

"I am not sure," Marietta murmured.

This was true; perhaps Australia would be no worse than Virginia, no worse than a hundred other strange, lonely places.

"But whatever has *happened*?" Agnes asked. "Why have you suddenly elected to leave?"

"Christopher and I have agreed to separate," Marietta replied, extracting her hands from her stepmother's painful grip.

"Separate?" Ambrose growled. "Despite your condition?"

"My condition doesn't signify," Marietta said wearily.

"It *does* signify, my dear; I should hope Lord Sheridan pledged sufficient funds to support yourself and a child as well."

"He pledged funds enough," Marietta said shortly.

"Excellent!" Ambrose beamed. "We plan to spend tonight in London, and at that juncture you and I shall discuss the situation fully. It is entirely possible that none of us shall have to venture to Australia after all."

Agnes brightened as well, but she was immediately distracted by a fearful crash behind them. The postboy—who, in the course of his smirking, had quite forgotten the luggage—was gazing down at a case which had tumbled onto the drive, and Agnes dashed over to scoop her underclothes back into the valise. Marietta, hoping to avoid a private conversation with Ambrose, hurried to the chaise and started to mount the steps. However, Roger had preceded her: he half-sat, half-reclined upon the seat—head laid back, eyes closed, possibly dead. He was occupying virtually all the available space, and Marietta belatedly remembered that under the best of circumstances a chaise was designed for only three passengers.

"It won't do," she said as the ubiquitous smuggler reached her side again. "We cannot all fit in the coach."

"You could occupy the floor," Ambrose ungallantly suggested.

"I shall *not* sit on the floor," Marietta snapped. "I shall have Grayson drive me to Chelmsford, where I shall hire a chaise of my own at the Crown. I shall send Grayson back with the barouche."

"Better still"—Ambrose beamed once more—"we shall take Lord Sheridan's equipage to London. An excellent idea, my dear; I regret I did not think of it myself."

Marietta had no intention of stealing Christopher's carriage and horses, but she decided not to argue. She walked back to the front doorway—where Crawford, trying and failing to be inconspicuous, was pacing about—and desired the butler to order out the barouche.

"Yes, ma'am." Crawford's eyes darted to the chaotic scene in the drive, and he nervously bit his lip. "And what am I to tell his lordship?"

Marietta suppressed an inclination to repeat aloud her earlier, unspoken sentiment—to instruct Crawford to advise his lordship to go to the devil. "You may tell Lord Sheridan that I am traveling to Australia," she said haughtily.

"Begging your pardon, ma'am, but I do not believe one can drive to Australia—"

"Just summon the carriage, Crawford!" Marietta stamped her foot again, stubbed her toe, gritted her teeth against a wince of pain. "At once!"

"Yes, ma'am." The butler negotiated a hasty bow and fled around the corner of the house.

Marietta surmised that she had, if for the last time, thoroughly terrified Crawford, for the barouche clattered into the drive under ten minutes later. The gap-toothed postilion, visibly perspiring now, was still wrestling with the baggage; and even as he started to tie down the first heap, April rushed out the front door.

"You left some things behind, Mrs. Hewitt," she called. "There are a number of gowns in the wardrobe in the bedchamber across from yours and a portmanteau on the bed. I daresay the gowns were packed in the portmanteau—"

"Well, repack them then!" Agnes interposed irritably. "You should have recollected that the wardrobe in our bedchamber was too small to accommodate my dresses. You should have *assumed* I'd move them across the corridor."

"Yes, ma'am."

April curtsied and retreated into the foyer, and Marietta could picture her racing through the gloom and up the curving staircase, running down the hall. Poppy would hear the abigail pounding by, would cock her head and lift her ears, would, perhaps, growl a bit

. . . Marietta's throat tightened again, and she shook her head; it was no time for regret.

"I fancy I should proceed ahead, Ambrose," she said. "I shall meet you at the inn."

"That won't be necessary." Ambrose shook his own bald head. "I shall drive the barouche myself; there will then be no need for Lord Sheridan's man to accompany us. We shall meet Agnes and Roger in London—"

He was interrupted by another great crash, and Marietta observed, to her relief, that at least half a dozen pieces of luggage had fallen off the precarious stack on the chaise roof and were scattered about the drive.

"No, it is clear that you must stay to supervise the postboy." She essayed a sigh.

"We shall *all* stay then," Ambrose said. "When the chaise is loaded, we shall leave together."

"No!" Marietta protested. "That is to say, I had no time for breakfast, and I am feeling quite faint. A symptom of my condition, no doubt." She modestly lowered her eyes. "I shall have a bit of breakfast at the Crown while I await you."

"Very well," the smuggler agreed dubiously. "But you are *not* to surrender the carriage."

"No, Ambrose, I shan't," she lied.

Grayson assisted Marietta into the barouche, and it occurred to her that, with any luck, she could elude Roger and the Hewitts altogether. She could dispatch Grayson back to Twin Oaks and be under way in her own chaise before the rest of the group reached Chelmsford . . . But her trunk, she noted, was at the very bottom of the pile on the chaise roof, and she dared not linger while all the covering baggage was removed, dared not risk an encounter with his miserable lordship.

"You may proceed, Grayson," she instructed.

The coachman clucked the horses to a start, and the barouche rattled down the drive and into the road. Grayson, evidently recalling their last journey to town, held the team fairly to a snail's pace, but Marietta perceived no reason to exhort him to greater speed. She did not suppose the chaise would be ready to depart for half an hour or more, and she had lied to Ambrose about breakfast as well. She was not in the least hungry; indeed, the very notion of food rendered her faintly nauseous.

Marietta rested her head against the seat and closed her eyes. She wondered if Ambrose had retained possession of Roger's note or had left it with Lord Cadbury. Perversely, she wanted it—the message which had initiated this sordid chapter in her life—to match the one, now tucked in her valise, which had ended it. At the earliest opportunity, she decided, she would find some clever, casual way to ask.

The barouche, still progressing very slowly, rocked gently from side to side, and Marietta felt herself slipping into and out of sleep. She would doze a minute or two, would dream a brief, vivid dream, would be jarred awake by a rut in the road, would watch the scenery a moment, would drift back into unconsciousness. She had repeated this cycle several times when she had a particularly realistic dream: a familiar voice, emanating from a considerable distance, was ordering the carriage to halt. To add to the realism, the motion of the barouche did seem to cease, and Marietta groggily opened her eyes.

She realized—coming instantly, totally awake—that the carriage *had* stopped, and she leaped to her feet and peered over the roof at the road behind them. A lone figure was racing toward the barouche, a man on a great black horse, and though Marietta could not discern his features, she knew with utter certainty that it was Christopher. He narrowed the distance between them to sixty yards, fifty, and Marietta whirled around.

"Continue, Grayson," she commanded. "Continue at once."

"But it is Lord Sheridan, ma'am—"

"I am quite aware of who it is!" she interjected shrilly. "Drive on!" The coachman, with visible reluctance, resumed their stately, leisurely pace. "Quickly, Grayson!" she snapped. "Proceed as quickly as you can!"

He glanced over his shoulder, gnawed his lip, returned his attention to the road, slapped the horses to a headlong gallop. Marietta was nearly thrown out of the carriage, and she spun round again, grasping the edge of the roof for support. Despite Grayson's efforts, Christopher had reduced the gap to perhaps twenty yards.

"Stop!" the Viscount roared. "I ordered you to stop!"

"Drive on!" Marietta screeched.

It was fruitless, of course: a barouche, drawn by the best of teams, could not outrun an accomplished horseman. His lordship continued to gain ground and soon drew abreast of the carriage.

"I wish to talk to you!" he shouted over the thud of his horse's hoofbeats, the clatter of the barouche.

"But I do *not* wish to talk to you!" Marietta yelled in response. "Turn back; do not impede my passage any further."

She feared that the force of her brave words was somewhat diminished when the carriage hit a particularly large hole in the road, she tumbled into the rear-facing seat, and her leghorn hat slid to a point just above her nose. Nevertheless Christopher appeared to take her seriously, for as she struggled up and jerked her hat back in place, she saw that he had ridden ahead and was now galloping along just beside the box.

"Stop!" the Viscount bellowed. "I demand you stop!"

"Continue!" Marietta shrieked.

The beleaguered coachman evidently decided to adopt the only possible compromise: he precisely maintained the barouche's speed, neither whipping the horses to a faster pace nor shortening the reins. Christopher remained abreast of the box for some seconds, then spurred the great black stallion forward until he was neck and neck with the team. They raced along side by side, and Marietta eventually perceived that the Viscount was moving steadily closer to the nearer of the carriage horses. He obviously intended to halt the barouche himself . . .

"Stop!" she screamed.

She could not conceive what had possessed her; she thought she should have enjoyed the sight of his lordship being trampled to well-deserved bits before her very eyes. At any rate, Grayson—his shoulders sagging with relief—reined in the team, and Marietta collapsed glumly back in her seat.

"Good morning, my dear," Christopher said politely, gazing up at her from the road. Marietta furiously noted that despite his exertion, he looked quite as immaculate as was his custom. "Would you prefer to talk inside the carriage or in the open air?"

"I should prefer not to talk at all!" she snapped.

"But talk we shall," the Viscount said, "and I daresay we should enjoy more privacy if we were to move away a bit."

He nodded toward Grayson, and Marietta could well imagine the tale the coachman was already concocting of Lord and Lady Sheridan's scandalous behavior. She sighed and permitted Christopher to assist her out of the barouche and lead her to a stand of trees on the far side of the road.

"I trust you were not injured?" The Viscount calmly straightened her hat. "Your stepfather has just advised me, with high indignation, of the possibility that you are in a delicate condition."

"Umm." Marietta peered studiedly at the ground and kicked at a patch of weeds. "I had reasons for leading him to believe so," she mumbled. She glanced back up at his lordship. "What . . . what did you tell him?"

Christopher's eyes swept her face, and she detected a light she had never seen before—a warm, dancing, mischievous glow. "I told him such a circumstance was *entirely* possible," the Viscount replied gravely.

Marietta's cheeks blazed, and she shuffled her feet amongst the weeds again. "I took your money," she said stiffly, "but I do not intend to keep it. That is to say, I plan to *use* it, but I view it as a loan, and I shall repay it whenever I can. And regardless of any statement Ambrose may have made to the contrary, I did not think to steal your carriage and your horses—"

"Do not speak to me of money and carriages and horses," his lordship hissed. "I don't give a damn for money or property; I've plenty of both. But I've only one wife, and I shall bear you forcibly back to Twin Oaks if I must."

"Indeed!" Marietta bristled with familiar anger, but from the corner of her eye she saw Grayson tilt a curious ear in their direction. "Indeed," she repeated in a whisper. "Then how your mind has changed in only a few hours. From the time you wrote your note, with two hundred pounds enclosed—"

"My note!" To Marietta's vague satisfaction, the Viscount blanched. "I wrote the note yesterday afternoon, after our quarrel. I gave it to Jack to pass to April, and I quite forgot it."

And April had forgotten it as well, Marietta reflected; Christopher's message was the "something important" the abigail had been unable to remember. "Then you *have* changed your mind?" she said aloud. She felt the first faint stir of hope, and she willed her heart to slow.

"Surely that does not surprise you." His lordship's eyes were dancing again. "A *great deal* has happened since yesterday afternoon."

Marietta attempted—vainly, she feared—to suppress another flush. "It isn't enough, Christopher," she said as levelly as she could. "You may find me . . . find me *desirable*, but you once claimed to have been seduced by a surfeit of summer darkness and champagne. It is not enough," she repeated.

She gazed down at her shoes, his white-tops, and his fingers gently lifted her face.

"I love you, Marietta," he said haltingly. "It is difficult for me to confess it, for I never thought I should love any woman. In fact, I placed a wager to that effect on my eighteenth birthday; I bet Mark a hundred pounds that I was quite immune to feminine charms. I was consequently compelled to ride to Purcell Abbey this morning to pay my debt, and when I returned, Crawford informed me you had departed for Australia. I really must insist you reconsider, for I shall be *most* annoyed if I have spent a hundred pounds for nothing."

He smiled, and she tried to smile back, but her vision was beginning to blur.

"Mark told me of your conversation," the Viscount continued, "and I daresay I can find it in my noble heart to forgive you both for scheming behind my back." He grinned again; she sniffled. "Speaking of which—scheming, that is—I must own myself extremely curious as to how you manipulated Roger and your stepparents and Uncle Ralph. Perhaps you'll tell me one day. In the interim, I wish you to know that I *do* love you."

Marietta erupted into a fit of sobbing, and as she had left her reticule in the barouche, Christopher was forced to root amongst his pockets for a handkerchief. He dabbed her cheeks very lightly, each touch of the linen like a caress.

"I *shan't* carry you back to Twin Oaks by force, Marietta, but I beg you to come with me. And I haven't begged for anything before, love, not ever." He swabbed each of her eyelids in turn. "I cannot promise you a bed of roses, for I suspect, once I have you in my grasp again, I shan't allow you out of my sight for months to come."

"Nor I you!" Marietta had intended to sound very forbidding, but her sobs had degenerated to hiccups. "If I did, I daresay you'd go . . . go . . ."—she seized on Ambrose's word—"go *disporting* about with Lady Winship."

"Ah." His lordship's eyes twinkled. "So I *did* make you jealous with my attentions to Elinor. Perhaps I'm a more accomplished actor than I fancied."

He chuckled, but Marietta's own laugh died in her throat.

"It is not a jest, Christopher," she said severely; "you must learn to trust me. Last night, for example: there was nothing between Roger and me. There never was."

"I know that." His voice was thick, raspy. "I knew it when I took you to bed. Clever as you may be, love, you could not have pretended *those* feelings."

Marietta blushed again, stared again at his boots; was she to spend the remainder of her life in this debilitating state of embarrassment?

"I *do* trust you," the Viscount said. "However, I may yet keep you imprisoned for some time." He once more tilted up her face. "If you *were* 'in a delicate condition,' Marietta, nothing could give me greater pleasure. Permit me to rephrase that." His eyes twinkled again, shone like brightest silver. "Nothing could give me more *happiness*. I do believe there is another activity which might afford greater pleasure."

"*Christopher!*" she gasped. Her cheeks were fairly aflame.

"In any event, I shan't let you out of sight just now. If you agree, I shall send Grayson back to Twin Oaks, and we shall follow at our leisure."

He granted her no opportunity to *dis*agree, but Marietta was far from wishing to do so. His lordship strode to the carriage and spoke with Grayson a moment, and the coachman—with a last, lingering, incredulous stare—turned the barouche around and clattered up the road. Christopher walked back to Marietta's side, seized her in his arms, and kissed her quite as thoroughly as he had the night before. At length, he raised his head, and his eyes, once more charcoal, devoured her face.

"I have wanted to do that since the first instant I saw you," he said huskily. "And now—"

He was interrupted by the drum of hoofbeats, the jingle of harness, and Marietta initially fancied that Grayson had returned. But it was the chaise which— overburdened as it was—lumbered toward them: and before the postboy could bring his team to a full stop, Ambrose leaped out and dashed across the road.

"We passed your carriage just a moment since, Lord Sheridan," the little smuggler panted. "I ordered your man to halt, but he most insolently ignored my instruction." Ambrose drew himself up to his full, inadequate height. "Well, I shall not have it; do you understand? *I shall not have it*. It is clear that poor Marietta has once more succumbed to your trickery, but you reckoned without *me*, Lord Sheridan." He squared his plump shoulders. "I *insist* that the barouche and team be made a part of Marietta's settlement. And I shall tolerate no delay; I demand that you deliver the equipage at once. When we reach London, I shall formulate the rest of our requirements, the additional details of the settlement—"

"But there is to *be* no settlement, Mr. Hewitt," the Viscount interposed mildly. "Marietta has decided to remain at Twin Oaks."

"Remain?" Ambrose paled, purpled, sagged against the nearest tree. "No . . . no settlement?"

"I fear I misstated myself," Christopher said kindly. "I believe the situation has been settled to Marietta's complete satisfaction, and you, Mr. Hewitt, have obtained a splendid new post. I *was* somewhat dismayed to learn that Mr. Lloyd may have miscalculated; our property may be located in the great Australian desert."

"The desert," Ambrose choked.

"I do hope such is not the case." His lordship sorrowfully shook his black-and-silver head. "But I am confident that you will succeed in overcoming any adversity, however forbidding it might at first appear." The Viscount's arm was still planted firmly round Marietta's waist, and he poked her in the ribs.

"Do write to us, Ambrose," she cooed. "Perhaps

Christopher and I shall visit one day. Christopher and
I and your grandchild," she added wickedly.

"Though, in view of the immense distance, I daresay
there may be grand*children* by then." His lordship
feigned an elaborate sigh. "Be that as it may, farewell,
Mr. Hewitt. And good luck to you."

Ambrose staggered away from the tree trunk, tottered to the door of the coach, stumbled up the steps,
pulled them in behind him, closed the door. The postilion whipped his horses to a start, and Marietta fancied he gave her a nod of amused approval as he
passed. She glimpsed Roger through the chaise window, not dead after all, examining them with bleary
eyes; and she thought Agnes was furiously berating her
husband for his latest, costliest error. But she could not
be sure, and she didn't care. She watched the carriage
until it had crested the first hill and disappeared. She
turned back to Christopher, and he pulled her close
again.

"As I was saying before I was so rudely interrupted,"
he murmured, "I have wanted to kiss you from the
instant we met. And now, my bewitching love, I want
a great deal more. So I daresay we should proceed
home at once, lest I drag you into the woods and have
my evil way with you."

"Christopher!" she chided. But she was no longer
discomfited: it was *right* that he should want her, that
she should ache with this deep, sweet longing. "Very
well; I shall get my things . . . My things!" She clapped
one hand over her mouth. "Good God, Christopher, all
my clothes are on the chaise. And Agnes may not notice till they've reached Plymouth. Till they've reached
Australia."

"Do not tease yourself about it, dear," the Viscount
said solemnly. "I doubt you'll have much requirement
for clothing in the immediate future."

"*Christopher!*"

But she was giggling as he led her to the black stallion and boosted her into the saddle. He mounted be-

hind her, and his arms went round her to take the reins, and she leaned against him, feeling the strong, steady beat of his heart upon her back. He turned the horse, and they trotted up the road to Twin Oaks. Up the road toward home.

About the Author

Though her college majors were history and French, Diana Campbell worked in the computer industry for a number of years and has written extensively about various aspects of data processing. She had published eighteen short stories and two mystery novels before undertaking her first Regency romance, *Lord Margrave's Deception,* available in a Signet edition.